Storm Brewing

Book Three The Rocket Series

Chris Dyer

Amber Martin, Contributing Editor
All rights reserved. © Copyright 2018 Chris Dyer

ISBN-13: 978-0692069905
ISBN-10: 0692069909

Monday Creek Publishing
Ohio USA

One precious gift given yet not owned
One to be cherished unselfishly
One minute missed a tragedy
One tear shed in joy is one tear worthwhile,
One thousand shed in sorrow are all wasted,
One heart that fills with love beats life,
One heart that fills with sorrow lies still,
One hand that reaches out succeeds,
One hand that stays does little,
One life is all we have,
One life too soon,
One love is given,
One love to fall,
One love forgiven,
One love took all,
Who shall remember me?

DEDICATION

For some of us love never comes; for some of us we are lucky to have found love. I dedicate this book to those who have been in my life. I would also like to make a dedication to those people who have, through no fault of their own, suffered at the hands of others in whatever form.

I find it such a shame that things that are really good have a habit of not lasting. The problem is that when it does go wrong it is for all the wrong reasons.

PREFACE

This is probably the strangest preface to a book that you will ever read but I hope you will read it and consider the contents!

As a writer (and many other things as well!) I use my limited imagination to weave my tales. I enjoy writing as I am now as the rain pounds the ground outside and my dog sits beside me head on my lap wondering why I am tapping away at these strange buttons rather than stroking his rather handsome head. It makes you think a little deeper, animals have such remarkable honesty. My horses are the same, each treats me with devotion even if I am stamping around blaming the world for my mistakes. Now what if we started to care about each other and this beautiful planet we are privileged to call our home? Imagine if everybody gave one penny everyday to a worthy cause, that would equal, assuming 40 million people in a position to do so in this country and remember it is just one penny. It doesn't sound a lot does it? One penny, but that equals about £2,800,000 a week! Which is around £109,600,000 a year! Now imagine if ALL the wealthier countries did the same... How much would that be...? Then imagine that the governments gave a little back... idealistic I know, but not beyond the realms of possibility, let's say a penny of every £100 tax collected. How long would it take us to stamp out poverty, hunger, abuse? In doing so it might even bring us all a little closer, so maybe there would be less war. I'm not talking about just humans, let's be honest we are one of the later animals to place our feet upon this Earth, I'm talking about helping everything; humans, the other animals, that dwell upon this earth with us and the earth itself. I'm no hippy. I'm not a vegetarian, before you all start thinking I'm some sort of religious nut, I have belief, but I'm not a religious fanatic. I do think we have a duty to stand together and protect that which we are guardians of! Don't forget our children inherit our mis-management! So, the next time you're stood fiddling in your pocket or purse perhaps you would give this some thought.

Oh, and one more thing, would all the fanatics and those with religious piety answer me a question or two? Why when you are all saying the same about God wanting mankind to be just and kind to each other are we kicking the shit out of each other? What makes you all so sure that you have the right religion and so don't those with different views have the right to those views, or do you just believe in dictatorship? I wonder what your God would make of it? When you've considered that think of this.

Listen to a playground full of children anywhere in the world, listen carefully... they all sound the same. Just remember the penny!

CHAPTER ONE

To say that Geoff Stokes was not a happy man was an understatement. Kate sat in the lounge looking at the magazine that was spread on the coffee table. The shots of her were revealing she had to admit they left very little to the imagination but she had to admit to herself they were incredibly sexy and she was more than a little turned on herself looking at them. She felt a tingle in her stomach as she scanned them with her eyes, remembering the moments after the shoot with Mike when everybody had left the yard.

"Are you just going to sit there and say nothing! You're a thoughtless fucking bitch! I told you not to do it and what do you do you go straight ahead and ignore me. This...!" He pointed at the centrefold where Kate was leaning back against Mike, her hips thrust forward as if the horse she was on was galloping across some field, showed her naked shaven body to the full. "And to top it all you're totally naked showing everything you have to a trainer who you fucking employ. I just don't fucking believe you, you, you... stupid cow!" Kate sat quietly as Geoff became even more agitated and offensive, his voice becoming louder with each word.

He walked over picking up the magazine and threw it at her.

"How the fuck can I show my face anywhere when a picture of my wife's fanny is stuck on every wall in the country!" Kate gave a small yelp as the magazine hit her face, leaving a stinging red mark where it had hit her.

She jumped to her feet, her own temper rising. "Who the hell gave you ownership of me? We may be married but you don't own me!"

"I've paid for you a thousand times over!" Geoff spat, regretting the words almost before he spoke them.

"You bastard! How dare you I... I..." Kate was speechless and close to tears. Geoff realised he had gone too far.

"I'm sorry!" He tried.

"So am I." Kate screamed and ran from the room.

Geoff ran after her, catching her just before she reached the stairs he grabbed her arm, swinging her round and as he did so Kate aimed a stinging slap to his left cheek. "Don't touch me!"

Geoff gritted his teeth drawing his hand back in automatic reaction managing to stop the blow aimed at Kate just in time. "I ought to."

"Ought to what?" Kate snarled. "If I'm that special to you what are you doing buying that magazine anyway? You ought to be proud I had the guts to do it and complimented that, so many men will find me so sexy! It's alright if it's someone else's wife and you're looking at her I suppose!" Her voice calmed. "Jealousy is nice in small proportions Geoff and a little jealousy would have complimented me, but to go off like a raving lunatic just shows me how selfish you are."

Geoff's anger flared again.

"I think most men would be pissed off seeing their wife stark naked on a horse with a fucking employee so tight behind them there wasn't room for a cigarette paper. Don't fool yourself, it's not jealousy... its fucking shame is what it is!"

Kate burst into tears and ran for her bedroom. She packed a suitcase, woke Becky telling her they were going to go away for a couple of days, packed her a case, and went back downstairs. Geoff was still waiting at the bottom. Without another word to each other, Kate passed by Geoff and walked from the house leading a confused Becky by the hand.

Mike woke head pounding. He felt ridiculous! He had not felt this way since his return from Spain. He reluctantly placed his feet on the floor, sitting on the side of the bed and holding his throbbing head in his hands. He slowly dressed and made his way downstairs to the kitchen.

"Right, sit down, and I'll get you something to eat… by the look of you you'll need something to soak up all that booze!" Vi tutted in her poshest and most matriarchal voice ignoring Mike's protestations. "I think you'd better tell me what's going on young man… we're all as worried as can be!"

Mike really didn't know 'what was going on'. He had always been a very self-possessed person, in the main able to ride any storm. He slipped when his relationship with Ann broke down, but he realised that was as much his pride as anything else if he were honest, he was hurt and felt alone but not like this.

This was different, he felt totally exhausted, empty. Life should be a breeze; he was famous, he was at last respected for being the exceptional horseman he was, he had taken on the world and beaten them with Rocket, even if he knew deep down it was the horse and not him. He was though fully aware that Rocket would never do it for anyone else.

So why did he feel so bloody awful? Vi looked at him sympathy showing in her face. "You ought to be the 'appiest man on this earth young man! Instead you're mopin' around like you've lost a pound and found a penny! You 'ave got to sort yourself out. I know your 'ankering after that girl, but you have to face the facts, her 'eart belongs to someone else." Mike sighed as he pushed the bacon and eggs around his plate. Slowly he looked up at Vi.

"What do I do? I try to think of something other than her but it all comes down to the same. Everything I do reminds me of her. The races, the horses, I go to town and I can smell her perfume, I see a child and I think of her. I just can't escape."

Vi put her hands on her hips. "Maybe you just needs a break, just a week or so away, even a few days find somefink you want to do and take the time to do it. 'Ave a word wif John, 'e's a sensible bloke, I'm sure 'e'll come up wiv sumfing. Now eat that breakfast an' get yourself in gear!" Mike had to smile, Vi was definitely a treasure, even her way was lovely from a very plumy accent to broad cockney all in the space of a few sentences.

Mike ate his breakfast, wandered down to Rockets paddock where the ever-present Nick stood watch over Rocket, Storm, and JC.

JC grazed contentedly whilst Rocket and Storm had stretched out beneath a broad limbed oak tree absorbing the morning sun. Normally a stallion is never run with his mares and certainly not foals, with Rocket it was totally different, but then so was Rocket!

Nick jumped up from where he was sitting by the two stretched out horses, one hand on each of their necks. "Sorry Guv I was jus' spending sum time wiv the boys before I got on wiv the fencing." Mike gestured to Nick that it was fine, Nick worked extremely hard for Mike and a few minutes enjoying what had become his charges was in Mike's book the right thing to do. "Its fine Nick, don't worry, I only came to see the boys myself. It's reassuring that you bond with them so well and that they are so well looked after by you! I'm taking a few days off, so I won't be around for a day or two."

Nick smiled knowingly.

"My Vi said she was goin' to 'ave a word wiv you. Right worried she was! Said you needed to get your 'ead straight, stop finkin' about that girl an' get to grips wiv fings. She finks the world of you Guv an' don't want to see you down in the dumps like. Reckon a few days would do you good." Nick laughed. "Blimey I know how persuadin' she can be when she wants. I was a bit worried when she said to me this morning, thought she might be over stepping the mark like, but my Vi says to me, some ones got to look after 'im proper like an' it's my job, I ain't gonna see 'im moonin' round the place that boy needs a break! She's always bin the same my Vi, like an ole mother 'en she is God love 'er."

Despite the grief Mike felt over Kate, and it was grief, he still felt a warm glow inside at the thought of Vi. It was great to know that you have someone that cares that much in a sort of motherly fashion.

Mike walked over to Rocket and Storm. Two voices rang in his head. "Don't be gone too long this time, just a few days, you've a lot to do, the boy is getting big enough to start soon!"

"Yeah," the lighter of the two voices rang, "and you're going to need to be on top form. I've a few tricks up my sleeve, but it'll be fun!" Mike groaned and smiled as he walked towards the garage.

He opened the F-type's door and slid into the contoured leather seat, turned on the engine and reversed out of the garage, turning the nose in the direction of the stud. The car burbled through the yard and as Mike reached the road, the car roared into action as he pressed the accelerator to the floor. He eased off slightly as the car's speedo leapt up to eighty in a few seconds. For Mike the F-type was nearly as exciting as a horse and he always enjoyed driving it, the admiring glances he received made the car just that bit more special. There was no doubt it was beautiful, a real head turner. Mike reached the stud and pulled up the drive, surprised to see John and Seamus sitting on the edge of Johns koi pond admiring the fish.

Both men smiled as Mike exited the car and wandered over to them. John jumped up and impulsively threw his arm around Mikes shoulder. "Come on let's go and have a coffee, we've a lot to talk about and as you're going away for a few days we just as well sit down now and sort things through!" Seamus took one more look at the fish and followed them into the kitchen.

Mike turned to them both. "Does everyone know what I'm doing before I do it, or is it just a select few?"

Seamus and John laughed, and John replied. "Vi phoned us, she said you were on your way and that she'd given you orders to take a few days off! If you ever want to get rid of her send her my way, she's worth her weight in gold that woman!" Mike had to nod in agreement.

They reached the kitchen and as they made themselves comfortable John brewed fresh coffee, the aroma drifting appealingly in the warm atmosphere around them. John finished making the coffee and placed the pot in the middle of the kitchen table for everyone to help themselves. He took a sip from his mug. "We ought to think about all the money we have in Andorra you know… and there is still the money from the bet - we have to decide what we are going to do with it… any suggestions?"

Seamus put his mug back on the table.

"I've an idea or two. The bet money I think should be divided up into three or four lots." Mike and John listened carefully. "Well I think that, as it is really down to Rocket, we ought to think about giving to one of the racehorse charities, another share I think should go to a local hospital for the kid's ward. I think Becky should have the choice of whatever charity she'd like to see benefit, seeing as how it was her idea," at the sound of Becky's name Mike visibly winced, it didn't go unnoticed by either Seamus or John, both saw the pain in Mike's eyes, "and last but not least, I think John's original idea should be put into practice. I know it's plagiarising on Alice and Ann's idea, but you have to admit it's a bloody good idea."

"Plagiarising? What did you swallow a dictionary before you came out?" Mike asked Seamus with a smile. "Well that sounds good to me, what about you John you happy with that?" John smiled and nodded. "Then if it's okay with you we'll leave you to deal with that?"

"No problem-o!" John answered with a flourish. "That just leaves the money we have in Andorra. I suggest that we either leave it all there for the time being or take out, say a couple each. That would leave us with well in excess of twelve million with the interest we've accrued. It would be nice if the three musketeers had a rainy-day fund in case one of us gets the urge to do something stupid again!"

"I don't think that'll happen again John, do you? Hopefully I've learned my lesson and so did you! All the same if it's okay with Seamus it makes sense. Unless you have a different idea?"

"It's funny you should ask!" Seamus grinned. "Since I became a bit of a millionaire meself like." He drawled in his richest Irish accent. "I quite like the feel of it, I was thinking that you two fellas' have come from nothing, me I got lucky having two very unusual bosses. Now that aside I think it would be nice and a bit of a challenge to start a little empire meself! Ideally I'd like for the three of us to go in on something together All For One and all that and I'd feel like I was contributing and not just taking."

"Neither of us has ever thought of you just taking Seamus. You've put as much into getting success for the horses as anyone.... So, you must never think that!" Seamus smiled gratefully as Mike spoke. "I have to say it seems like a good idea to me, how about you John?" John looked to be deep in thought and hesitated for a moment before answering.

"Bloody good idea I think." He suddenly burst out. "In fact, I think I've got just the thing to interest us all. It's a little idea I've been thinking about for a while now. We'd have to use some of the bet money.... But don't worry this idea would give us the chance to not only make a great deal of money but also help under privileged kids, the disabled, old folks, in fact anybody we wanted!" John looked really smug.

"I hate it when he does that don't you!" Mike said tongue in cheek to Seamus, who readily agreed.

"Come on then clever clogs… spill the beans I want to go on my holiday!" Mike had cheered up a great deal talking to his friends. He still ached inside but Seamus and Johns company lifted his spirits somewhat.

"We set up a theme park!"

"What!?" Mike and Seamus said in harmony.

"A theme park, think about it, we have all the normal stuff that any other theme park has but with a twist. We put a night club on the perimeter, we can call it the Jockey Club! Good ehh! The theme park can be centred around racing, we can have everything made 'horsey', the possibilities are endless. We can put in a petting zoo for kids as well, maybe even a working show farm for town kids to see and have all the rides that are normally associated with theme parks. I think it would be brilliant! As I say the possibilities are endless, endangered breeding programmes, rescue, education and imagine the employment we would create. Well, what do you think?"

Mike spoke first. "I think the ideas superb, but I see a stumbling block...... where are we going to site it. Let's be honest it isn't going to be that easy to gain planning permission for something like that and finding an actual site won't be easy either!"

"I didn't say it would be easy. Nothing worth having ever is! It is possible though, especially as I think I know of the perfect spot. Oh, and I've bought Mrs. Canning's place next door, the relevance of which you will see in a moment." John smiled smugly.

"I agree," said Seamus looking at Mike. "I hate it when he does that as well!" Everyone chuckled.

"Mike, how would you fancy selling your satellite yard, the one you use for youngsters and for stalling out of work horses?"

"I wouldn't mind John, but I still use it, not often mind you but occasionally it comes in real handy. Have we got anything there at the moment Seamus?" Mike tried to stay focussed at the mention of his satellite yard, it was the yard where Kate had done her glamour shoot and the mere mention of it brought her beautiful face and body vividly to the front of his memory. Seamus had shook his head.

"How about we go halves on the Canning place? It's much bigger so there'll be plenty of room for the stud to expand. We could split it down the middle. What would you say your yard was worth?"

"Off the top of my head around £900,000 I suppose."

"How many acres is it?"

"Roughly two hundred and fifty, but of course there's no house with it. Just the yard and that's fairly run down still."

"Okay! If we could get a theme park on it, it would be worth fortunes and it is in the right place. No neighbours and its three miles to the nearest town. So, the possibility of any objections are lessened. Say we were," John continued indicating Seamus. "to give you £2,000,000 from the bet money," John put up his hand to stop interruption.

"In truth it has cost none of us, with each of us having a third share, and we still couldn't lose because if we didn't get the theme park we should have no bother getting planning for at least one house, so the value would still be fairly good. If we fail... well we could always set it up as another yard again, or something? However, if we succeed, bingo! You have had a serious result and so have we. Even more so, so will those we are trying to help. If you're worried about losing the usefulness of having the yard like I say, you can buy half of next door. It's only another five minutes away and with half the staff here most of the time it works out better for you. I gave three million for it, which is an absolute bargain, even though it's run down. You give me one and a half and you end up with an extra seventy acres on what you have now, more buildings albeit run down but with half a mill to play with and a third in a potential theme park on land that you'll still own a third of! What do you say do we give it a go?"

Seamus and Mike looked at each other for a while, then Seamus put his hand on John's, which was already resting in the centre of the table. Mike looked at them both then smiled placing his hand on top of the others. "All For One!"

"All For One!"

Mike left the kitchen bidding John and Seamus farewell and telling Seamus he would only be gone for a few days, ten at the most, if there were any problems Seamus was to ring his mobile, if it was something he could sort out don't.

Mike felt as though he was leaving a huge mill stone behind him as he drove towards the main road. He still hadn't decided where he was going and casually followed his nose. The car reached the A303 and Mike decided he turned the nose of the car towards the M3.

CHAPTER TWO

Kate sat with Becky in the hotel dining room, Becky looking rather cross. "Mummy? Why are we staying in a hotel?"

"Becky I've told you we're just treating ourselves for a few days. I just don't fancy cooking and doing housework, so I thought we'd have a break. Why don't we go and have a swim after dinner, maybe we should make use of the gym as well."

"Mummy I thought we said we'd always tell each other the truth… I'm not silly you know and now that I'm eight I think I'm pretty grown up don't you! I know something's wrong between you and daddy I heard you shouting!" Kate couldn't help but smile at her young daughter. As with most children innocence is a gift, with Becky her innocence was tempered with a logic far above her years. She looked into the small face staring intently at her now.

"You're right Becky you are a bright girl and you do deserve the truth. It's always better to hear the truth at the beginning that way it is never quite as painful."

Becky's face took on a worried expression at the seriousness of her mum's voice. Both looked around the dining room to see who was within earshot but apart from two couples that were sitting at the far side of the room there was no one. Kate reached down into her bag and pulled out a glossy magazine and carefully showed it to Becky. Becky's eyes widened as she looked at the pictures of her mother naked on the pages. Kate did not say anything, she took back the magazine and waited for Becky's reaction. Becky giggled.

"They're very rude mummy!" She finally said after a minute or so. "You look very pretty, much prettier than the ladies in daddy's magazines. Why is Mike in the pictures with you? Is daddy cross because you took your clothes off? You used to do that when we were in Spain and daddy never minded. Is it because Mike's in the pictures? Wow I bet your really famous now if you're in a magazine!" The words came out in a rushed jumble Becky looking directly into her mother's eyes.

"Anyway, I think you look very pretty, which horse is that you're riding I haven't seen that one before?"

Kate laughed at her daughter's reaction, seeming to lift a heavy weight from her shoulders, it was her turn now to answer Becky's questions and to try and explain the situation.

If only life could always be seen through a child's eyes, how honest and simple it would be. As she started to answer she wondered how turning eight had made Becky this wonderful, logical, worldly wise little creature. As she went to speak Becky interrupted.

"Do you like the pictures mummy?" She asked very seriously.

Kate thought for a moment before answering. "Yes, I do. I don't see anything wrong in them at all. As you rightly say, I take my clothes off on the beach and if people think I look pretty I think that's rather nice! I think it's a compliment that people want to buy a picture of me." She smiled conspiratorially and lowered her voice further. "Even if I don't have any clothes on!" Both mother and daughter giggled furiously. "Any way daddy wasn't very happy and called mummy some nasty things but then grownups do that sort of thing. I'm sure that after we've both had a chance to cool down things will get back to normal." Though in her heart Kate was not too sure her words were true. Geoff would need to do an awful lot of creeping to put things right again and Kate knew that it was not Geoff's way, he was far too stubborn to admit he was even partly in the wrong.

"I'll tell you what, we'll give daddy a ring just to let him know that we're okay and then how about we drive to the airport and catch a flight to Spain, we can soak up some sun at the villa for a few days?"

"Can we go to Mike's first so that I can see Sunrise? I want to know how Cloud, Dusk and Dawn are. I'll have to stop and buy them all a present on the way, but I do have some money." Becky delved in her pocket and pulled out what looked like a roll of at least a thousand pounds. Kate gasped.

"Becky where on earth did you get that money?"

"Granddad gave it me, he said I should buy whatever I wanted," Becky said a little defensively.

"There must be a thousand pounds there!" Kate continued. "Do you know how lucky you are to have a granddad like yours?"

"I do, and I love him very much and it's one thousand five hundred pounds." Kate marvelled at the matter of fact way Becky treated having so much money and not seeming to allow it to bother her at all. It wouldn't it seemed have mattered if it was one pound fifty it would still have received the same gratitude from this remarkable little girl.

"I think I'd better look after that young lady. I know what you're like for losing things and that is an awfully large amount of money." Becky passed the money over without question.

"Granddad said it was for spending not for saving!" Becky exclaimed in an effort to reinforce her idea of buying something for the horses.

"Okay you can spend a hundred pounds and no more on the horses. They really don't need anything though with all the stuff you've bought them… or should I say granddad has ended up buying them lately." Becky grinned. "The rest you can use for a spending spree in Spain!" Kate put her arms around Becky and gave her a long loving hug. "Let's order I'm starving then we'll have an early night, get up nice and early and go and see the horses then we'll get to the airport and go get some sunshine!"

"Yippee!" Becky squealed with delight, though Kate knew it was because she was seeing her precious horses and not because they were going to have a few days away.

Mike booked himself into the Heathrow Hilton, the porter took his bags up to his room and Mike tipped him a twenty-pound note. "Thank you, sir," the porter said gratefully. "I hope you don't mind my asking but aren't you the chap that trains The Rocket?" Mike smiled, the porter was only in his late teens but 'The Rocket' was said almost with a reverence. He told the porter he was. "I know it's a bit cheeky sir, but do you think I could have your autograph."

Mike had to admit to himself that he had never quite got used to people asking for his autograph but when they did it not only made him feel warm inside but brought the realisation of how lucky he was.

"Of course." He said. "Are you a race fan then?" The porter nodded his ascent, expressing in no uncertain terms that he was and always had been a fan of The Rocket, even giving Mike a very accurate account of Rocket's career. "I'll tell you what then, write your address down and not only can you have my autograph, but I'll send you Rockets and one of his shoes." The porter was absolutely thrilled scribbling his address as quickly as possible just in case Mike changed his mind. Mike laughed.

"Don't worry, I won't forget," he said as the lad handed him his address.

"Anything you want sir you just ask for me 'Justin' and I'll make sure you get it. Thank you very much sir." And he exited the room with a spring in his step. Mike picked up the phone and called Seamus knowing that if he didn't organise his promise to the young lad he would probably forget, then in six months he'd find the lads address in his pocket and wonder for weeks who the hell it belonged to. Seamus promised he would deal with it, assuring him that all was well at the yard and Mike placed the receiver back in its cradle and headed down for dinner.

He stopped at reception and asked the girl behind the desk if she would be kind enough to book him a flight to Malaga, club class if she could and having done so went into the dining room.

He didn't feel much like eating sitting on his own and the glances he kept getting from the other diners and whispered comments started to make him feel a bit paranoid. He had not bothered to change for dinner and was still in his old jeans, deck-type shirt and cowboy boots.

He started to look down at himself thinking why he hadn't taken the trouble to change but then a flash of the real Mike came back thinking 'what the hell, I'm as good as anybody in jeans or in designer trousers!'. His thoughts were interrupted by the waiter. "Excuse me sir but before you order I have several requests for you to accept drinks."

He leaned forward and spoke quietly. "In fact, I don't think there's anybody here that doesn't want to buy you a drink. But then you do look remarkably like the chap that trains that famous horse The Rocket!" Mike was sure he heard laughter deep inside his head. The waiter had said it almost apologetically, pompously, as though it were some sort of insult, though to whom he thought this Mike couldn't quite make out. "I suppose I look like him because I am!" he said louder than intended. The whole dining room was silent as the waiter was talking to Mike. Spontaneous applause started and within a couple of seconds the whole dining room exploded into applause, standing up to face towards Mike.

It had been a long time since Mike's face had been red with embarrassment, but it was now. He smiled weakly at the applauding diners nodding as he did so. It ended up being a long night for Mike as more and more people pressed him to allow them to buy him a drink. His throat was raw from telling the tale of Rocket and his antics. The only person who seemed content to sit on the periphery was a large well-muscled man in a grey suit who Mike had noticed had not allowed his eyes to stray from him all evening but as, of yet had said nothing or made no approach.

Mike felt the hackles rise on the back of his neck and his jaw muscles start to tense.

"Slow down!" the voice of Rocket popped into his head making him start. "It's not what it seems, just ignore him. He'll make himself known soon enough." The voice was gone leaving Mike looking totally bewildered. "You all right buddy?" One of his new found friends, a smartly dressed American with a southern drawl asked. "You look like you just seen a ghost!" Not waiting for a reply now that he had Mike's attention, he raved on about Rocket. "Best damn horse I ever seen, jeez you should bring him over to the States. Hell, they'd probably make him President! He'd probably have a lot more sense than the one we've got now!" Mike laughed along with the throng that surrounded him.

"I hate to be a party pooper but it's three o clock and I've a plane to catch at nine… and I'm not sure I'll be sober by then!" Mike laughed again and so did his compadres. He made his excuses and made his way towards the reception feeling like a rock star that had just played the best concert ever. His feeling of elation and his head swimming with alcohol, exacerbated his start when the strong hand grabbed his shoulder. It was the man that had been watching him so intently in the bar. Mike spun round and the man quickly put his hands up. "Sorry I just wanted a word. Didn't mean to startle you! Didn't want to interrupt your fans!" He smiled, and Mike relaxed a little.

"Look I know you said you've got a plane to catch in a few hours, but I'd be real grateful if you could spare me half an hour of your time." The man looked at his watch and smiled again. "After all it's hardly worth going to bed now and you can always have a couple of hours sleep on the plane! I assure you, it will only take half an hour and I would be very grateful." Mike looked at his own watch it was three thirty now.

He shrugged resignedly and moved towards the armchairs that were situated in the reception. The man that had stopped him turned to the receptionist.

"I'm sorry to be a nuisance but do you think you could organise some coffee for us?" He turned back to Mike grinning. "From what I've seen tonight I think another Irish and you might turn into a leprechaun!" Mike smiled back but did not speak. "I believe you have a foal that you're rather fond of and think might just emulate his father?" Mikes face took on a tense look. "Sorry I don't seem to be starting this very well, do I? ... Let me start again, I realise that the foal must be a bit of a touchy subject especially after all the problems you had with him being stolen but I can assure you I mean no harm to you or the foal. Have you named him yet?"

"Storm." Was all that Mike replied.

"Sounds rather apt seeing as his father... and his trainer have kicked up such a storm over the last couple of years! I've followed your career and your horses for the last few years. I have to say that you seem to have a touch of genius where horses are concerned, which brings me to why I'm here! I've owned horses for a long time... Don't look so worried, I'm not trying to get you to take on my horses, they are only average and I'm quite happy with my trainer. He's only small but he's a genuine sort of chap and has always been as straight as a die with me and gets me wins with horses that others would have struggled with. He's well in his sixties now and in truth only has a couple of owners apart from me, which is really all he can manage. The poor old chap loves what he does and if I moved my horses it would put him out of business. I couldn't do that to someone who has been good to me for years. Apart from that I am not a wealthy man, just comfortable and I'm pretty certain I couldn't afford the sort of fees you can command. Anyway, I digress! I'm proud to say that I have a pair of twins, sixteen they are and you'd never think it but they're both as skinny as a rake and strong as an ox. Like their mother God rest her soul. Anyway, the pair of them...".

He pulled a photo from his wallet of a young lad and girl each sitting proudly on a horse. Mike thought they both looked like they belonged. It's unerring a good horseman can tell you if someone will make a rider just by seeing them on a horse. Mike's old guvnor always used to say to him 'it's in your blood boy or it isn't there at all' and his words rang through Mike's head now. "The thing is they were born dumb." He paused it seemed to gather himself. "I don't mean stupid, far from it the pair of them are as bright as buttons, they just can't speak.... It makes life really difficult not just for them but for everyone around them. Can you imagine what it's like not being able to communicate easily? I have so much sympathy for anyone that has a disability but when it's your own children you really can't imagine." Mike was tired and the worse for wear with the amount he had drunk, but this man had his undivided attention. He felt so humble that he could have cried. How could he feel sorry for himself when this poor man and his children were going through this! He felt angry that the world could deal such unfair blows not just on this man's children but on tens of thousands. The man continued. "Look I don't wish to burden you with my problems, but it is so hard to find anyone that will give them a chance... most people just think they're being ignorant because they don't answer and of course they can't tell you an opinion verbally, everything has to be written down by them. The old chap who has my horses would take them on in a flash, but I don't think it's fair on him or them. They're bloody brilliant around and on horses and deserve a chance in a decent yard... I ...wondered if you'd consider giving them that chance... it wouldn't be easy mind it can be very frustrating for all concerned, but I know they would work hard and I'm certain they're determined enough to make the grade. With your profile at the moment I'm sure that if you thought they were good enough you could get them a license." He hesitated, waiting for Mike to speak. Mike could see the agony on his face as he waited for a verdict.

"Does anyone know why they can't speak... I mean is it something they can pinpoint like a disease or something... I'm sorry that sounds dreadful, I really didn't mean...".

"It's okay I've asked the same question a hundred times myself and no one seems to have an answer... they just don't know, everything seems to be okay physically, but they have never uttered a sound since the day they were born!"

"You said their mother has passed away?"

"Yes." Mike could see the pain and grief in the man's eyes. "She died giving birth, never even got to see them." He looked at the photograph again. "And Mel, that's my little girl." He smiled at the photo lovingly. "She's the absolute spit of her mother. Mark... that's my lad, he looks more like me but with his mums build."

Mike involuntarily looked at his watch, it was four-thirty, he would have to soon make a move if he was to catch his flight. "I'm sorry." The man's face fell. "I'm going to have to make a move but..." he reached into his pocket withdrawing one of the stud cards. "Give this number a ring and ask for Seamus... tell him you've spoken to me and explain the situation, just as you've told me, he's a really nice guy, tell him if it's okay with him we'll give them a try... No allowances where they're work is concerned mind you, they'll do the same as everyone else. If he agrees, tell him I'll sort it all out properly when I get back in a few days, they can start then." For a moment Mike thought the man would burst into tears.

"Thank you, thank you so much!" Mike rose to leave.

"By the way, how on earth did you know I was here?"

"Please don't say anything but Justin the porter who took your bags up... he has a real soft spot for my daughter... he rang me and said you were here... I only live twenty miles away, so I jumped in the car and came straight here." Mike smiled at the man again and held out his hand.

"If you want to know the truth I'd have done exactly the same... by the way I didn't catch your name."

"Sorry, it's Kevin Stokes." Mike did a double take. Could there be a connection? He looked again at his watch, he had to go. Any questions would have to wait.

"Look, you have my number. I'll be away for about ten days. Give me a ring around then and we'll meet up and have a chat. In the meantime, I'm afraid I have to go or I'm going to miss my flight!" Mike said a hurried goodbye and rushed over to the reception desk. He had already arranged for his car to be left in their secure covered car park, organising to stay the night of his return, he asked if they would be kind enough to have someone bring the hotel transport to the front entrance to take him to the airport and raced upstairs to get his holdall.

It was fortunate that Mike had made arrangements, if he had taken his own car, by the time he had parked it, he would never have made the check in. As it was, he made it with only minutes to spare. He was the last person to board. He settled himself into his club class seat and thought it was nice to remember being on the plane, which was more than he did of his last sojourn to Spain. He smiled to himself thinking that he would this time have a look around properly and see some of the sights.

He ordered a small beer when the stewardess came, sat back and opened the magazine he had bought earlier. He turned the pages skimming over the contents when suddenly his eye caught a face he recognised. It was the American that had been talking to him the previous evening, he started to read the article...

Roy Winston is one of the biggest names in Holly-wood, asked what his next project would be he answered he had plans to make a movie that would not only rival Seabiscuit but would outshine it.

"*Seabiscuit*," he said, "was an amazing film which really didn't get the credit it deserved. My film will be something that, like *Seabiscuit*, we can all relate to but with a difference." Asked what the title of the film would be and its subject he replied. "It's going to be called *Storm Brewing*... the subject, well you'll see soon enough. Let's just say when I do announce it officially you'll see a firework display like you've never seen before!"

Mike read on, the article telling of the countless films that Roy Winston had backed and had made fortunes with at the box office. "Well, I'm damned." Mike unwittingly said out loud. "You never know who you're talking too!" Everybody in club must have heard him and Mike nearly had a heart attack when he heard his name screamed joyfully as Becky came running down the aisle and leapt onto his lap. Becky went straight into verbal mode and asked Mike about twenty questions before she took a breath, or he managed to get his. He didn't bother to answer any, but instead asked Becky, as she finally paused for breath, his own question. "What on earth are you doing here?"

"Mummy and I are going away to Spain for a few days. Isn't it exciting! We can do things together now... that would be fantastic!"

"Becky! What do you think you're playing at? Get back to your seat straight away.... No arguments. straight away!" Kate's voice held an icy edge but even so Mike's heart missed a beat as he looked at her face.

"Please Kate, she's not hurting."

"Since when have you had parental responsibility for my daughter? You train our horses nothing else!"

Mike couldn't have been more hurt if Kate had thrust a dagger into him. Becky looked shocked and ran back to her seat crying. "Now look what you've done!" Kate spat at Mike, her face as cold and hard as steel. She turned and walked back to her own seat leaving Mike feeling like a crumpled wreck.

The plane landed and Mike watched as Kate dragged Becky behind her, carefully avoiding any contact with Mike at all. Becky however was not to be totally thwarted and as they stood waiting for their luggage she mouthed at Mike the name of the hotel they were staying at, pulling faces at the same time making Mike laugh. Kate snatched at her hand nearly pulling her from her feet as she realised what she was doing. Becky managed to mime *see you on the beach* before her mother grabbed their luggage and quickly exited the airport building.

Mike waved as Becky turned to wave goodbye, herself miming back himself, *ten o'clock tomorrow*. Kate's ice-cold reaction to him had really taken the enjoyment off the start of his break. He had come away to try to come to terms with the way he felt about her and here he was facing her in person in a way he would never in a million years have thought she would be, somewhere a niggle started at the back of his head. Becky was his saving grace, her happy little face and chirpy way brought him a warm feeling. It made him wonder what it must be like to have a child, 'that little girl' he thought, is a gift from heaven.

Mike couldn't believe it when he went down to lunch. As he entered the dining room the first person he set eyes on was Becky standing at the grill bar holding a plate that contained a steak almost as big as her. "Do you really think you're going to manage to eat all that… and save room for pudding, remember!?" Mike said to the back off Becky's head.

"Ooh! Mike!" she squealed with delight. "Are you staying here as well?" and when Mike confirmed that he was, rather than the villa, went straight into the 'Becky jig'. It didn't last long as Kate suddenly appeared back from the dining area, obviously concerned at what was taking Becky so long. "Why is it that whenever I turn around or wherever I go, you seem to materialise? Kate sneered at Mike. Mike had just about reached the end of his tether where Kate's attitude towards him was concerned, he was just about to fly into a tirade at Kate when he looked into those big blue eyes. All the tension went out of him and he found himself saying "I guess you're just lucky!" albeit with a sarcastic edge.

Becky giggled and blew Mike a kiss before walking towards their table. Kate stood stony faced for a moment, then couldn't help but smile herself for a second. Regaining her refrigerator repose, she snapped at Mike "You're intolerable!" and flounced off to where Becky sat.

'In for a penny, in for a pound' thought Mike as he hurriedly grabbed himself a large steak, fries, a side salad and moved across the dining room past several empty tables to where Kate and Becky sat. He smiled cheekily at both Kate and Becky. "Is this seat taken…. would you mind if I joined you?"

Kate didn't even look up at him. "Do we have a choice?" she asked.

"Everyone has the choice!" Mike replied rather pointedly. "I could go and sit somewhere else, but it does seem rather churlish when we know each other, and it will give me a chance to bring Becky up to date on her horses, you could treat it as an employee bringing the bosses up to date… we don't seem to have seen much of you lately!"

Mike almost enjoyed the fact that Kate had been cornered. It wasn't that he relished her being uncomfortable, but he did enjoy getting his own back just a tiny bit. He sat down and started eating, totally ignored by Kate. Becky rattled on about everything and everyone, questioned Mike regarding the horses, the yard, Anita and the others, Mike answering her between mouthfuls. There was not so much as a glance or a word from Kate until Mike asked what they were doing there. Becky began to answer, with absolute honesty and innocence, as only children do, she had managed 'Mummy and Daddy had a massive argument. They don't know I heard them'. Before Kate interceded, stopping Becky in mid-sentence. "Becky that's enough!" she snapped, then turning to Mike her voice as cold as ice. "What gives you the right to ask questions of us? We are none of your business." Her voice lowered a menacing quality on her face. "I told you I want nothing to do with you. Stay away from me and my daughter." She grabbed Becky's hand and dragged her from the table, turning about two steps away. "And I'll be arranging to move Becky's horses as soon as I return."

Mike was furious, he couldn't understand why Kate was being so horrible and as he saw tears in Becky's eyes welling as Kate proclaimed the horses would be moved, he could hold back no longer. He was about fifteen paces behind Kate and followed her towards the reception. She entered an empty lift and before having chance to stop him, Mike ran in behind them. The doors closed. Becky stood wide mouthed as Mike threw a verbal tirade at Kate. "Now you look here you spoilt little mare! Just because you want an excuse to attack someone to relieve your own guilt doesn't mean you have an absolute right to do so. You're always telling this little girl about manners. Well it's a shame you don't practice what you preach! Now if you have a problem that's genuine, fine, but being self-serving is not going to do anyone any good including yourself... now I suggest that you find someone to watch over little one this evening so that you and I can talk this over like two grownups..." Kate had not said a word.

"Right I will meet you in reception at eight-thirty!" the bell sounded on the lift and the doors opened, both Kate and Mike got out.

"Amazing!" said Mike to himself. "I travel all the way to Spain in an attempt to come to terms over her and not only is she in the same country, in the same hotel, but she's on the same bloody floor!" Mike strode off towards his room. Kate watched his back and Becky watched her mum, she saw how her mums face softened when Mike wasn't watching her. "Why are you so cross with Mike mummy?" Kate shrugged pulling a resigned face.

"Do you know sweetheart I'm not really sure of that myself!"

CHAPTER THREE

For such a huge man Nick could move exceptionally quietly. The smartly dressed man that was standing in front of Rocket's box didn't realise Nick was even there until a massive hand gripped the back of his neck and he was lifted with ease so that his feet dangled uselessly about two feet from the ground.

There was no subtlety in Nick's demand to know what he was doing there but there was on the other hand no way the lifted man could answer; Nick's hand was so big it encircled his neck and had cut off his air supply.

"Nick, it's okay, put him down!" John Cullen's voice rang down the passageway. Nick looked at John Cullen, then at Seamus who were now hurrying toward him and without speaking released his grip on the lifted man's neck. He crumpled to the ground gasping and coughing. John and Seamus were both apologising to the man profusely as Nick looked on totally bewildered. The man slowly rose to his feet aided by John and Seamus. "Jeez! He's one helluva strong fella! I gotta have him!" Nick pulled his shoulders back which only served to make him look even bigger and more ominous. "I work for the guvnor I ain't goin' to work for no one else not for nuffink… anyway." Nick said puffing his chest out. "My Vi loves it 'ere an' loves Mike so I ain't goin' no where's!"

"It's alright Nick." Seamus reassured him. "That's not quite what the gentlemen meant!"

Nick looked even more suspicious. "I ain't fightin' no more!" he stated emphatically.

"it's alright Nick… he didn't mean that either. It really isn't anything to worry about, I'll explain it all later. Now you go make sure Vi isn't over doing things and get yourself some lunch…. I'll make sure the boys are okay!" Seamus added and Nick looking at the stranger with suspicion slowly moved out of the stable block looking over his shoulder as he did and then made his way to the house.

"Where the hell did he come from? Christ I've got ears like a bat, but I didn't even hear him, he's gotta be one of the biggest fellas I've ever seen. I can't believe he held me in the air like that, just like I was a feather!"

Seamus laughed, "It's a long, long story! That's our Nick he's a bit impressive, isn't he? You wouldn't want to be trying to do anything to them two fellas!" he pointed a finger at Rocket and Storm. "Not even an insult, and God only knows what he'd do if you ever did anything against Mike. Mary mother of Jesus, I shudder to think. It'd be better to be trampled by a herd of wild elephants! If you think Nicks forbidding, wait 'til you meet Vi!" The now grounded man gulped! John was laughing uncontrollably, tears running down his face, Seamus had gone straight into Irish mode, broad accent, his tale slipping easily from the tongue.

"Seamus," he said gaining control of his laughter. "You do exaggerate. Don't look so worried Roy, Nick's actually a real pussycat. He's as gentle as a baby when you get to know him!"

"I think," the man said rubbing his neck. "I'll air on the side of caution in that matter. Seamus from my perspective makes much more sense!" But he too was now smiling.

John and Seamus, with Roy following, entered Mike's kitchen where Vi was busying herself laying the table with a prestigious display of her culinary skills. She placed one of her now infamous chocolate cakes in the centre of the table, which already seemed to be groaning under the strain of her baking prowess. "Don't you go telling young Michael that I've been baking chocolate cake when he's not here or he'll have a fit. One can't get this sort of thing when on holiday you know!" She said in her best voice. Nick was standing in the corner of the kitchen head down looking like a scolded schoolboy.

"Haven't you something to say to the nice gentleman?" she asked looking towards him.

"Sorry, I 'ope I didn't 'urt yuh! I fought you was after me boy's."

Roy grinned at Nick. "No harm done... well nothing permanent anyway! Though I hope we never have to go through an action reply. You've got to be one of the strongest men I've ever met!" He stuck his hand out and Nick shook it warmly. "Jeez! I'd like some knuckles left!" Roy winced, looking at the food on the table he added in the direction of John and Seamus. "No wonder this fellas so big, it would take an army to eat this lot, which." he supplemented in Vi's direction, "looks delicious!"

"You gentlemen sit down, and I'll make you some tea." She looked towards Nick. "You'd better sit down as well, you big lummox... If that's okay with Mr. John and Seamus?" Nick grinned not waiting for an answer from the two men and tucked straight into a slice of cake that nearly covered the plate.

"Nicholas!" Vi protested. "Where?" as Nick looked suitably rebuked, then, "are your manners, you should offer the gentlemen first." John and Seamus burst out laughing when Vi's back was turned as Nick pulled a face and grinned. "And you can stop pulling faces too!" she said without even turning around. "Men! I ask you!" and she carried on with her tea making.

"Nick." Said John "What you are about to hear you are not under any circumstances to discuss with or tell anybody... okay?"

Nick almost looked offended. "You knows me better than that Mr. Cullen. I don't tell no one nufink, especially when it's to do wif Mike or the yard. Gawd they could stick 'ot pins in me eyes an' I wouldn't say one word! As long as it ain't nufink that would 'urt the guvnor… That would be different." He said pulling back his shoulders and puffing his chest, which would be sufficient for anyone to realise that no one was going to do anything that would hurt Mike.

"Mike doesn't know anything about this meeting…. We thought it best to keep it under our hats for the time being. There are two reasons really. This first is that unless Mike has something like this landed on him without too much warning, he has a tendency to go modest, and secondly we thought it might be a nice surprise for him, take his mind off other things for a while!" Nick nodded understandingly.

Roy Winston cleared his throat. "Well gentleman as you know I believe there is the potential for a blockbuster movie. Your horse has caused one heckuva stir over the last couple of years. I did an interview for a magazine a couple of months ago and in truth I thought I'd said too much! Thought I'd let the cat right out of the bag, or the horse out of the stable in this case! Anyway, *Seabiscuit* was an amazing film and as I said in the article I still don't think it gained half the credit it deserved, but Rocket, now he's got the advantage because people still know him, possibly they can, if they were lucky enough touch him. With *Seabiscuit* they were working with memories, history… so though it made a fantastic film, most people didn't have a clue who or what it was about. I shouldn't think that there is anyone that doesn't know who The Rocket is! Jeez if you went to the outer Himalayas and asked some hundred-year-old Buddhist monk who Rocket was I bet he'd tell you every race he's run! As I see it the biggest problem is going to be getting Mike to go along with the idea of making a film about him and the horse!"

Both John and Seamus smiled. Roy was quite right, Mike would be their biggest problem, but they hoped that with both of them in support of the idea Mike just might be persuaded to at least assist. They had already suggested that if Mike could be persuaded Rocket might even be the star of the film himself. There was so much detail to discuss that it was decided that they would have a wander around the yard and the stud so that Roy could evaluate whether he thought it would be suitable for filming. John pointed out that they had just bought the next-door farm as well and had formed a partnership on Mike's old satellite yard. "It's early days yet but we were thinking about going for development."

"Wow, if you get permission to build houses here... and they're nice, you can put me down for one. Hell, I could save myself a fortune in hotel bills and it's always nice to have your own things around you!" Roy spoke enthusiastically as if owning a piece of something in the English countryside was all he had ever wished. It amused John the man was probably wealthy enough to buy England let alone a house just to save on hotel bills. "We're not intending to develop it for housing Roy. We were intending... if it comes off to build a theme park based on The Rocket and horseracing. We've quite a few ideas planned already if we gain the correct planning permission." John and Seamus both saw the reaction in Roy's eyes, like someone had just given him a diamond as big as a bucket!

Mike opened the mini bar and moved the small bottles around until he found a bottle of whiskey, taking one of the glasses from the top of the cabinet that contained the refrigerated bar, he emptied the bottle into it, topping it up with a can of dry ginger ale. He walked out of the French windows and on to the balcony breathing in the warm Spanish air, his afternoon wander around the town had relaxed him and he had bought a few interesting little nik naks to take back as gifts. Looking down at the glittering water of the swimming pool he heard a splash accompanied by a giggle. "Little toad! You just wait!" the voice was light hearted and the reply he recognised straight away as Becky. "You've got to catch me first!" and there was another splash as Becky curled in a ball and dive bombed her mum. There was a lot of spluttering interfaced with giggling. Mike watched for a few minutes as Kate and Becky chased each other through the water, admiring Kate's body as she glided through the water before walking back into his room feeling a twinge of guilt for looking as the two of them interacting. He finished his drink and laid himself on the bed deciding to doze for an hour before readying himself for his dinner date with Kate wondering just what he was going to say as slowly he drifted into a half sleep. The voice in his head sounded, "I'm going to be a film star!" He wasn't sure if it was for real or whether his sleepy imagination. He looked at his watch it was seven-thirty, time for him to have a shower and get ready. He remembered feeling like this once before - it was the time just before he had answered the phone to John Cullen and he had walked across the yard feeling like he was walking towards the gallows. Then the outcome was positive.... This time he wasn't so sure it would be! He stood in the shower, the warm water falling against his skin and started to feel a little better about the whole situation. At least she hadn't refused his dinner demand but then on the other hand he hadn't really given her the opportunity. He stepped from the shower, dried himself and pulled on a pair of cream trousers and a light pale blue shirt. He had bought a pair of deck shoes and he plumbed for these, looking in the mirror he was quietly pleased with the result, smart but casual, expensive but simple look. "You'll do!" he said aloud and made his way down to the reception.

It was eight forty-five before Kate appeared and when she did it took every ounce of breath from Mike's body. She wore a figure hugging La Perla dress in black with lace sides. She looked absolutely incredible. You could hear the intake of breath from each male she passed as they stared in her direction with obvious desire. The dress was not particularly revealing but was unbelievably sexy, tantalising with a show of naked flesh through the lace that formed both sides of the dress. Mike stood and greeted Kate but did not even attempt to lean forward as one would normally and kiss her cheek. Kate's eyes were stony and in her return greeting made it perfectly clear that she did not relish sitting down to dinner with Mike. He took the bull by the horns. "Okay I suggest we get a drink... if you've no objection to my buying you a drink." Mike rarely succumbed to sarcasm, but Kate's attitude had goaded him to such a degree that he was finding it hard to control his temper. At least his sarcasm gave him a small outlet. "Then perhaps," he continued, "we could sit down and talk like two adults instead of behaving like children."

"You can do what you like.... Burn in hell for all I care.... But if you so much as look at me wrong I'll call the police! Just hurry up and say what you have to say, and no you can't buy me a drink! I already have one." She held up the glass that was in her hand, though Mike did not have a clue what it held but whatever it was had certainly done its job by the look of the glow that was creeping over Kate's face.

"Why are you being so destructive?" Kate's eyes hardened even more, her mouth curled into a cruel smile, Mike almost stepped back it took him so much by surprise, it was like looking at a different person, not the beautiful, gentle, caring Kate he had grown to know. There was a cruel malevolence in Kate's posture, like a cat playing with a mouse. "Whatever, if that's what you think, what I do has nothing whatsoever to do with you and just remember neither does my daughter."

"Now hang on Kate whatever problem you feel you have with me shouldn't be taken out on the little one. I've become really fond of Becky and I think she has of me, I think it would be very unfair if you stopped us having a friendship."

"How dare you tell me how to treat or bring up my daughter... you asshole! Fuck you!" Kate was wide eyed with rage, the alcohol stoking the fire. Before Mike could stop himself, the words were out of his mouth, his temper taking control.

"You already have in more ways than one!" he thought for a moment Kate was going to strike out at him her teeth clenched as did her hands, instead she seemed to steady herself and holding herself upright said. "Yes, I did," she said haughtily, "and I have to tell you it wasn't very memorable!" The cruel smile returned momentarily before she turned and walked away, taking a stool at the bar to order another drink. Mike nearly rose to his feet and followed her as four young chaps who had watched Kate since she had entered the reception area immediately rose and sat next to her at the bar. His jaw muscles spasmed and his fist clenched so tightly that he actually drew blood on his palms as his nails dug into the flesh. Kate turned, looked at him the cruel smile back then laughed tossing her hair flirtatiously as she put an arm around the waist on the young man closest to her. Mike felt as though the very life blood had just flowed out of him, he rose and walked out of the hotel.

Mike walked along the deserted beach wondering how the hell he had allowed himself to fall for Kate in such a big way, knowing it was an impossible situation before it even started. He knew that falling in love with someone wasn't a matter of choice, it wasn't something that you went out one morning specifically to do. You didn't say to yourself. 'ah ha today I shall go out and fall in love', it just happened. It just seemed at that moment as he stared up at the stars listening to the gentle lap of the waves on the shore it was different for everyone and at that precise second it was something that he wished had passed him by altogether. Mike had no desire for plain sex, sex is a hollow thrill without emotion. To reach the real highs you need that heart stopping feeling when you're close to the person you feel true affection for. Mike rose somewhat wearily from where he had sat to ponder life, or rather the mystery that surrounded his life, and started back towards the hotel. It was with heavy heart that he walked through to the bar ordered himself a drink sitting in the corner before hearing Kate's laughter. He looked over in the direction of the laughter and his heart plummeted to his boots. Kate was sitting at the other end of the bar, he was uncertain if she was aware he had entered the bar but whether she did or didn't, Mike couldn't believe it. It just wasn't the Kate he knew, she moved onto the lap of the chap whose waist she had put an arm around her skirt riding high up her legs. She wriggled around seductively as the young chap's hand stroked her thigh. Mike could bear no more and left the bar for his room. He sat on the balcony unable to sleep surrounded by the small empty bottles from the mini bar he consumed without feeling any effect. He heard voices and looking over the balcony saw two figures at the side of the pool. It was Kate and the young man. Kate peeled her dress off and as the young chap reached for her dived into the pool. Mike walked into his room, closed the doors and started to pack his bag. It was a haggard looking Mike that went down to breakfast that morning and within seconds of him seating himself at a table, Becky plonked herself down opposite him, her huge smile was, even in Mike's current state, like the sun coming out on a cloudy day. "Wow! You look tired! You and mummy must have talked all through the night... did you make friends again... you must have or you wouldn't have stayed talking for so long!" Mike felt awful, he didn't have the heart to tell Becky that he hadn't been with her mother, he had been alone, she was so full of hope that everything was okay again. In desperation he lied. "Mummy and I talked for ages!" he said, "but I'm afraid it wasn't much good. Mummy's still really cross with me. That's us grownups for you! We get cross with each other over the silliest of things, then we forget why we are still cross, then it gets harder to put things right. That's grownups for you, we really are very silly you know!" Mike tried to make it sound as amusing as he possibly could. "Anyway, where is your mum?" he was looking around waiting for the verbal onslaught from Kate for having her daughter sitting at the same table. Becky was looking thoroughly disappointed. "She hasn't woken up yet.... she didn't come to bed until five o'clock... she thought I was asleep, but I wasn't... anyway you know."

"Of course," Mike replied even though his throat had formed a lump, he tried to regain his composure.

"Look, what say we grab a quick breakfast and go for a swim? I wouldn't tell mummy I'm going to be there though." Becky seemed quite okay with Mike's explanation and they finished breakfast and went up to their rooms to change into swimming costumes.

Becky told Mike that her mum was still fast asleep and so rather than wake her, she had changed and come straight down to the pool. Just for a while Mike forgot his heartbreak as Becky's infectious laugh and smiling face took him back to being a child himself. He couldn't remember when he had enjoyed himself more. Mike made a complete fool of himself and it wasn't very long before several other grownups with children joined in. Becky became Vengeful Vera the scourge of the seven seas and the dozen or so children that had joined them became her pirates. Mike and the half dozen grownups were the 'soldiers' that had to try and capture Becky and her pirates and for an hour everybody had an absolute whale of a time. Mike bought Becky an ice cream when the kids had totally exhausted the adults and they had one by one given in. "Sweetheart," Mike turned towards Becky, her ice cream covered face looking back at him with affection. "I'm going to have to leave today," he saw tears welling in the bright little eyes that stared at him.

"Ohh, please don't go. I know you and mummy will make friends again. Please don't leave yet, we have such fun." It was all Mike could do to stem a tear himself. He just couldn't do it, looking at this child he had to find a way around the problem.

"Okay. Here's what I'll do... I have to go to a meeting, it's very important, about the horses." He lied.

"But I promise you I'll come back tomorrow and we'll have another go at sorting things out!" Becky cheered up straight away.

When Mike left the hotel, he didn't have a clue where he was going to go for the next 24 hours or so. He decided he would try to catch a flight to Aero Puerto de la Seu and from there get a taxi to take him into Andorra and check on the account. He telephoned John to tell him of his intentions and after assuring John several times that he was fine, despite sounding down in the mouth as John put it, told the taxi to take him to the nearest airport. It wasn't long before Mike found himself being flown along in a chartered helicopter, something he had never experienced before and although it was strange in comparison to flying in a fixed wing, he enjoyed the feeling of freedom it gave. He found it difficult to come to terms with the fact that a journey that would by any other mode of transport take hours was reduced to minutes. He laughed to himself as he thought 'time flies when you're travelling by air'. After they had landed, Mike made arrangements to be collected the following afternoon, paid for his charter and found his way through the airport and into a taxi. The journey by road would take as long as the journey in the air, so Mike also had the forethought to take the mobile number of the pilot just in case he managed to find somewhere he could be 'picked up' from in Andorra itself. His mobile rang and it was John. He didn't even wait for Mike to say hello. "Are you sure you're okay?" Mike laughed, it was a great feeling to know that you have friends, especially when things are running awry.

"Honestly I'm fine...... no really I'm fine.... Seamus needn't worry any more than you, I'm fine. I hope you two aren't going to phone me every five minutes to see if I'm okay. I'm meant to be on holiday!" Mike could hear the relief in John's voice knowing that his friend was okay.

"Mike are you in Andorra yet? Good, look as soon as you told me that you were going, Seamus and I faxed instructions to Sue Parker arranging for the availability of the two million. She said she would either give you a banker's draft or preferably talk you into opening a personal account. Anyway, that's your decision. Look, have a great time and forget all your personal problems. Come back refreshed, we've a lot to bring you up to speed on when you get back."

"What are you two reprobates planning now?" Mike asked jovially.

"Nothing much.... I'll tell you all about it the moment you're home. Take care and have fun!" Mike bade farewell to John and realised the taxi was pulling up outside the entrance of the bank. He paid the driver and made his way through the front door and walked up to the enquiries desk. The young man who greeted Mike picked up his phone and spoke to the manager, after a minute or so Sue Parker came out into the reception, shook Mike's hand, greeted him warmly and invited him into her office. Mike had to admit she was bloody good at her job having obviously researched him and his partners business very well. She spoke in very knowledgeable terms of the horses, which Mike trained and owned, especially Rocket. Mike had already decided what he was going to do with the money John and Seamus were transferring to him. He told Sue his intentions and she immediately put everything as he requested. One and a half million into a personal account and half a million that was to be divided into two halves, one going to the rehabilitation of racehorses and the other half to riding for the disabled. Feeling as though he had achieved something, he excused himself and left Sue Parker to deal with his requests, safe in the knowledge that she would handle everything both efficiently and discretely. Mike decided he would have a look around and wandered around the streets until he found a pleasant looking café where he sat and enjoyed a simple but very pleasant lunch. His mind was working overtime as he ate, even if the subject was one that he tried hard to obliterate from his thoughts. Kate! He was, he decided, so much in love with her that he didn't know where to go. He also decided that his love was totally fruitless, he even managed a smile as he thought it was like sowing grass seed on concrete, the chances of it germinating were little to none. "Oh well." He said aloud causing the other people to look round in his direction sharply. Mike nodded towards his unexpected audience as if in apology. His thoughts became his own again. Mike was an impulsive, often doing something without ever thinking it through and always aiming his basically generous nature towards others. He flipped open his mobile phone and dialled the number of his local garage. He asked to speak to Simon who ran the sales and who he had bought his car from. "Hi Simon, it's Mike Willett…. fine thank you…. good…. look I have a favour to ask. I want an F-type and I want it in metallic purple…. wait a minute, I haven't finished yet! I need it ready for delivery in a fortnight and it has to be in pristine condition… I know, but you would be doing me a real favour if you could." It went silent for a moment then Simons voice came back. "Alright, I'll see what I can do…. I'm not making any firm promises mind you and if I do manage you'll have to give the garage a mention when your next in the paper."

"That's great, I'll let you know where it has to be delivered in the next few days and if you ring me and let me know how much, I'll wire you the money." Mike pressed the red button on his mobile and sat back looking half satisfied and half concerned with what he had just done. Finishing his coffee, he looked at his watch and decided it was time to make a move. He thought about ringing the pilot but determined it would be more leisurely to be driven back to Aero Puerto de la Seu if he could persuade the taxi driver to keep his speed under a hundred miles an hour! After showing the driver a fifty euro note, which would be a bonus if he adhered to Mike's appeal, the journey back to the airport over the mountain pass was quite enjoyable, giving Mike time to take in the spectacular scenery rather than worry whether there was a vehicle approaching at the same breakneck speed as they traversed the narrow road and sharp bends. He reached the airport in a relaxed and happy state, alighting on to the helicopter for the rapid flight back to his hotel. Becky was ecstatic as he walked into the dining room to have his evening meal. She rushed over and hit him with her normal verbal onslaught ending with. " …. I thought you weren't coming back until tomorrow. It's great, there's a disco tonight and mummy's going to take me, you can come too… we'll have great fun." She did a little twirl revolving so that she ended up facing Mike again. "We can rock the night away kiddo!" she said, and Mike felt such joy at this tiny ball of enthusiasm that he burst out laughing before agreeing to go to the 'disco'. Kate stayed at her table not even acknowledging Mike and though he brimmed with pleasure at Becky, his heart felt heavy at Kate's snub.

Mike walked into the 'ballroom', which he had to admit to himself was quite impressive to the bright flashing lights and sound of the Black-Eyed Peas, wearing his trademark cowboy boots, blue jeans and a sleeveless tee shirt, several women turned their heads as he walked by only to pretend they were looking at something else when their boyfriend or husband scowled at them. The same was true in reverse the moment Kate stepped up onto the dance floor with Becky both being unaware of Mike's arrival. Kate looked like some higher being had taken all the film stars there had ever been and mixed them altogether, not only was she breathtakingly beautiful but she just oozed panache. The dress she wore was gathered in what almost looked like a knot about six inches above her knee, clinging tightly to her slender body everywhere else. If Mike had made any progress at building a wall of defence, it had just had an atom bomb placed right underneath it and it had gone off with an enormous bang. He stood mesmerised, as did every other man in the room as Kate sensuously swayed her hips to the music which now played, then as the tempo of the music quickened she became almost wild, though every movement remained controlled, by the time the record had ended she was the only one on the dance floor apart from Becky and there was not a man in the place that wasn't going to get a real verbal battering when they finally got back to their room. Mike rose and was made to walk over to where Becky and Kate now stood, surrounded by an expectant male audience all waiting for the next record to start. He had almost reached them when a young man walked arrogantly from the crowd and put his arm around Kate's waist pulling her close and kissing her. Becky was furious and pushed the man away. Kate, though surprised, didn't react immediately, it was the young chap Mike had seen with Kate at the pool. The young man pushed Becky away and she fell, it didn't appear that he was being aggressive, just boisterous, but Kate fell on him like a tigress, slapping his face with such force that it silenced the chatter in the room, he returned the slap instinctively, it seemed, and Kate staggered back. Mike was there before anybody else could intervene, unfortunately his anger at seeing the man that had been with his dream the night before rose from the ashes and he cracked his fist into the man's face. The man staggered back falling to his knees and Mike side kicked him in the chest and as the man fell backwards dropped onto his ribs with his knees. It was like watching a horror movie as Mike slammed his fist time and time again into the unconscious face of the young man. It took five fairly hefty onlookers to finally pull Mike off and subdue him by which time the police and an ambulance had arrived. Mike was carted off to the local police station and the hapless young man was carried off to the local hospital to have several stitches implanted, his bruises looked at and a couple of cracked ribs wrapped in bandages.

Mike sat in the cell subdued and angry, though this time at himself for losing control. His holiday had turned into a disaster. He heard Kate's voice and a very insistent tone of a shorter person. What Mike assumed was the equivalent of an English sergeant came to the cell door and unlocked it gesturing him to come with him. Kate stood at the front desk of the police station, one side of her face red from the slap she had received and a worried looking Becky stood by her side. "I've spoken to the officer and explained what happened and he is quite prepared to accept you were doing what any gentleman would do… even if you did it with rather too much force! Anyway, you are free to go but he says if you misbehave in any way whilst you are in his town he will put you in a cell and forget you are there." She said something to the police officer in Spanish, he replied, and she told Mike to follow her as she had a cab waiting outside ready to take them back to the hotel. Becky didn't say a word until they were safely in the cab and on their way to the hotel. When she had been an onlooker to the battering that Mike had given out, it had frightened her, now it seemed it had become something akin to a movie. Even her mother could not quiet her as she relived the dance hall scene, probably with a little artistic licence to say the least. "Wow! Then you spun in the air and kicked like a horse and he fell to the ground……." Mike rose and made as though he was listening but was not, he felt ashamed that he had resorted so easily to violence in front of this young girl, but it would seem that the legend that was Mike had grown in her estimation. After a few minutes Becky had finished her rhetoric and Kate spoke. "I'm not saying that what you did wasn't way over the top but thank you for protecting my daughter…. And me." Mike beamed, he would have killed for such meagre praise. They arrived back at the hotel to find Becky's opinion of Mike was not unfounded as it seemed everybody wanted to either buy him a drink or talk him through his earlier event. He couldn't believe it when a pretty young Spanish girl approached him and asked if he would give an interview to her paper. It seemed Mikes incognito had escaped and he was back to being the volatile trainer of the famous Rocket. Things from then became manic even though all Mike wished was to sneak away, he could find no opportunity to do so. Becky, however, revelled in the attention she was receiving now that she had also been recognised as the leader of the almost as famous as Rocket 'Becky's army' albeit without the fancy dress. Becky spoke in her poshest voice to a rapt the audience that surrounded her. "Of course." She said, "I wouldn't allow anyone else to train my horses and as we are all good friends it was lovely when Mike came on holiday to Spain and we all met up. He's very good fun you know and he can talk to horses. I've seen him do it loads of times. He can teach them tricks if he wants to and they do anything he asks. Of course, he's very shy about that sort of thing when he's talking to people, which I think is silly because if he would say more he'd be even more famous than he is now. Mummy's not very happy with Mike at the moment… I don't know why but I think it has something to do with the photographs they were in… I don't think daddy is very happy… though I think mummy looks very beautiful even if she hasn't got any clothes on." Kate dived in and removed her daughter before she could say any more. The Spanish reporter shouted to Kate. "Meesus Stokes is eet true that you have fallen out with your husband over your friendship with Meester Weelitt? Are you and Meester Weelitt seeing each other? Are you lovers?"

"No, I am not! No, we are not!" Kate shouted back at the reporter as she hurried to reach the lift and make her way to the safety of her bedroom. Mike quickly followed her trying to make a clear passage through a growing crowd of questioners. They reached the lift and both let out a sigh of relief as the doors closed.

Kate turned to Mike though there was no anger in her voice or her face. "Why is it that my life has turned upside down since

I met you?" her voice was close to plaintive. Mike's flippancy came out.

"My natural charm just brings out the worst in people."

"You're impossible!" she retorted, this time it was her turn to be the little girl lost and she burst into tears muttering something under her breath like 'what am I going to do.' Mike enfolded her in his arms and held her tight trying to console her, he looked down at Becky who was smiling broadly and put a thumbs up.

CHAPTER FOUR

Mike's mobile woke him at seven-thirty the following morning. It was John. "What the hell have you been up to now?" he didn't wait for a reply. "I've had the Jockey Club, television, *Racing Post*, those bloody awful parasites at the Racegoer and uncle Tom Cobbly on the phone. All hells broken loose here, the yards under siege. They're saying that you've been in some sort of serious fight, been arrested and that Kate is there with you and has told the papers in Spain that you're lovers! More to the point if you have been in a fight are you alright? Apparently, its front-page news in all the tabloids!"

"Oh fuck! Kate's going to be bloody furious! That's not what she said at all."

"Are you okay? What's this about a fight? Is Kate there then?"

"John give me an hour to get showered dressed and get some breakfast. I'll have woken up then and have had a chance to see the papers myself. I'll ring you back.... And thanks, I'm fine so don't worry."

"Alright, I'll speak to you in an hour, it'll give me a chance to go to the newsagents and get copies to see what they're saying. Bye." The phone went dead. With a certain feeling of Deja Vous, Mike rose from his bed, showered, dressed and went down to breakfast. The hotel appeared to be surrounded with journalists. Mike had a feeling of being trapped and the warm lazy days of his break in Spain started to lose its allure and he found himself wishing for the security of his home.

John couldn't get out of his drive there were so many cars, vans, cameras and people at the end of it. He went back to the house and called the yard. It was quite amazing how room was made as the towering figure of Nick standing in the back of the pickup driven by Seamus, made a now unhindered entrance to the stud. Nick offered to 'move 'em on a bit' but though the idea was sorely tempting it was decided that Nick be kept as a last resort and John called the local police, who it turned out were only too willing to help. Within half an hour the lane was clear again and two policemen were sitting at the kitchen table enjoying bacon and eggs. One of them spoke up between mouthfuls. "He's a bit of a lad that Mike, isn't he? You would think he'd learn, keep his temper in check a bit. Might save himself all sorts of bother!"

Nick jumped to his boss's defence. "'e's a good man the Guvnor, an don't you let me 'ear no one say no different or they'll be speakin' to me!"

"It's okay I didn't mean any offence." The officer said quickly looking at the huge bulk of Nick now standing at the table. "But he does have a bit of a temper, you have to agree. I'm only saying he would be better to think before he goes off on one!" John interceded putting a hand on Nick's shoulder and gently putting pressure so that he was reassured, and sat back down much to the relief of the two policemen. "It's okay Nick, nothing bad was meant." And Nick smiled at the policeman. "But the officer is right, Mike really has got to find a way of controlling his temper, it gets him in to so much hot water. Anyway, I think for the moment we had better wait until Mike rings us and we find out the truth rather than speculating on the rubbish that's printed in these." He pointed at the papers that were strewn on what space was available on the kitchen table. Alice having not lost the theory that she should prepare to feed the whole of the English

Constabulary, just in case they decided to turn up on mass!

Further conversation and the consumption of the prodigious fare was halted when the telephone rang, John jumped up as though he had been electrocuted uttering a frantic hello down the mouthpiece of the phone. Mikes voice was at the other end. John fired several questions at Mike but was halted as Mike interrupted and recounted the tale of his misdemeanour. John recounting every word to the eager ears of his friends and the police officers that had come to help with their journalistic problem. The conversation was not that long but sufficiently detailed to relieve the worries of all in the room. Nick was the only one that spoke saying he knew the 'Guvnor' would have a good reason for 'beltin' someone and smugly informed the police officers, even though there was no reason too, that the 'Guvnor' was always a gentleman. The irony of this comment after Mike had, according to the papers, very nearly wrecked a hotel; and half of Spain drew a great deal of merriment!

Mike sat at the poolside watching Becky splash around, filling the surrounding air with spray and laughter as she slapped her hands on top of the water in an effort to spray her mother. "You little minx!" Kate said with mock severity and grabbed her daughter pushing her to the side of the pool.

"Why you nearly drowned me!" A comment which only drew more amusement from Becky who squirmed delightedly in Kate's arms. "Come on Mike don't be an old grumpy, come on in it's lovely!" Mike walked over to the side of the pool and bent down to feel the water, he smiled at Becky and not wanting to encroach between mother and daughter found his excuse as lame as it was. "I'll come in later when the waters a bit warmer." Kate reached out and grabbed his arm before he could get himself out of the way. "Don't be such a wuss!" Kate shouted and pulled him headlong into the pool. Mike came up coughing and sputtering, which brought gales of laughter from both Becky and Kate, he reached forward in an effort to grab hold of Kate, but she eluded him by diving under the water. Coming up inches from where Mike stood, she leaned forward and pecked him briefly on the lips. "Friends?" Mike's smile needed no words to reinforce his thoughts.

Dinner that evening seemed like a culinary delight to all three. In truth the food was no different than anything they had eaten before, it was just the atmosphere was so pleasant and relaxed. Conversation was constant and it was with a feeling of absolute euphoria that Mike took Kate on to the dance floor and Kate led her head onto Mike's chest for a slow dance. Mike caught Becky's eye as they were dancing and received a wink and a thumbs up. "Told you you'd make up didn't I." She mouthed smugly. Mike had a dance with Becky, then a dance with both and came off the dance floor ecstatic but exhausted. When they walked upstairs and Mike reached his room, he thanked Kate and Becky for a lovely evening and was rewarded with a kiss from them both. As he closed his door a happy man, Kate and Becky walked the few steps to their own door - he overheard Becky say, "I really like Mike mummy!" and Kate replied, "I know darling, so do I, that's half the problem!" Mike poured himself a drink and went out to the balcony to enjoy the warm Spanish night and to gaze at the stars a smile bigger than a Cheshire cats, Becky pulled her covers up to her chin confused, wondering why liking someone was a problem.

The holiday for Mike came to an end all too quickly and despite the pleadings of Becky, knew he had to get back to the yard and make sure things were okay. He knew they would be under the watchful eye of Seamus and the protective bulk of Nick, but self-reassurance puts the mind at rest. He managed to sooth Becky marginally by saying he had to go back and make sure Sunrise was alright and ready for her next race. He left with the lingering taste of Kate's lipstick and a promise they would come over as soon as they returned in a week. Mike relaxed on the plane, happy in the knowledge that there had been a complete breaking of the ice on the relationship he and Kate had, and that there was, it seemed, now a reason for hope.

He landed at Heathrow and hailed a taxi to the hotel where he had stayed before leaving for Spain and to retrieve his F-Type that was parked there. "Jesus!" the cabby said as they pulled up outside the hotel.

"Must be a rock star or something staying here… look at that lot." Mike felt that all too familiar sinking feeling deep down in his stomach as he recognised some of the reporters that stood outside the hotel. The moment he saw Claudia Jansen of the *Sporting Weekly* he knew why the reporters were there, even worse when he noticed the sleazy figure of the one reporter, he truly despised from the *Racegoer*. He didn't recognise many other of the throng and he assumed they were from the daily tabloids. He paid the cabby, who sat wide mouthed as the herd of reporters, seeing that it was Mike sitting in the cab, surrounded the vehicle trying to open the doors and shouting questions. Mike casually stepped out of the cab, shouted no comment and before any of the reporters realised had sprinted into the hotel. Mike had no delay as he had already left more than enough money to cover his car parking and with the journalists believing he was going to stay at the hotel for at least the night it wasn't too difficult for him to set up a small diversion and make his escape. The porter that had informed the father of the twins helped by putting on his normal clothes, the reporters knowing that he worked there and making as though he was going home. Mike found it quite amusing as the young lad probably made more that day in 'bribes' from the eager journalists than he did working for a month. Mr. Willett, he told them, was staying at the hotel for the night before driving back to his home at mid-day tomorrow. He was tired after the fight and did not feel like facing the crowd, he would though, the lad assured them, be easy to catch up with the following day as he himself would give them the nod when he was leaving. Mike gave it an hour and with the reporters relaxed and unwary he roared by them in his F-Type, leaving behind him the curses and shouts at his trickery from the eager pen holding mob. Mike arrived home in exceptionally good spirits, the journalists having not bothered him as they normally would, his thoughts were of Kate and the last few days of his holiday. Kate's beautiful blue eyes sparkled in his memory, the smell of her perfume, her lithe body as she walked around the edge of the pool laughing at Becky and Mikes' antics. Violet was like a mother hen deciding that he had to put his feet up and be fed, having lost weight according to Violet, Mike had to laugh to himself as she berated 'them foreigners' for not looking after him properly. Mike decided that even though his holiday had turned out to be spectacular it was good to be home. He slept soundly that evening and walked into the yard cheery and alive. The old Mike was back yet again and everyone was ecstatic to have him there. John had come over to see him and even though he was concerned over the innuendos that had been written in the daily rags he only skipped over it telling Mike it was important that he come over to the stud with Seamus to discuss some business. Seamus spent the rest of morning stables whistling happily and avoiding Mike's questions. Even as they drove towards the stud and their meeting with John, all Seamus would do was grin broadly as Mike badgered him as to the reason for the 'important meeting'. As the F-type burbled the curving drive to John's, Mike saw the black limousine that was parked directly in front of the house. "We going somewhere posh or something?" but again, all he received from Seamus was an all-knowing very self-satisfied smile. "You could become very annoying this morning you know!" Mike said slightly exasperated, which only brought forth a merry chuckle from Seamus.

They wandered round to the kitchen door and entered. Sitting at the table was John and a man who Mike immediately felt he recognised but couldn't quite place. The man rose and warmly shook Mike's hand firmly. "Nice to see you again," he said with a southern American drawl. Mike hesitated for a few seconds then his brain clicked. "The hotel? We met in the hotel?"

"I'm impressed... I'm not sure I'd remember anything if I'd have drunk as much Irish as you that night!" It was said with a great deal of humour and everybody joined in the fun.

"Jeez, I'm Irish meself and I can't keep up with me boy here!" Seamus exclaimed.

After they had all settled, John introduced the American. "This Mike, is Roy Winston."

Mike almost feel off his chair. "*The* Roy Winston?... the film director?"

"In the flesh and twice as ugly as my photos!" he said, and Mike liked him from that moment.

"Look, let's not mess around John, and Seamus here told me I would have to approach you with a bit of caution. Not because of your temper mind you," Roy added quickly, "but because you're a stubborn old bugger was I think how Seamus put it! That said, I have to say that I have never heard two men speak so highly of another." Seamus and John looked slightly embarrassed that their compliments had been passed on. "I want to make a film about Rocket, and furthermore John and Seamus have told me about your plans to build a theme park and I'd like a part of that as well! Furthermore." He continued before Mike could interrupt. "I'd like you to play yourself in the film and, of course, the Rocket would play... well the Rocket!"

Seamus couldn't help himself. "Jesus lovey, I'll have to be buyin' you a chiffon scarf so I will!"

Mike didn't know whether to laugh or be angry, he sat silent for several minutes before anyone else spoke. It was Roy who broke the silence. "What d'yuh say. Will yuh give her a try or do I call in some wishy-washy actor that don't know one end of a horse from the other."

Mike smiled then. "You're assuming I've agreed to let you make a film about my boy." The voice in his head rang loud and clear. "You let him make the film, I'll be fantastic!"

"Bighead!" Mike said out loud, then realising, made a quick apology assuring everyone that the comment wasn't aimed at them. Seamus looked at Mike quizzically. "The boy?" he asked and Mike nodded. "Come on now Michael, you have a chance to go down in history... Jeez, you'll be immortal!"

"I've got a funny feeling that this is all because you two want your ugly fizzogs on the silver screen! Alright I'll give it a try if we can agree on the finances, and if we do and I don't like it, then you'll have to get some actor in... okay?" They all smiled in acknowledgement and the discussions started in earnest on what the film was worth and how much it would cost Roy to invest in the planned theme park. The figures that were discussed were so huge Mike thought it was like playing monopoly when you had all the hotels, houses and held all the money. It became obvious that there was going to be the need for some peripheral input. It was decided that Sue Parker from Andorra would be invited to aid in the negotiations along with, if she could be persuaded to agree, Kate. This stunned John and Seamus a little but Mike insisted that he thought her to be judgmentally sound, trustworthy and even more important to be honest in her opinions. So it was agreed that they would try to make a meeting which would include the two 'arbitrators'.

They made the phone calls whilst Roy was there. Sue Parker, as Mike had rightly gathered, was only too pleased to come over when required, her financial brain could almost be heard whirring down the phone. Kate took a lot more persuading, but after being excitedly plagued in the background by a small but very astute young lady who could no doubt already see her name rolling by on the credits, she agreed. A meeting was planned for the following day and it was with an air of great optimism that the kitchen table was evacuated. Mike and Seamus went back to the yard driving sedately in the Jag and as they did Seamus asked Mike. "He spoke to you, didn't he?" Mike tried to look innocent. "Who?"

"You know who I'm talking about... Rocket!"

"Yeh," Mike said a bit casually. "Reckons he'll be fantastic in the film... Can you believe it!"

"Mike!" Seamus said solemnly. "The way you are with horses, if you told me that one could fly I'd believe you.... And don't forget I was there with you and Rocket when you found Storm and if I needed proof that was about as good as it gets." They pulled into the yard to see Geoff leaning casually against the bonnet of his car. "Oh dear! Looks like someone's been reading the papers and has heard you're back!" Mike stepped out of his car and strode purposefully towards Geoff with Seamus hurrying beside him. "Don't you go doing anything stupid now Michael!"

he whispered as they became closer to Geoff.

"Geoff!" Mike greeted. "How are you?"

Geoff looked like a man on the edge but managing to control what little command he had left over his emotions. "I'd like to have a word with you in private," was all he replied and Mike invited him into the house asking Vi to go and see what Nick was doing and to get him to take her into town shopping.

Mike had to admire Geoff's self-control, he was so obviously fuming but kept not only his cool but his manner as well. He knew if the roles had been reversed he would be kicking Geoff around the room at this moment without waiting to discuss the matter and find out the truth. Geoff took a long breath and then spoke. "I like you Mike, can't say that I don't but when I saw this..." he took the magazine that showed the pictures of Kate and himself and threw it on the kitchen table. "I was pretty pissed off too say the least. I didn't react too well and that is why Kate walked out.... But now I'm faced with this!" The newspaper he had also been clutching was thrown beside the magazine. Geoff's voice began to rise slightly. "Every fucking front page in the country very nearly, not only reminding me that my wife has done a nude romp with an employee." Mikes jaw muscles began to knot. "But has just had a holiday in Spain with him and not even bothered to attempt to conceal the fact...." Mike had heard enough.

"Just hold it right there Geoff," Mike growled. "First and foremost, I am not one of your employees and never will be.... Clear? Secondly, I didn't have a nude romp with your wife I supplied a venue for her photo shoot and ended up in one of the photographs, and thirdly I did not go on holiday with your wife. It was pure coincidence, that's all nothing else." Mike stopped, he wanted to say that he had fallen in love with Kate but knew she would never forgive him if he did, he started to feel guilty, he hadn't lied in what he said, but he desperately wanted to blurt the truth out in full. He didn't. Geoff stood for a few seconds without saying anything, just looking at Mike. "I'm not stupid Mike! I can see you've fallen for her... well I believe what you've just told me but I still think there's more to this than meets the eye. If you hear from her, tell her to get in touch, there's a lot to sort out." There was a long pause before Geoff spoke again, then turning to leave he spoke. "By the way, you're welcome to her. You're not the first and don't fool yourself you won't be the last." And he left. Mike wasn't sure how he felt. Guilt for what he'd done, sadness for a man he liked and joyous that the main competition had just, it would seem, left the playing field. Kate was coming to the arranged meeting the following day. What the hell was he going to tell her? He looked at the magazine admiring her photos, her lithe body, her face seemingly alive in the picture as she posed for the camera without inhibition. He put it back on the table and picked up the tabloid to read the front-page story.

There was a picture of him leaving the Spanish police station, Kate and Becky walking beside him looking concerned. The headline was as they normally are - exaggerated and misleading.

MIKE WILLETT PLAYS HAPPY FAMILIES AS HE LEAVES THE SPANISH JAIL WHERE HE SPENT THE NIGHT.

Mike Willett was arrested after an unprovoked attack on a young man, smashing a hotel ballroom and leaving the man senseless and requiring hospital treatment. This is not the first time Willett has been in trouble for losing control of his temper. To the rescue comes Kate Stokes, wife of wealthy businessman Geoff Stokes, whose empire includes property, the biggest plant hire company in Europe and a computer company in greater London, to name but a few. You have it the wrong way, Willett, it's the man whose supposed to do the rescuing! Sources close to the couple (Mike noticed they put couple to strengthen their innuendos) say that romance has blossomed since Willett allowed a nude photo shoot of Mrs. Stokes to be shot on his property, even managing to talk himself into one of the photos holding a naked Mrs. Stokes as she rode one of his horses. According to our source, the photo shoot was the beginning of the end for Geoff Stokes who on seeing the photographs threw his wife out of his house. Neither Willett nor Mrs. Stokes would comment on the allegations but have been constantly in each other's company for the past few months.

The article did more mud throwing, but Mike couldn't bother to read on, he threw the paper back on the table. He really didn't care one iota what the papers said about him, it was water off a duck's back, but he was deeply hurt that Kate had been brought into the fray and worried over her reaction when he collected her from the airport the following morning. It was with a feeling of trepidation at her possible reaction and excitement at the prospect of seeing her again that Mike faced the rest of the day. Though his burden was eased slightly by the support of the stable staff and by the time nightfall came he was feeling a little better. Surprisingly he slept quite soundly.

CHAPTER FIVE

Mike cringed as he walked into arrivals at the airport. There were reporters everywhere. He was mobbed. In fairness to Mike he kept his cool and through all the jostling he received did not say a word. The airport staff kindly ushered him into the club class lounge so that he could wait in peace. Kate and Becky arrived and he went to meet them followed by what looked like a swarm of flies as reporters tried desperately to photograph and question him. The appearance of Nick and Seamus soon gave him space. The formidable bulk of Nick causing without exception the paparazzi to fall back to a safe distance. "Not that I'm not pleased to see you but what the hell are you doing here?"

"Vi decided that it might be wise for you to have some help considering the hornet's nest the papers are kicking up. She thought you might have a welcoming committee! Clever woman is Vi. Nicks here to keep them off you," Seamus smiled, "and I'm here to keep me laddo on a leash." Mike laughed out loud, it was strange to think of the diminutive Seamus keeping the huge bulk of Nick in tow. Though he knew that Seamus seemed to be able to calm Nick down quicker that anyone…. Apart from Vi. "Vi's given Nick strict orders he's to listen to me and behave himself…. Just be a deterrent she said…. Make sure they don't bother my boy. Jesus, I'll tell you she's one hell of a lady."

Cameras were still flashing though now at a respectable distance the rapid-fire questioning having stopped after one glowering look from Nick. Becky spotted Mike first and ran down the corridor throwing her arms round his neck and planting a kiss on him. "Missed you it was so boring not having you to play with! How are the horses? When are we going racing next? Do you think Sunrise will win again? How are all the others? Can I ride Rocket?" Mike was stunned but not surprised as Becky threw questions at him quick fire but more stunned by her last question, asking to ride Rocket. More to his astonishment was Kate who walked up to him, kissed him and put her arm through his. "Shall we go?" she asked and manoeuvred him towards the exit. Mike had never felt as proud in his whole life as he did that moment - arm in arm with Kate, Becky holding his hand tightly on the other side, and his unusual 'bodyguards' flanking them all. They reached the car without incidence and sped off leaving the reporters looking confusedly for Mikes F-type, Mike having borrowed Johns new Aston Martin to collect Kate and Becky. "This is such a beautiful car," Kate said, sinking into the sumptuous leather seats, very sophisticated. "You like my car though, don't you?" Mike asked almost school boyish, remembering that he was having one delivered for Kate that afternoon. "Of course, it's stunning but they're completely different aren't they, one is a classic four-seater luxury performance car, the other is a luxury out and out sports car, a bit of a beast with manners." Mike couldn't help but laugh, Kate had just spoken as knowledgably as a car pundit. Look to your laurels Jeremy Clarkson he thought! "You're very knowledgeable on cars!" He said it was framed as much as a question as a statement. "Living with Geoff you pick a few things up. There really isn't many cars he hasn't owned over the years and his expertise would frankly take some beating. He could probably tell you details the manufacturers don't even remember about most cars!" They pulled into the yard followed shortly after by Nick and Seamus. Becky was desperate to see her horses, which was just what Mike had hoped for. He had the F-type he was going to give to Kate parked in the wide central passage of the American barn where Becky's horses were kept. "Wow!" shouted Beck's. "Look mummy, Mikes got a new car and its your favourite colour!"

"Oh, that's not mine, I'm just storing it. It's a present for someone very special…. To say thank you for just being them really."

"Ooh, they must be very special… it must have cost a bomb, who is it for?" Becky was so excited and curious.

"Well actually it's for the most beautiful woman you could ever imagine." Mike replied and as he did so he tossed the keys nonchalantly towards Kate, she caught them automatically.

"Mike… it's an incredible thought but…"

"Please don't offend me by saying that you can't accept it. If I hadn't of met you and Beck's I'd still be rolling around Spain drunk as a skunk… and I certainly would never have raced Rock's again, in truth I wouldn't have raced anything. So, this is my way of saying thank you." Becky was beaming looking over the car with a critical eye.

"Mummy this is so cool, my friends at school are going to be *so* jealous!" she said with glee. Mike walked up to her kneeling down to her level. "As for you young lady! I've a lot to thank you for as well. When you're old enough to understand you'll realise that without you as well I would never have found my self-esteem." Becky's little face tried hard to take on an expression of understanding but Mike knew it would be a few years yet before she really came to grips with how big a role she had played in his life. She had become the child he had always wanted, no one would ever convince Mike that biology was important. He had decided that any fool could be a father but it took a man to be a dad. He would have died for Becky just as he would for Kate and as far as he was concerned Becky was as much his daughter as she was Kate and Geoff's. He saw the irony of it as well, he was just someone on the periphery, but he didn't care, but then love when it comes never does. "You had better come with me a moment because I have something to show you. He took Becky's hand and led her to the far end of the barn opening the last stable door. "Go on, have a look. I'd like to know what you think of her. She's probably too small to make a decent racehorse but she's as kind as a Christian, I'm interested to know what you think. Becky looked in the box where a small but very pretty bay filly stood, she shone like a pin. She walked over to inspect Becky. "She's beautiful Mike." Becky said running her hand over her sleek neck. "I think she likes me."

"Good I'm glad because she's yours and when you've learnt to ride properly you can ... if it's okay with mum, take her up the gallops with the others." Becky didn't say a word, she jumped into her mum's arms and cried. "I think your gifts a hit!" Kate said smiling.

"Oh, nearly forgot... you'd best take a look at the new peg in the tack room!" Becky released her mum and rushed into the tack room situated in the middle of the barn. In the corner was a brass plate on which was engraved *Becky* underneath it a brand-new race exercise saddle, bridle and just about every gizmo ever invented for the horse. It took an awful lot of persuading to convince Becky that she wouldn't be able to 'ride work' the following morning but would have to be patient and learn to ride properly before it was even considered. "I'll get Seamus to give you a lesson tomorrow, he's a good teacher and a better rider than I've ever been or ever will be." Becky was placated.

Kate agreed to go to the house for coffee and a bite to eat after Mike agreeing that she would pay for a takeaway to be delivered. "Look, why don't you stay the night..." Mike asked and seeing the uncertainty in Kate's eyes added. "I've plenty of room, you can either share a bedroom with titch or have a bedroom each."

"Please mummy, can we stay? It would be a real adventure!"

"I don't know sweetie. We really should find a hotel somewhere!"

Mike jumped in the conversation. "It seems silly that you find a hotel when you're going to be back here in the morning for our meeting. Apart from that, Vi will love having someone else to fuss over when she comes in in the morning. You'll be doing everybody a favour!" Becky looked up longingly at her mum. "Okay but just for tonight."

"Excellent! Come on, let's go inside and sort things out."

Mike telephoned the local Indian restaurant and after they had gorged themselves on the huge selection Kate had insisted they ordered, Becky was taken to her room and fell asleep before the covers were pulled over her. Mike and Kate went down to the lounge sitting in front of the fire that roared in the grate, a glass of whiskey and a glass of wine respectively. They sat at each end of the couch, Kate with her legs tucked under her facing Mike and talked. There was no depth to their conversation, it was just a mixture of the horses they had watched race together, life, friends, a little bit of everything. It was comfortable and relaxed. Kate said that she really had to go to bed as tiredness had overtaken her and it was with no little regret that Mike told her, her bedroom was adjoining Becky's. Kate kissed Mike on the cheek and walked across the room, Mike admired her as she did, her taught bottom and slim waist hugged by the short pale blue dress she wore, he could just make out the silhouette of the tiny g-string she wore beneath. She turned as she reached the door to say goodnight and Mike could see the outline of her round breast and pert nipples. He sat alone reaching for the Jameson's bottle that sat waiting in the coffee table and poured himself a night cap. He hadn't even taken a sip when Kate appeared back in the doorway. "I don't suppose you'd have a spare toothbrush, would you?"

"There should be one in the bathroom cabinet I think."

"You obviously have guests often!" Kate said a teasing smile spreading across her lips.

"No, I just happened to have bought a pack before I went on holiday."

"Are you going to sit here all night?"

"No, I thought I'd just have a night cap."

"I feel awful leaving you here having a drink on your own… pour me a small one, I'll join you before I go." Mike poured Kate a glass of wine and she sat beside him, he could feel her warmth, smell her perfume, she sipped her wine putting her glass back on the table turning to say something, her lips moist from the drink. Mike tried to stop himself from leaning forward, but it was impossible, she was so beautiful, he touched her lips gently with his and she responded. Mike pushed her back so that she was lying across the couch, her short dress rising up as he did so revealing her slender legs as far as the black crutch of her g-string. He held her breast squeezing tightly and Kate let out a low moan, her hips moving rhythmically against the couch. Mike reached down undoing his flies releasing his erection he pulled frantically at the crutch of Kate's pants, pulling the material to one side not bothering to remove them. Her clean shaven womanhood revealed he thrust his penis into her. Withdrawing, he turned her over so that her legs were now over the edge of the couch and kneeling behind her he took her again. Kate moaned as he hammered into her she could feel his body slamming against her and her body shuddered as she reached a climax. She sighed and went limp as Mike's movement became more frantic and she felt his hard cock pumping as he ejaculated filling her already wet womanhood with his sticky fluid. Mike at that moment thought he would never be whole again without Kate. They laid in each other's arms, Kate falling into a deep sleep as Mike stroked her hair and just enjoyed watching her stunning face, finally falling asleep himself clinging tightly to Kate.

"I knew you two would do that!" the small voice rang in their ears. "I said to mummy that you'd end up falling asleep if you spent half the night talking." Then forgetting her 'telling off' moment she shouted 'YAHOO' as loudly as she could and jumped on Mike nearly knocking the wind out of him. "Becky!" Kate said firmly but with a hint of laughter as Mike gasped for breath. "Oh, he's alright mummy! He's as tough as old boots… Seamus told me!"

Mike smiled. "Come on let's go to the kitchen and get some

tea before this puppy…" he poked a squirming Becky in the ribs. "Chews this old boot into pieces." As they walked into the kitchen the smell of bacon assailed their nostrils and Vi was standing busying herself at the Rayburn. She immediately left what she was doing making a beeline for Beck's, her face alight at the sight of her. She looked her up and down critically. "Have you had a wash young lady…?" and Becky looked surprisingly guilty. "I thought not… right, as soon as you've had your breakfast your straight upstairs and in the bath. I'll put you out some clean clothes, I'm not having you walk around like an old scruff bag!" She turned back to her cooking and they all smiled hunching their shoulders and pulling a serious face. "And you can all stop pulling faces…. There's strong coffee on the table for you two," Vi said, turning and raising an eyebrow at Kate and Mike giving them the feeling of being naughty children.

Mike and Kate walked off towards the barn Kate having decided that as Mike had given her such a wonderful gift it was only right and proper she use it. Becky waved as she stood in the kitchen door holding Vi's hand. Vi having insisted she look after her whilst Kate and Mike attended their meeting. They arrived at John's to find Sue Parker already sitting at the lounge table pouring over a pile of papers, Mike assumed they were from Roy. She looked up and greeted him briefly before waxing lyrical over the potential of both the film and the theme park idea. Kate sat next to her saying that if she was going to contribute she needed to know what she was talking about. Sue willingly went through the papers pointing out what she thought was positive and which in her opinion was negative. The two seemed to have an instant rapport and much to Mikes surprise heard them discussing the photo shoot Kate had done, he heard Sue say, "Not only do I think you were brave to take off all your clothes but I think you have a very sound financial mind to have negotiated such a deal. If you ever need a decent bank overseas, please give me a shout, I'd be more than happy to have you as a client."

"I might just take you up on that…. Between you and me I've been offered a fortune to model a new range of extremely sexy underwear and a contract to promote a very well-known companies perfume." Kate giggled and Sue joined her. "It seems that for a few sexy shots of me cradling a bottle of perfume with no clothes on, tastefully I'm assured, the skies the limit. I never realised that advertising was so lucrative! I'll talk to you about it after the meeting if that's okay." Sue was more than happy to agree knowing just how much money is involved in an advertising contract. Another good client to add to her list could only favour well when she went to her board.

Mike, John, and Seamus had been thinking in terms of several millions but when Sue opened the meeting all three of them fell silent their mouths wide open. Kate casually added her agreement to Sues opening gambit. "Whilst I appreciate the theme park has not yet gained any formal permission the initial enquires to the planning authority have been met with a degree of enthusiasm. I also appreciate that it is a virgin site but an assessment has to be made on the potential. It is gentlemen vast. I believe that should the park be realised the rewards will far outstretch anything that you considered originally. Now if you take this along with the planned film, which I hasten to add neither Kate nor myself think Mike should star in, maybe a cameo role but nothing more in our opinion, you have something totally unique. Not only do you have a film but a park dedicated to the star of the film, Rocket!"

"I like this girl!" the voice in Mikes head rang.

"Add to that you can utilise the props, special effects, the broader spectrum of horse racing in general, and most important of all the star of the film and his following generation… I think you are talking more in billions than millions." She didn't wait to see if anyone else wished to have an input though she did glance at Roy Winston noticing his face held a worried 'this is going to cost me more than I'd bargained for' look, then turned to Kate, who immediately took over where Sue had left off.

"Sue and I were brought here to arbitrate and to take part in these negotiations. Well, on a personal level, I don't see that there should be any problems. If the film is a hit, and from what Mr. Winston predicts in his resume it would appear he believes it will be a blockbuster, I think the figures that have so far been bandied about have to be thrown into the bin where I have to say they belong. A figure of three hundred and fifty million plus 15% of the net earnings from the film would be closer to the mark considering the large sum of money that will be required to develop the theme park, the income that will be generated from the film, and the potential earnings of the theme park itself when developed. Sue and I both agree this would need to be divided as follows - 200 million to develop the park, 20 million each to John, Seamus and Mike, leaving 90 million, which should be divided as follows - 10 million to charity, the remaining 80 million should be deposited as a slush fund to cover any unforeseen circumstance. The fifteen percent would of course go to Mike, John and Seamus directly." Even Roy Winston who was used to dealing with such massive sums of money was left speechless for a few minutes. The four men stared at each other, then Roy spoke. "Hell!" he said, his southern drawl seeming more pronounced. "I can see why you wanted these girls along Mike!"

"That's as maybe Mr. Winston, but you haven't responded to our proposal."

"Honey I ain't man enough to take you two on! What the hell, let's give her a try. You draw up the papers and I'll sign 'em! And I don't mind tellin' you this is the fastest meetin' I ever bin to an' for sure as hell the most impressive." Kate and Sue smiled sweetly at Roy Winston and the meeting was over. After a further hour of general discussion in which time Roy had passed on the details of his lawyers to Sue as she was to deal with sorting out the finer details of the contracts they went their separate ways, agreeing to meet in a weeks' time to visit Mikes old satellite yard hopefully with the local planning officers in tow. Roy would bring along an architect who had done similar types of proposals in the past. He would get him, he said, to visit the site prior to their meeting and draw up a few sketches if that was okay. John said he should liase with Mike as his knowledge of horses would prove useful in the early stages of planning.

Mike drove gently down the drive back towards home.

"Bloody hell Kate! You were amazing! Don't suppose you'd be interested in working for me?"

Kate looked wistful. "That's a really nice offer Mike but at the moment I'm not sure what I want to do. In truth I'm getting loads of offers and the way my life is I'm at a bit of a loss which way to go." Mike understood. After his conversation with Geoff he could see it would make things difficult for Kate but then on the other hand so it would if Geoff realised that Kate had stayed with him. He hoped secretly that Kate stayed a lot longer and wanted the world to know, not just Geoff. He had a sudden thought that might just offer a reasonable compromise for Kate allowing her to maintain credibility and some semblance of self-respect. "Look this is just a suggestion." Mike stared tentatively. "You know the track that forks off my drive? Well there's an empty cottage about two hundred yards up there. It's been empty for a year and I keep saying I'm going to get it sorted out and don't. it would take two or three weeks mind but if I ring our builder today I'm sure I could get him to make a start on it straight away. He's pretty good to us but then we give him a lot of work," he added knowing he would have to threaten the builder with a competitor to get him there. "You'd be doing me a favour if you moved in there when it was done and ..." he decided to play the trump card even though it gave him a feeling of mild guilt, "Becky would love it being so close to the yard. You could stay at my place in the meantime, your own room of course, no strings attached, and in two or three weeks you'd have total independence." If Mike could have crossed his fingers without being seen he would of. He waited breathlessly as Kate turned to look at him he had unknowingly slowed to about twenty miles an hour.

"Mike." His heart he was sure stopped beating. "It's a wonderful offer." His breathing stopped as well. "if you don't put your foot down we'll never get back and I won't be able to look at this cottage because it will be dark so I won't be able to make a decision!" Mikes foot hit the throttle of the Jag leaving black lines behind him as the wheels span and they were thrust back into their seats. Kate laughed and Mike thought of the first time he had heard that laugh in Spain it was still like bells tinkling in his head running right down to his stomach and now the effect was even greater. Kate reached over and grasped his hand, Mike felt as though he ruled the world.

Becky skipped the two hundred yards up the track to the cottage urging Mike to skip along with her, which he did rather clumsily much to Kate's amusement. "You're as daft as each other," she said, and Mike felt such a warm glow inside, feeling like part of a family for the first time in his adult life. Deep down the old saying 'what fools believe' rattled around his brain trying to take away the moment, it didn't manage Mike deciding that something as precious as he felt at that moment couldn't be destroyed. Becky fell in love with the cottage, it was very pretty with its clematis growing wildly across the front walls. The stone that could be seen looked warm and the garden though overgrown gave an inviting feeling as they walked towards the front door. Becky rushed inside not waiting for Mike and Kate, sprinting up the old oak stairs and exploring. "Mummy." She shouted. "Can I have this room it's wonderful. I can put all my horse posters along this wall and I could have a really neat stereo in the corner, my TV here and…" Kate smiled at her enthusiastic daughter. "Just slow down I haven't even decided if we're going to take Mike up on his offer yet!"

"Please mummy, PLEASE, it will be a real adventure…. and I could spend holidays and weekends in the yard… I'll have loads of time to spend with Seamus learning to ride properly…and… and Vi's really good fun and very nice… she said I could help her anytime I wanted!" Kate couldn't help but smile at her daughter, Mike felt butterflies whizzing around in his stomach to his chest as he watched her face light the room up with that one smile. 'God' he thought 'she is so beautiful'. Becky was dancing from one foot to the other in excitement as Kate considered whether or not to take Mike up on his offer. She turned to Mike that devastating smile still in place. "No strings you say." Mike nodded.

"Well if we reach some financial agreement then okay." It was all Mike could do to stop himself from joining in with Becky as she ran around in circles shouting joyfully. "Kate, I don't think there is any need to talk about finances you have made me an absolute fortune with the way you handled Roy Winston! I think I owe you more than free rent on a cottage!"

"Alright we'll call it quits… especially as you bought me that gorgeous car."

They left the cottage with Becky racing headlong down the track. "I'm going to tell Vi we're staying," she shouted over her shoulder. "You know I think Vi is going to be almost as happy as Titch," Mike said, and they walked back each wondering where this was going. The next few days past in blur of activity and Mike wondered whether he would cope, there were papers to sign for the deals with Roy Winston, races to plan, though fortunately Seamus dealt efficiently with most of the yards administration, the cottage to oversee, planning officers, builders the list seemed endless. Then it all seemed to fall into place and became relatively simple when everyone knew exactly what they were doing. Becky spent her days helping Vi, wandering around the horses with Nick keeping a watchful eye on her. Mike's relationship with Kate was friendly and he kept his word avoiding even a casual brush of their hands, though the room to anyone on the periphery was charged with sexual tension. They were sitting chatting about everything and nothing after dinner when the phone rang, Mike picked up the walkabout from the coffee table and answered. "… Oh, hi Roy, where are you?… Yes, everything's going really well…. Yes, she is." Mikes voice took on a surprised tone obviously at Roy's last question. " Yeah… I'll just pass you over." Mike held the phone out to Kate shrugging his shoulders to her mime of 'why does he want to speak to me'. Kate held the phone to her ear a look of intense concentration and surprise showing in her eyes. She raised her eyebrows in shock. "But I've never done anything like it before… surely there must be someone who is not only better known than me but better qualified… Well I don't suppose it would hurt to give it a try… HOW MUCH?…

Alright I'll be there in the morning." Mike looked at Kate with a puzzled expression. Kate did not speak rising from the couch she walked out of the room, stood at the bottom of the stairs and called Becky to come down, then returned still without a word and sat back on the couch looking very smug. Much to the irritation of Mike. Becky entered the room still trying to rub the sleep from her eyes, flumping down on Mikes lap. She yawned and stretched nearly removing one of Mikes ears as her arms shot upwards. "Becky," Kate said soberly. "I would like you to listen to what I have to say very carefully because it's very important that you understand what I am about to say means and because I would only consider it if you think it is okay!" Mike and Becky both looked at each other seriously, wondering whatever was coming next. "You know the film Roy is making about Rocket?" Understanding started to dawn on Mike. "Well Roy wants me to take a major role, he wants me to play myself in the movie!" Becky leapt from Mikes lap, winding him in the process. "Wow! My friends are going to be really jealous. That's wicked Mummy." She chuckled loudly. "My Mummy's a movie star!"

"Calm down!" Kate urged Becky. "I haven't said yes to Roy yet and there is a lot to consider. Firstly, I have to consider Mike in all of this, certainly as it was Sue and my suggestion that he should not take part in the film itself other than as an advisor." Mike went to interrupt but Kate stopped him. "I know that isn't an issue with you Mike… it was the sensible course of action… God knows how you'd react if some camp actor tried to chat you up!" Becky squealed with laughter.

"Oooh mummy, he'd probably spark them out." Mike and Kate couldn't help but smile at each other.

"She's spending too much time in that yard!" Kate said towards Mike. "Back to the point! I would also have to do a nude scene… a replay of my magazine shoot…. well some of it anyway," Kate said, rather coyly to Mike. "It would mean rather a lot of money and with the possible cosmetic company contract that I'm negotiating it would mean a serious amount of money." Becky was still jumping up and down with excitement. "You can do it mummy… it's no different really than taking your clothes off in a magazine… and I bet you'd make a fantastic you!" Mike didn't say anything whilst Becky jumped around excitedly and stayed smiling though quiet until Becky had been put back to bed. Whilst Kate was doing this he poured a Jameson for himself and a wine for Kate. "You're very quiet?" she questioned as she sat and picked up her glass of wine.

"I was just wondering what sort of reaction you're going to get from Geoff? From what you said he was pretty upset about the magazine and from my brief meeting I can concur with that completely." Mike didn't want to say it the words almost stuck in his throat but he knew he had too or he would never live with himself, principles mattered he reminded himself even though his had fallen by the wayside big time of late. "If you don't speak with Geoff about this there'll be no going back for either of you. You know how I feel about you and because of that I think you should speak to him for your own peace of mind." Kate sat silently a pensive look on her face, sipped her wine then answered.

"Mike Geoff was… is still really the love of my life…" Mike's stomach dive bombed. "But I can't see there being any way back after his reaction to the photo's let alone if I do a nude scene in a film. I will speak to him, but I can't see it doing any good, he's a very stubborn man and I am, if I'm honest, enjoying the financial freedom I now have, if all the things that are in the pipeline come off I'll never have another financial worry, I'll be financially independent for life… I can't turn an opportunity like that down because the man I love wants everything his own way!" Mike's stomach sunk again at the words 'the man I love' but he didn't show his feelings. Kate stood up and came over sitting beside him. She gently kissed his cheek and made to snuggle into him. Mike felt confused, one minute she was talking about 'the man she loved', which wasn't him, then without warning started to flirt with him. He felt used a feeling he found hard to bear. "Coffee?" he asked jumping up.

"What's wrong?"

"Nothing!"

"Oh, come on Mike you don't normally pull away from me."

"I'm not I just thought you might like a coffee."

"Mike I'm not stupid, you did a pretty good impression of a stone likeness when I tried to cuddle up to you!" Kate's voice took on an edge.

"Alright…" it was Mikes voice turn to be edgy. "You've just sat and told me about 'the man that is the love of your life', which it would appear has made you feel either insecure or saddened so to make up for it you take what's available to make you feel better… Me! And if we end up making love, which it is too me but obviously not to you, I'll end up feeling all moon struck and guilty all at the same time and you'll end up telling me it can't happen again making my guilt even worse…. Making me feel like I've used you for sex when in truth it's the reverse. I'm not prepared to put myself through it anymore. You know I love you I've admitted it, hook line and sinker but I have, to protect myself. The cottage will be ready in a couple of days and I think you should move in straight away!" Kate never said a word, no sign of affection she simply rose and walked from the room. Mike slumped in his chair and fitfully fell asleep. In his dreams he heard the words from a song 'Love can tear you apart' and even in his state of unconscious he thought what a good job it was doing to him. He woke at around six going into the kitchen to make tea, it was just starting to get light and he could see the stable lights were on. Seamus was already putting out the morning feeds. He stared towards the lights thinking that perhaps his lot was set, maybe he was destined never to find unconditional love. Lady luck had shone down on him, but had it seemed pulled the rug right out from underneath him again. He would have given anything to have his love for Kate returned but at that moment felt it would never be. He wondered what he was going to do. He drank his tea and pulled on his work boots and wandered across to the yard wallowing in the sound of horses quietly munching on hay or their breakfast. Listening to those awaiting food, stamping impatiently and whickering at Seamus to hurry up and get to them. Mike was suddenly stunned into standing stock still and watching, walking along next to Seamus was Becky carrying a bucket and chatting nine to the dozen as usual. Seamus was smiling quietly to himself as he listened to the figure that walked confidently beside him. "I'll give Sunrise her feed, you do Dawn and then we'll go and get the feeds for the others." Mike couldn't help himself, he laughed out loud, both Becky and Seamus jumped. "What are you doing here young lady?" Mike said as severely as he could between chuckles. "And why are you telling my top man what to do?" Becky looked suitably abashed but managed to bring herself back to an apologetic air of self-authority. "I wasn't really telling Seamus what to do, I was just helping, mummy said I could help feed one morning and as you were both sound asleep I didn't want to wake you to say I was going to this morning!" Mike was amazed at how someone of such tender age could be so astute.

"I don't think you'd better tell your mum that you came here off your own back young lady... I think you might find yourself grounded for the next ten years. We'll say you came with me okay?... and no repeat of this in the future... alright." Becky nodded agreement and rushed off to feed her horse.

"That, Michael, is one hell of a young lady... and the makings of a bloody good horseman, bright as a button and cute to boot!"

"You're certainly not wrong there Seamus... You know it makes me realise just what I've missed by never having my own children. She's an absolute treasure." Mike wandered into the feed room after asking Seamus which horses still had to be fed and collected the buckets, it felt good putting the horse's food in their feed bins and watching them dive their noses into it keenly. A simple task, but rewarding and effective, dissipating the gut wrenching feelings, if only temporarily, from the previous evening. Mike and Becky walked back to the house hand in hand with Becky animated by her early morning visit to the yard. "Seamus says if I keep going as well as I have for a couple more days... and listen to him without arguing, I might be able to have a go up the gallops with Anita."

"I think you'd better run that past your mum first... and if I were you, I'd pick my moment, catch her when she's in a really good mood." Becky squeezed Mikes hand and skipped along her excitement almost at boiling point. Mike hoped her mum would give her the chance. They entered the house through the kitchen door. Becky immediately flicked the switch on the kettle. "Tea?" Mike smiled.

"I'll make one for mummy and take it up to her." Again, Mike wondered how a child of such tender years had gathered such a worldly knowledge and knew how to put it to use!

Mike started at the sound of Kate's voice. "And why would you bring me a cup of tea in bed young lady? What are you up to? I'm sure that you're something to do with this as well Michael Willett so spill the beans you two!" Mike was more surprised at Kate's upbeat manner, after she had gone to bed without a word the previous evening and his reaction to her advance he had expected to be greeted at best with silence, certainly not a cheerful and happy nature. Becky took the bull by the horns and explained much to both of their surprised Kate agreed. "I can't say that I'm not nervous about it because I am, but I knew it would eventually come and Seamus has taught her well. There is however a condition." They both waited for the Coup de Gras and were both amazed when it came. "You lend me a horse and I ride as well, just so I'm close at hand if anything should go wrong." Mike looked flabbergasted. "Don't look so astounded I can ride you know," she said to Mike. "Becky close your mouth darling, it's very rude. Mike I'd like a quick word with you in private. You make the tea Beck's, we'll be back in a couple of minutes." She walked off into the lounge, Mike following with a feeling of utter dread from his head to his feet. Kate sat down on the couch and Mike sat in the chair opposite.

"I've thought long and hard about what you said last night... and it's not true... I've never thought of you as just sex... I've had to be honest with myself and it is hard for me to admit but I realise now that I love you and I think if I'm to make a new life, I just as well start now. I'll have to discuss it with Becky because she's the most important one in all of this but if she's happy and it's what you really want I'll stay here…. I suppose what I am saying is we'll have a go at living together." Mike leapt from his chair threw his arms around Kate and kissed her. "There is nothing on this earth I would like more," he said. They sat at breakfast, Vi doing her normal feeding of the five thousand act and fussing over Mike like a broody bantam hen, even though he had taken second place to the attention Becky received. With breakfast over and Becky off to her lesson with Seamus, they decided to drive over to the theme park site, Vi having left strict instructions with Nick that the moment Becky had finished her lesson he was to bring her back so that she could fluff her feathers and fuss her some more, though not in those words. Nick was more than happy to oblige, for one thing he worshipped the little one and the other it would most probably mean Vi would bring out the cake. He said it worked out well because he needed to mow the lawns and tidy up around the garden though Mike was pretty sure after looking at the lawns on his way to get the car it was in the hope that Vi would let him take Titch off with him for an hour when he went to check the fences and to go and see Rocket and Storm. On the way to the site Kate said she thought they should sit Becky down after dinner and find out what she thought about the idea. She intended to phone Geoff or go and see him to try and get back on amicable terms, she did not intend to tell him of her plans just to attempt to sort a few things out.

The site was unrecognisable, there was pile upon pile of concrete blocks, steel girders, roofing sheets, machines and concrete lorries everywhere. It was amazing how much progress had been made in just a couple of weeks. Mikes old stables and barns had been carefully dismantled and he had organised to have them re-erected on the new land he had bought from John. Much to has astonishment he was told this had already been done and a road and yard laid. He walked quickly around the site with Kate as he was keen to go and see what sort of job had been done. A massive portacabin had been brought onto the site to act as both a rest room for the men and adjoining office for the site manager and foreman Mike made his way over and entered. The site manager was a stocky man with weather beaten face showing he had done his fair share learning his trade before moving on to management he looked up from the plan he was studying and held out a calloused hand. "Morning, nice to see you both, what do you think of the progress?"

"Bloody amazing, I can't believe it, especially as one of the lads has just told me you've already put my buildings up to boot!"

"I think you'll be pleased they made a really nice job of it. The big fella that works for you."

"Nick?"

"That's the chap... Christ, he's some size... and strong. I certainly wouldn't want to get on the wrong side of him, frightened one of my lads half to death, he found a young hare in the corner of the field and was going to knock on the head to take home to eat... Jesus, you're bloke picked him off the ground and shook him like a piece of rag! It was bloody lucky that little Irish chap turned up and told him to let go. He dropped my bloke without a by your leave, picked up the little hare, which was cowering in the grass. I'm not sure from the sight of your chap or my blokes intentions mind you!" They all smiled. "Then without a word to anyone, except your Irishman, he walked back over to the corner of the field, put the hare as gentle as you like back in the grass, said 'don't you worry, if anyone comes near you I'll deal wiv 'em'. I don't think you could have given any of my chaps a year's wages to even look at that part of the field!" They all chuckled. "Anyway, he's done all the fencing and put up all the gates, even did some planting. Made a marvellous job."

"Nick and Seamus, you say.... They never said a word to me, wait till I see them."

"They did, it as a surprise, wanted to see your reaction after you first saw it. I tell you this, I could do with as many like them as you can find me! Anyway, I'm glad you came because we hit a bit of a problem. The entrance building has had to be relocated because we hit a spring. I've had word with the planners and they've okayed it. You can see here." He pointed to the plan. "I've drawn in on the general site map where we've re-sited it, works quite well really." He poured over the map with Mike and Kate looking intently at what he pointed at. "Here's where it would have been, this is the fence line for the actual theme park. What we've done is move the building back to here, which will actually, work out better because it brings it into line with the rest of the building, cafes, gift shops, that sort of thing. Really it should have been there in the first place in my opinion not stuck out here all on its own. We've moved the fence line out to here and I thought we'd dig a lake where the spring is. We can run an outfall into the ditch just over the rise, landscape the surrounding area and you could do all sorts there. Put in some seats, a little coffee shack or ice cream stand, it'll also give an area where kids can play, run around a bit." They left the cabin and walked around the site with George the manager, Mike was amazed at how big the car parking area was it must have covered forty acres, but then he knew that if it was as successful as they hoped they would need every space. George walked them to an area that was not only cordoned off but hidden behind large screens. "What the devil have you got in there?" Mike asked, George grinned.

"Ah ha, this is the Rocket. The engineer got the idea after watching your little girl at the races," he added to Kate, "even the plans are held in here so that no one can get hold of them." They walked behind the screens to see a hive of activity that paled the rest of the site. There was a smaller more robust portacabin that looked as though it would take a tank to get into. As they moved nearer a uniformed security guard came out with two massive German Shepherds, both snarling and baring their teeth. "They're quite friendly really," the security guard said. "But they know their job. Sit!" And both dogs sat straight away. "Just come within reach and let them say hello." Mike and Kate moved a little closer if a little cautiously. Both dogs immediately rose from the sitting position. "It's alright boys, friends." The security guard said softly to the dogs and they reached forward to sniff the hands that Kate and Mike held out. Within seconds they were being stroked and leaning against the legs of their new friends. "Mind you!" the security guard added. "If I don't tell them you're friends they're a completely different ball game. Let them on someone without telling them and they'll take chunks out of them," he said with obvious pride in his boys. In the middle of the screens was the half completed 'Rocket'. George started to explain how it worked, the structure vaguely resembled the outline of a horse. "It starts there," George said. "You'll notice it's shaped like the back leg of a horse, the end product will have a face that is an image of your horse. It shoots up the back leg, that's where your daughters performance comes into being because when it's about twenty feet off the ground it sets off a small charge that gives the same effect as your daughter's costume, sparks come flying out behind the cars as they race up the leg. Then it slows down and goes over what will be the rump, though it'll be plenty fast enough to turn your stomach over, it then goes along what represents the back, up the neck, over the head, upside down under the neck and down its front leg, it then goes along the ground at incredible speed and back to where it started!" Mike looked queasy just getting Georges description but Kate was full of excitement. "Wow I can't wait to have a go, when will it be finished?"

"It'll be at least another three months before it's done and passed all the safety checks."

"Mike, we have to have a go first, it looks amazing." Mikes face showed panic as he looked at the massive structure under construction in front of him. He could handle most things but thrill rides were definitely not one of them! Kate spent the journey to Mikes new yard enthusing about the ride which only made Mike look forward with impending doom on its completion. He knew he would go on it even though he was near to petrification just to please Kate. They reached the new yard and Mike forgot all about the ride, Nick and Seamus had ensured the job was done superbly. The drive was magnificent and had been planted with young copper beech trees, the yard itself had been laid with red non-slip tarmac and there was a circular pond in the middle with a bronze fountain, there were flowering plant pots everywhere. It looked fantastic. Kate smiled at Mike, the look on his face speaking volumes. They walked over to the stables, which had not only been re-erected but totally renovated, on the door was a note it read... *On us! For all you have done for us both. Your friends...* it was signed Seamus and Nick. Mike felt a lump in his throat. He opened the door of the stable noticing that the inside was as pristine as the outside. He walked inside slowly turning around to take it all in. Kate stood framed in the doorway; the balmy warm late summer suns haze made her form radiate a golden glow. She very slowly started to undo her shirt and Mike almost fell over in his haste to reach her. "Uh uh, you just stay where you are until I tell you 'my little stable boy' - I have plans for you." She ran the tip of her tongue over her lips. "By the time I've finished, I want you so ready... this!" she reached forward slightly running one finger over the lump in his jeans, "...is on fire... and then Michael Willett, I am going to fuck you like never before!" She touched Mike on the shoulder, firmly pushing him to his knees as she slowly, tantalisingly undid the buttons on her jeans and slid them down her tanned slender legs. She stood before him naked from the waist down, her shirt open revealing her perfectly shaped hard nipples. Slowly, very slowly, she moved towards Mike until she was touching his upturned face. She gently cupped his head in her hands and he buried his face between her legs, his tongue darting out to enter her. She moaned pushing her hips forward, her naked flesh grinding against his face. She stepped back slowly, peeling the shirt first from one shoulder then the other. Mike made to stand up and move towards her. "No touching unless I say!" Kate said, a wickedly sexy smile spreading across her face. Mike stood still grinning like a Cheshire cat. "Keep your hands where they are, remember no touching until I say you can!" Kate ran her finger nails lightly under Mike's tee shirt, moving down and sliding her hands into his jeans, he gasped as she grabbed his manhood and began to massage him. When they finally exited the stables, they were both exhausted and Mike was wondering if his legs would hold him upright long enough to reach the car. They drove away, both giggling like children and both a step nearer to being one.

CHAPTER SIX

Seamus knocked the door flanked by Nick, both men looking very smart in suits and ties. "We're all loaded Guv, will you be coming with us or travelling later?" Seamus said, his accent strong.

"I'll see you there, I don't need to come to the stables with you there so I'll meet you in the owner's bar. If you don't mind, I'd like to help saddle up, it's been a while since we've raced and you forget how much you miss it!"

"Well it'd be a fine guvnor you'd be if you didn't. Don't forget we've two of little one's fillies in the same race, and the other in the race after." Seamus was grinning as he spoke. Nick stood behind him, a grin from ear to ear. "Go on you reprobates, bugger off I'll see you there."

"Fine way to be talking to his bestest men now don't you know," Seamus said to Nick as they walked away, both men threw a huge grin over their shoulders. "Oh, should we take Vi or will she be riding in style with the royal party?" Seamus was in fine form, racing brings out the best in any yard.

"She can come with us, we don't want her mixing with you serfs!" Mike replied, Seamus grin grew wider as did Nicks and they disappeared towards the already loaded lorry. Mike had invited Seamus, his wife, Nick, Vi, John, Alice, Anita, and her boyfriend back to supper after they had finished racing. He had a surprise for all of them and hoped they would like it. He telephoned John and told him they would pick him up in an hour having insisted it was time he supplied the transport instead of John. They hadn't seen much of each other over the last few weeks and it was Mikes turn to be worried about his friend rather than the reverse. He asked Kate if she would amuse everybody for half an hour, so he could have a private word with John at the races and find out why he hadn't been around. Vi appeared and though she was excited to have a day off she was still pretending to be cross with Mike because he had employed caterers to prepare the meal that evening, Kate felt a little miffed when he told her of his plan as she and Vi had already secretly planned the meal. Still as Mike said, he couldn't have the hostess and one of his guests running backwards and forwards to the kitchen all night. Instead he employed an enterprising Thai couple who did everything from laying the table, cooking and serving the meal to the washing up. Not too hard as Mike had a huge dishwasher. Mike had also planned a surprise for the children having arranged for them to have their own 'dinner party' though party being the more descriptive word. The limo arrived to collect them all and Becky sat biting her nails and throwing questions at Mike for the whole journey. Sunrise was running in a listed race and the stable had high hopes for her chances. Becky was thrilled Sunrise was to race in the second, the listed race, and Dusk and Dawn in the fourth, a fairly good maiden. Mike thought they could be lucky and be placed, there was little to choose between the pair, Dusk probably being the more forward of the two. Becky was postulating on not only the chances of her horses but also the possibility of anyone else ever having had such a good idea as to name their horses as she had, and certainly she explained to her captive audience they would never have had them all running at the same meeting! They arrived at the racecourse and Mike found himself having to go to the stables, not because of any specific reason but just to see the horses for himself. Satisfied, he returned to the owners and trainers bar where Seamus was looking very pleased with himself. "Good man Michael! You just won me fifty quid!" Mike looked confused. "I bet old Bert on stable security that you wouldn't be able to help yourself... you'd have to have a look at the horses even though you said you wouldn't bother!"

"I wondered why he started cussing when he saw me." A round of drinks was purchased and they sat round a table. Kate winked at Mike and said, "Why don't we all go and have a look around the stalls. I noticed there were quite a few. You never know there might be a bargain. It'll give John and Mike a chance to catch up." She raised an eyebrow. "If I know men, they won't want to come... but you Seamus can come and spoil Mary for once!"

Mike and John were left alone, Mike didn't waste any time and straight away asked John what the problem was. John acted puzzled, there was nothing wrong he told Mike, why did he ask? Mike explained his reasoning, he did realise that he had been quite tied up himself for the last couple of weeks but normally there was not a day that went by when one of them phoned or popped round. Mike had tried several times to get hold of John over the previous couple of weeks but received neither joy nor response. John, spoke. "After you guys stood by me over the gamble...." He put up his hand to avoid interruption from Mike, "I know everything thing turned out really well in the end but you still stood by me and I don't think it's fair to burden you with my problems... especially when I know you've had such a hard time emotionally of late. Though I have to say you look happier than I've ever seen you before. Things seem to be going well with Kate."

"Better than I could hope for." Mike replied but then his tone changed it bordered on angry. "I'm not talking about me though. I'm talking about you. We're friends that's why Seamus and I did all we could when you were having problems... that's what friends do and it's what they're there to do. John if it wasn't for you I would be nowhere, Seamus would probably had to find himself another job. You didn't only give me a chance financially, but you gave me friendship too so if you have a problem I'm here for you. So, spill the beans!"

John rubbed his chin. "It's stupid really! Not really anything! In truth I don't know why it has even bothered me."

"For God's sake spit it out!"

"Alice's mother is seriously ill. That doesn't really worry me there has never been any love lost between us, but I like the old feller and he's taking it really hard. I don't know what to do to help and then of course there's Alice. She was so excited to be back in the family fold so to speak. I'm frightened to death that the old girl will tell her how I got them to contact her. If she left me I just don't know what I'd do."

Mike ran his hand over his face. "John, I know you said she was a malicious old cow but do you really think she'd stoop so low even on her death bed?"

"Yes!" was the short reply.

"Then don't try to hide things you think are going to hurt the ones you love… I've made that mistake and probably still do even though I know it's misguided. You should talk with the old chap… you've told me often enough how well you get on and if what you've said is true not only has he done a fantastic job turning the estate back around but wouldn't want to take the chance on losing his daughter again... And let's be fair it was his doing not yours… Okay you may have taken advantage of the situation but you have to ask why… because you love Alice and her father knows that. You gave all of them a second chance… we don't get too many of those in life and you did it solely for selfless reasons. Jesus man, they should be fucking grateful! Go and speak to him then you should sit Alice down and tell her... she's a star and you know it. She'll be far more understanding than you think I'm sure." John looked a little more at ease and they got down to racing, John asking Mike what he thought the chances were for Becky's horses. "Pretty good I'd say. Sunrise won't be a very big price but you might get five to one on her with a bit of luck… it's just unfortunate that the horse she beat at Salisbury has produced so well it makes her form look pretty good... personally I'd say she be there at the shakeup. Dusk I reckon will take some beating if she runs as well as she works at home but Dawn hasn't really come in to herself, good horse at home though I think she'll need time, I think the razzmatazz of the races might just be a bit much for her first time. She'll improve for the run though and given a couple of races I think she'll get a win or two under her belt. Best left alone for this one put a couple of quid on Dusk she'll be worth a shout."

The others came back loaded down with carrier bags. "Bloody hell! We'll need to hire another lorry to get this lot home!" Mike said and was rewarded with a poke in the ribs from the girls.

"I didn't think Bert could really afford to lose fifty quid so I bought him this jacket... he was telling me about when we arrived, poor old sod said the extra fifty quid he'd win off me would give him enough to buy it. Insisted I took the money though, so he did. He's a good old boy I didn't have the heart to walk away with his money!" Seamus said almost as if by excuse. The chatter turned back to racing and Seamus went off to saddle up. As always, the girls had done a marvellous job of preparing Sunrise she looked absolutely amazing, coat gleaming, muscles rippling as she jig jogged round the saddling area the specially made bridle that matched the colours of the jockey silks adding to the grace of this beautiful creature. This is where it starts to become serious for all involved, the banter stops and the looks upon the faces of the lads and lasses become concentrated, concerned, expectant. There isn't a person leading a horse up that isn't going over the race in their mind or in their horse's ear. It is a sport of love not of kings. Even if it costs a king's ransom. The bell rang and the jockeys were called out, a separate parade of colour and banter. Seamus now in his second role was joking with the jockey of the favourite, race tactics having already been discussed in the weighing room. Often jockeys will decide who will make the running, who will settle their horse in behind another, each trying to give their particular horse a good chance. Even the horses that have no chance are taken into consideration, the horse that at least gets a mention or two during the race can give an owner the pleasure that has cost him so dearly. The jockeys mounted and Mike legged up Seamus, each man simply nodding to each other both knowing the horse and needing no discussion as to how the horse should be ridden. As Seamus turned to walk, the now excited filly onto the course he turned to Becky. "Get mum to put a couple of quid each way princess, she'll give you a good run today." Mike and the others that stood in the owner's enclosure had to stifle their laughter as Becky answered, "Okay Guv!"

The horses cantered past the winning post as they must and after a few minutes they were circling behind the stalls waiting to be loaded. Sunrise was third favourite though the betting market seemed uncertain as to her real chances, her odds fluctuated from five to eight to one. Becky asked her mum to place a bet for her and Kate asked Mike if he would mind taking Beck's as she was busy going over the dinner party plans. Though why, Mike didn't comprehend as it was all organised, including the 'extra' surprise party for the children. Mike led Beck's over to the bookmaker's stalls and was more than a little surprised when Becky took out a hundred pounds to place fifty each way at seven to one. "Are you sure it's okay to put that much money on? I don't know if your mum will be too pleased with me if I let you."

"It's okay, this is some of the money that granddad gave me to spend on the horses. They've got everything they need so I thought I'd spend it on the horses still but in a different way!" Mike didn't know how to argue against such logic.

"Okay I'll let you do it but on one condition... if she loses I'll pay for the bet. It'll be much easier than explaining to your mother!" they agreed, and Mike made Becky put twenty-five each way on with one bookie and twenty-five each way with another putting the same on himself with two more though he had to take lesser odds in doing so. John joined them both and they moved over to the rails knowing that had they placed their intended bets prior to Becky the odds would plummet. They placed their bets each putting ten thousand to win doing the same bet for Seamus…... Sunrise went odds on favourite. Mike, John, and Seamus had agreed that should the horse win they would give their winnings to three separate local charities. They had decided on the special baby care unit, a small animal sanctuary, and a little riding for the disabled yard that struggled to survive. By the time they had placed their bets the horses were loaded and they hurried back to watch the 'off'. Becky held tightly to Mikes hand as they grabbed a place by the winning post. The big screen panned to the stalls, jockeys eyeing each other like boxers entering the ring, reins were held tight, a handful of mane grabbed as they waited for the crash of the gates as the starter prepared to release fifteen surging power houses each weighing half a ton. The jockeys concentration became total as they watched the starter. "JOCKEYS!" and the gates flew open releasing the energy of fifteen highly strung balls of muscle. Becky screamed in excitement. Sunrise was one of the first to break Seamus holding her hard and settling her in to third spot half a length off the leader. "And it's Red Dragon that holds the lead by a neck to Golden Chime, Sunrise is laying half a length off the two leaders and they're going at a blistering pace, the leading three have opened up a gap of ten lengths to the field who are struggling to get on terms. Golden Chime takes up the running as Red Dragon starts to fall away, Sunrise is looking for a run on the inside but Golden Chime holds the rail 'O' Malley brings Sunrise out and its neck and neck, Golden Chime is scrubbed along 'O' Malley starts to ask Sunrise, he's driving her hard and it's Sunrise, Golden Chime, Sunrise stretches for home." "GO ON SUNNY!" a diminutive little voice rang over the screaming crowd making Mike jump. "GO ON YOU CAN DO IT!"

"And it's Sunrise that crosses the line to win the valuable listed race here at Windsor today by half a length, Golden Chime second, and a long way back Red Dragon third the rest of the field tailed off."

Becky was doing a little dance which looked like something out of *Saturday Night Fever*, singing at the top of her voice… "Do a little dance… sing a little song… she's won again!" The crowd were as fascinated with Becky as they were the race and once again the photographers were pointing cameras at Becky rather than the horse, the headlines in tomorrow's papers would no doubt feature the already fast becoming famous face of Becky Stokes. They walked over to the winner's enclosure where a television crew were waiting to greet them. Seamus jumped off Sunrise he was gasping for breath from the exertion of racing. Anybody that thinks riding a horse in a race is easy should try it… you have, to be as much of an athlete as the horse. "Well done Seamus, absolutely bloody brilliant ride." Mike gushed.

"Mike we're going to have to talk about those twins… I'm getting too old for this… we need some young blood!" Seamus smiled.

Becky rushed over to where Seamus stood throwing her arms around his neck and hugging him impulsively. "You're the bestest!" she enthused. "I've won……. How much have I won Mike?" she said releasing Seamus and turning her attention to Sunrise.

"Roughly four hundred and thirty pounds plus your stake back." The smile on Becky's face told its own story, she had no need to speak.

Seamus was not riding either of Becky's other runners and so after weighing in and taking his memento for the race they moved to the owner's bar leaving Anita and the girls to deal with the other two horses. Seamus was surprised that Mike had insisted Anita saddle up for the race without one or the other of them being there, but he was sure that Mike would reveal why in his own time. Mike sat at the table with the others sipping his scotch as Becky enthused over Sunrises win going through the race with amazing accuracy much to the amusement of the other owners as she imitated the ride by Seamus. In seconds of finishing her re-enactment she was badgering Mike to take her to the bookmakers so that she could place a bet on Dusk and Dawn. Mike resignedly dragged himself from the comfort of his chair and moved off towards the bookmakers with Seamus and John following Mike with an animated Becky hopping along beside him. Becky was slightly disappointed that the odds she obtained on her horses were fairly short, 4 to 1 on Dusk and 5 to 1 on

Dawn. Mike explained that with the stables horses being in such good form it was in fact fairly generous. Becky placed five bets of twenty pounds each way on Dusk and five bets of five pounds each way on Dawn. Mike was a little reluctant to let her place what for a child was a considerable bet but capitulated after Becky calmly explained to him that she would still be over two hundred pounds to the good from her winnings on Sunrise and she emphasised was not even touching her original stake money. Bets placed they walked across to the paddock standing in the middle to await the call for the jockeys. There was a large field for the race with 18 entries and Mike cast an expert eye over the horses as they were paraded around. Seamus had done a marvellous job and Mike felt himself swell with pride as he watched his own entries jig jog by. The girls leading up rightly looking proud of their charges. Anita walked across from the saddling boxes where she had 'tidied' up the horse's kit before coming over. "Well Guv. What do you think, look well don't they? Dawns sweating up a bit though… finding it all a bit hard to cope with… still she'll get used to it, she's a bit of a baby still I reckon." Mike answered saying he was pleased with the job Anita done but apart from reminding her not to be late that evening said little else. He could see that Anita was disappointed in his casual reaction and smiled inwardly. "You've a wicked side to you Michael Willett." He said to himself. The jockeys mounted and the horses made their way to the start.

The sun made it difficult to see the big screen on the side of the course properly and so Mike and his party made their way back to the owner's bar to watch the off. Dusk walked in the stalls like a true professional Dawn had to be blind folded and was obviously stressed as she fidgeted in the stalls. The gates crashed open and the horses leapt from the stalls. 'It's Dawn that leads the field as they move towards the rail, Seven Up tucked in behind her, Celestial…. Forward Thinking, Herbal… Mukbil,.. Cost A Packet… Almera,.. and Dusk sitting at the rear by five lengths. "Look at Dawn go!" Becky shouted. Mike looked at her seeing the enthusiasm and love for horses in her eyes, it was like looking at himself at that age, he idly wondered if he had met Kate in a former life and Becky was really his own. "She's running on adrenaline sweetheart... don't get too excited she'll drop away in a furlong or so." Becky's face showed her disappointment. "Don't look so sad, she'll take two or three races to get the hang of it, you keep your eye on that other filly of yours she's hacking along."

'Four from home and Dawn is starting to fall away Almera making good progress along the outside, Herbal starts to weaken, Celestial making headway, Seven Up takes up the lead,' Becky was jumping up and down on the spot, ' Dusk finds space and is pushed up to third, Dawn seems to have found her second wind and is racing after her stable mate, Dusk hits the front but Almera comes to take her on, it's Dusk by a neck, Almera fighting hard Almera takes the lead, Dusk comes back again, Almera, Dusk, Dusk Almera and they cross the line together... too close to call, it's one for the judges, Seven Up closely followed by Celestial then half a length to Dawn, Herbal... the commentators voice was drowned out by the ecstatic screaming of Becky. "Did she win, did she win." Becky screamed.

Her joy was contagious and Mike, John, Seamus and Kate were trying hard to control themselves, Mike drew breath. "I don't know sweetheart but I think Almera might have got it on the nod! Mind you she's a good horse and she's run three times before and been placed second every time out against some decent horses!" Mike added trying to make Becky's potential disappointment should her horse have been beaten into second a little easier.

"She jolly well maybe a good horse but she's nowhere near as good as Dusk." Then with a sensibility that stunned even her mum she continued. "If she is second it doesn't matter, she ran an absolute corker, especially first time out, so whatever the outcome I'm well pleased! As for Dawn I think under the circumstances she ran really well and I agree with you." She looked directly into Mikes eyes, "She'll need another run or two and then I think we'll have a decent horse." Mike turned to Kate.

"I think your daughter is far too clever for someone of such tender years and is going to stun the horse racing world if she sticks to her guns and does take up training when she's old enough."

Becky looked at Mike very seriously. "I will be the best, but I'll never be able to do what you've done… no one will!" Mike found he had a lump in his throat, he looked around and guessed from the look on everyone's faces that they felt the same. 'What an amazing little girl' he thought and not for the first time. The tannoy whined "The result of the fourth race dead heat, dead heat, Seven Up two lengths, Celestial a neck, and Dawn by a length. Becky went straight into her wiggly little dance routine singing 'Do a little dance sing a little song we've won again' flashes from cameras lit up the room from professional photographers and other owners. It looked suspiciously like Becky's fame was to get a serious injection as Derek Thompson from channel four racing hastened towards Becky for another interesting interview. "Where's the man that wears the funny hats, too? And all those silly rings? He made me laugh when I came on your show!" Now she had made the TV crew laugh and Derek, through his own merriment, asked Becky if she thought her mum would bring her to the studio again for Saturday's morning line as it would be nice to have them both on the show again as they could talk to her about the horses and mum about the film. She assured Derek that she could after asking mum, Kate having no objection, she excused herself very formally saying that she had to go to the winner's enclosure to collect the trophy with Mike. Mike smiled at the camera crew, shrugged his shoulders and walked off being hurried along by the tiny hand that gripped his. Derek Thompson turned to the camera almost lost for words, he shrugged his shoulders. "Bloody amazing!" he said and the action went back to racing, leaving even the most hardened bookmaker shops customer hoping that for once racing would take the back burner and the interview with Becky would continue. Saturday morning would bring channel fours biggest viewing figures.

If you ever have the opportunity to ride home in a horsebox in which there is a winner, especially when there are two and one in a listed race... do so... you'll never see such elation anywhere else, they should make all drug addicts do it, then they'd realise that there are bigger buzzes!

Mike walked into the dining room and very nearly burst out laughing, Vi was standing in the middle issuing orders to a Thai couple who were doing the catering. Mike was certain that they had everything under control but looked totally flummoxed as Vi stamped her authority on the situation. Mike diplomatically steered Vi from the potential fray explaining that she ought to go and sort out Nick, who he told her was still in the yard fiddling about. "Big lummox!" she said. "I told him to make sure he was home and getting ready on time.... I suppose I'll have to go and sort him out.... !" and with a last glance over her shoulder at the activity in the dining room reluctantly left her domain in the hands of the caterers.

Even Vi had to admit that the dinner was faultless, the food excellent and the service provided was superb. Mike thanked the caterers giving them a tip of fifty pounds and an assurance that he would be using their services again. Everything having been done they retired to the lounge and relaxed knowing that even the dishwasher was empty and its contents packed away. Mike poured drinks for everyone whilst Alice and Kate went to check on the 'kids party'. Becky sat in the middle of the floor with a rapt audience, even the child minder was enthralled as she told her tale of Rockets race soon to be followed by a re-enactment of her own horse's races. They quietly closed the door and made their way back to the lounge. "Well I guess you're wondering why I've suddenly come over social? Well I've an idea or two I'd like to put to you!"

Seamus Irish lilt interrupted. "And there we was tinkin' the Guvnor was being nice!" The whole room laughed.

"Seriously," Mike said gravely. "I've been doing a lot of thinking lately and I think it's time I took more of a back seat... I haven't been too involved of late and in truth I've quite enjoyed the break. It doesn't mean I won't be involved still because I will it's just that I think that I should pass a bit more responsibility to those who after all have been dealing with it of late and have stood by me. So, here's my plan, when I've finished you can tell me what you think." Mike sat down leaning forward in his chair sipping his Jameson before continuing.

CHAPTER SEVEN

Mel sat on a straw bale in front of Storm, Mark never far away stood in the corner of the stable both stared intently at Storm then at each other. Storm moved across to where Mel sat putting his nose against her shoulder and pushed. Mark smiled and the twins looked hard at each other, Mark nodding as though knowing the question that seemed to be forming in all the occupants minds in the stable that evening. Mel raised herself to her feet and walked out of the stable coming back through the door after only a couple of minutes holding a bridle and saddle. Slowly the two walked up to Storm, who stood calmly looking from one to the other. Mel ran her hand over his handsome head and down his sleek neck to just behind his withers then patted him firmly. Storm did not flinch. Moving slowly, she put the bridle over his head and placed a thumb in his mouth pressing down on his tongue so that his mouth opened wide enough for her to slide the bit in. Again, Storm did not move but stood patiently taking all in his stride. With Mark holding his head and gently stroking his neck Mel moved to his side with the saddle slowly but firmly placing it on his back. Storm did not move. She reached underneath him and pulled the girth into place and apart form a small snort Storm still did not object. For a few minutes they walked Storm around his stable and when he did not seem to have any objection to either the saddle or the bridle the twins smiled at each other and nodded. Mark hurried across to the indoor school and switched on the floodlights, Mel followed holding Storm. They stood in the middle of the school and Mel walked to the front of Storm as Mark held him, reaching up she stroke his face kissing his velvet soft nose, he whickered softly. Again, the twins smiled and nodded to each other and Mel moved back to Storms side, Mark still holding the bridle. Mel bent one leg and Mark put his hand underneath her knee lifting her into the saddle. Storm still did not object.

"Right first and foremost," said Mike, "well done for today… Anita you know that we've built a new yard, which I must add you two reprobates have done a marvellous job on!" he looked at Seamus and Nick who chuckled conspiratorially to each other. "Well I'd like you to consider taking charge of it…. We'll make you assistant trainer and though you will still be responsible to Seamus and myself to all intents and purposes you will operate the yard off your own back. If you take it on I'll expect you to do everything, including staffing, dealing with the owners and there are plenty waiting to move horses to us, keeping the books and records straight, again you'll be responsible for finding the right staff to do it. In short it will be your yard to run and race from and of course there will be a substantial pay rise if you choose to take it on. Seamus and I will always be around if you need advice or have a problem. Oh, one more thing I'm having the old house renovated and you would of course be expected to move in. we can put a couple of decent mobiles up there for staff until we sort out some permanent accommodation for them. Well what do you think because if it's a yes you had better get up there tomorrow and have a word with the builders to sort out what you want in the way of kitchens and decoration!"

Anita jumped to her feet emotion overcoming her. "Thanks Guv!" she said sobbing with joy. "I promise you I'll make you proud!"

"You already have sweetheart," Mike said smiling at her.

"Right now to you, you big sod!" Mike looked at Nick who blushed as all in the room looked at him.

"You've done a bloody marvellous job for me all round but I think you need to take things a little easier!" Everyone in the rooms face dropped, Kate went to say something to Mike but Mike raised his hand to stop her, Nick looked petrified as did Vi. "So, I've decided that you should take on two or three staff to do all the gardening, fencing and maintenance work you do… you'll be in charge and I don't want you doing all the work because you're now management! It will also give you more time to spend with Rock's and Storm. There's one more thing I'd like you to do though. I want you to watch over the twins, Seamus said they are seriously good around the yard and horses but they're still having trouble getting things across to others, Seamus tells me you've built up a bit of a rapport with them, so I'd like you to try to help them a bit. It seems you appear to understand what they're trying to get across. Oh, and as you are now management there will be a pay increase for you as well!" Nick was lost for words and Vi beaming proudly for her man hugged Mike. "If there isn't a saint Michael there bloody well should be and I'm proud to say I know him. Thank you, Michael, you're a good man with a heart as big as… well you know what I mean!" she broke off.

"Me? I'm just a bloody old fool!" Mike replied to all the compliments he was getting. "Anyway, you might live to regret it because the Irish raider is still your boss!"

"And bollocks to you too!" Seamus shouted with everyone guffawing.

"John, Alice could I speak to you in the office for a moment… if you'll all excuse me that is?"

Alice looked slightly bewildered, as did John and as soon as they had entered the office and closed the door John asked what was so important that they had to leave the party.

"It's about our conversation at the races!" Mike said and John went ashen faced. "I know I'm not the best diplomat in the world and my tact leaves a lot to be desired but the quicker you say the sooner it's mended if it needs mending at all that is. I know how much this is worrying you and we're friends so if you don't tell Alice the story I will!" John's face was a cross between fear and anger he knew Mike was doing what he felt was best but feared his wife's reaction.

"Will someone tell me what the hell you two are talking about!" Alice said quite calmly.

John told her everything, how he had managed to get Alice's parents back in touch with her, he spared no detail and as he spoke Alice stood calmly listening intently to all he had to say.

"John Cullen," she said quietly, "do you honestly think that my father and I don't communicate? I'm not a fool and as much as I love my mother I know what a stubborn stuck up mercenary woman she can be. Daddy told me what had happened shortly after little Mike was born. He shouldered the blame rather than you I have to say though, and let's be honest it was him who was stupid! He knew mummy would have to try and stir up trouble at some point... it's just her way and he not only thinks quite a lot of you but also has great respect for you. You did in a roundabout way give him back not only his daughter but his estate. So, let's say no more about it shall we and get back to the party!" John was gob smacked at Alice's reaction and even more so as she, it seems, knew all along, he walked over and kissed his wife lovingly and the three-wandered back to the lounge all looking very pleased with themselves. As Mike passed the front entrance a gleam of light caught his eye and on entering the lounge he turned to Seamus. "Shorty!" he joked, "good guvnor you are you left the lights on in the indoor school!"

"I'm big enough to put you over me knee you young whipper snapper!" Seamus retorted, "You're seeing things no one's been in the school today." Mike looked concerned, Storm's abduction never left his mind. It appeared that the same was true for John, Seamus and Nick for they all rose quickly from their chairs. "All for one!" Seamus said, and apart from the three friends everybody looked puzzled.

"Only thing is," Mike said, trying to keep a little levity on their unspoken concern, "is that there's four of us now... and from what I've seen of the film he looks nothing like d'Artagnan!" He threw a glance at Nick. "Though in truth I know which one I'd plump for.... Come on let's go have a look."

"What's going on?" Kate asked.

"Nothing to worry about someone left a light on is all."

"Do I look that stupid Michael Willett?!" Kate added sarcastically.

"From here you look like heaven sweetheart," Mike said turning quickly before there was time to answer. "Just be a minute!" he threw over his shoulder as they went out the door.

"Men! I ask you... come on girls," she said noticing that Anita's boyfriend who was only slightly smaller than Nick had somehow managed to creep out with the others without being noticed. "I think we'd better go and see what they're up to!"

Mike and the others stood silently peering through the partly open door of the indoor school. "Well I'll be damned!" whispered Mike.

"You will......"

"Sshh!" Mike went stopping Kate from speaking further then beckoning her and the girls forward, she saw why. Mel was sitting on top of a very proud looking Storm trotting around the school. Seamus whispered to Mike. "I tried to put a felt pad on the little fella two days ago and he was an absolute shit, I can't believe what I'm seeing. You'd think he'd been doing it for months. Look how responsive he is too her!" There was no doubt to what Seamus said, as Storm broke into a canter with Mel making him change legs as he did a figure of eight around the school. Mel looked up and saw the faces peering through the door, her expression turned from exaltation to fear as she saw her bosses. Nick stepped forward straight away walking over to where Storm now stood still awaiting Mel's next command. He put a reassuring hand on her arm. "It's alright the guvnors not mad." Mel took out a pad from the inside pocket of her jacket and frantically scribbled something. Nick read it aloud. "She says she's sorry Guv, she just wanted to see if he would let her ride him." Mike couldn't help but smile. "Mel what you've done is very impressive but in future make sure there's someone like Seamus, Anita, or myself around as well… just in case anything goes wrong." Mel beamed. "now put him back in his box and go to bed." Mel gently slid from the saddle with Storm still standing stock still and with a shy smile at the others walked Storm back to his stable with Mark by her side.

When everyone had settled themselves back into the house the conversation turned inevitably to Storm and Mel. John was already picking up the prize for the Derby, Diomed Stakes, St Leger, Guineas, in fact just about every prestigious race there was, Seamus had fallen as well and was enthusing about the Melbourne Cup, Kentucky Derby with the Triple Crown in his sights. "For Christ's sake you two the horse has only just been sat on…. Look let's all calm down a bit shall we… we don't even know if he's any good!"

John and Seamus spoke as one. "Any good! Any good…. He'll be better than good he'll be bloody brilliant… he's the son of The Rocket."

"Exactly and just remember what a cantankerous little shit he was!" 'Thank you very much!' the voice in his head interjected. "Sorry!" "Apology accepted" Mike found it very confusing holding two conversations at once.

"Ahh, but the big fella showed 'em all in the end so he did!"

"I know Seamus but please I had enough of you two with Rock's to last me a lifetime, let's just take it a step at a time… please!"

A voice from behind Mike interrupted. "Sorry I'm so late… goddamn plane was delayed." It was Roy Winston. "What's going on have I missed something. I heard Seamus saying about the Kentucky Derby… is Rocket going for it?" Seamus was quick with enthusiastic help from John to explain all that had been seen and discussed. Mike sat down heavily with a resigned look on his face. Kate walked over to him cupping his face in her hands and kissing him. "There, there sweetheart!" she cooed and everybody laughed.

"Hell boy's that's a fucking good idea…. We could announce

it in the press… imagine what it'll do for the theme park and the film! Jeez you couldn't get better advertising."

"Look hold on we don't know if the horse is any good yet." Mike repeated. "And if he goes out and fails we'll look like a total bunch of idiots… now surely that isn't good advertising?"

Roy and the others thought for a second. "Good point. Maybe Mikes right… let's wait and see what the horse can do…. Then I'll go to the papers… and if he fails then well we'll say he's biding his time just like his old dad did!" Mike looked a little more relieved at Roy's last comment. A little bundle flopped into Mikes lap. "Why is everybody so excited… I was asleep but you lot woke me up!" the bundle complained in mid yawn. Mike tried to explain briefly what had happened, then carried Becky back to her room and settled her back in bed. "Now you get some sleep you've a long day tomorrow… superstar!"

"I know it's very hard being so popular. I suppose I should go back to sleep I want to look my best for my interview…. And don't you keep mummy up too late either… remember she's on the telly as well tomorrow!" Mike smiled at Becky walked to the door turned and noticed that Becky was already sound asleep.

The chatter about Storm went on for another hour before everyone slowly filtered towards their own homes. Mike and Kate went to bed hand in hand and by the time Mike had cleaned his teeth and made his way to his side of the bed Kate had joined Becky in the land of nod.

Roy had generously organised a helicopter to fly his new film star to the interview which was to be held at the newly built Newbury racecourse in the hope that it would generate further interest in the film of Rocket… not that it really needed any more advertising it had been the talk of just about every TV show and every paper for the past few weeks. If fact the announcement of its making had left Roy's desk heaped with offers from those wishing to take a role in the film and from those wishing to become involved financially. The film was already a success and they hadn't even started on the first scene!

For Kate and Becky it meant that the trip to the racecourse

was simple, it would take only thirty to forty minutes rather than an hour and three quarters and be a lot less tiring that driving. Becky looked very smart and grown up in her newly purchased trousers and matching top, despite her mother's protestations that she should wear a dress. Becky would have none of it, far to girly she told her mum and after all it was the racing channel not some silly fashion show! Kate gave way and in truth, it didn't matter because Becky looked a star anyway. Kate was stunning she had chosen a short dress in blue that showed off her long slender legs and highlighted her amazing eyes. There was no doubt thought Mike that all eyes would be firmly affixed to her gorgeous lines and he would have placed a bet that the camera strayed as often as possible to catch a glimpse of her legs and braless bust whose nipples seemed absolutely determined to break free from the tight jersey dress. Kate smiled at the approving look she received from Mike as she came down the stairs. She walked over kissing him on the cheek.

"Now you be a good boy and watch the show… oh and don't forget to record it for Titch… see you later." And with a wave from Becky they went out the door to strap themselves in the seats of the helicopter that awaited them. Mike was slightly puzzled at Kate saying 'watch the show', it was after all just an interview with her about the film and Becky simply because she was such an amazing personality. Mike was certain there would be record ratings for the Morning Line yet again. It was the way in which Kate had said it that caused him to wonder, as though she had some surprise in stall. He walked back to the kitchen making himself breakfast before wandering into the lounge and settling himself on the couch, breakfast on his lap remote control by his side and recorder running. The Morning Line theme blasted out of the speakers and Derek Thompson's face appeared on camera. "This week's guests are as you will no doubt have read… as it seems to be in every paper in the country, are the delightful Becky Stokes and her beautiful mother Kate Stokes." The camera panned to where they both sat on opposite Derek and his cohorts. Mike dropped the bacon and eggs he was eating on the floor as the camera panned. The camera man must have fallen over because the camera was suddenly filming the ceiling, another camera took up filming quickly directly in front of Derek and his companions who had all dropped their clipboards and sat open mouthed, the camera panned back around to where Kate sat. "Something wrong boys?" she asked demurely as she again uncrossed and crossed her legs. Mike burst out laughing. "I'll bet everything I own that every bloke in the country wishes they were recording this and those that are will make a fucking fortune! Sharon Stone you've just been upstaged. What a bugger you are Kate Stokes a beautiful, clever, bugger. I'll bet Roy Winston is already counting the cash for the release of the film!" Channel Four studios were pandemonium as camera crew, lighting technicians, sound men and presenters all tried to compose themselves, Mike was in hysterics as he watched the TV, even though he felt a certain sympathy for the occupants of the studio knowing how devastating Kate could be under normal circumstances without trying! Becky brought about respite from the ogling at Kate in her normal fact of the matter way. "I know my mummy's very pretty but if you men would all stop gawping at her then perhaps you could ask some sensible questions…. I do have something very important to tell you, you know!" Derek Thompson cleared his throat, digging John Francombe in the ribs as he did so as he had slid forward on his chair to such a degree that he was in danger of ending up on his knees. After a few humms and hahs Derek managed to address Becky.

"Quite right young lady. We're just not used to interviewing beautiful film stars now what is it you have to tell us?" Becky almost took exception as Derek had unwittingly started to talk to Becky as though she were a child. An understandable mistake but one that Becky was not going to put up with.

"Firstly I think you should be honest and apologise to mummy for trying to look up her skirt!" the camera man obviously found this highly amusing as the camera started to wobble uncontrollably.

"And you can stop laughing!" Becky said to the camera. "you

are just as bad!" It was a good few minutes before order was restored and the Morning Line was back on track. Kate now looked very demure and seriously smug, knowing that her little performance would bring about an unbelievable reaction.

"You were saying you had something important to tell us?" Derek asked in his most formal interviewers voice. Mike looked at the close up of Becky and at that moment knew she was not going to be upstaged and his stomach churned as he considered what he thought she was about to say.

Becky's face took on a serious and concentrated look, making sure that she had the attention of all in the studio. The camera panned back slightly so that viewers had a view of the whole studio.

"Well I shouldn't really tell you this because it's sort of secret... well not really secret but no one else knows anything about this at all! In fact." She continued. "If they hadn't made so much noise I wouldn't have woken up and even I wouldn't know... can you believe that!" Becky had captured her audience. Mike looked at the TV. "Please Beck's please don't say what I think you're about to!" but he knew exactly what Becky was about to say.

"You know Rocket?" Mike cringed. "Well he has a son... I expect you've heard about him... well you might not have because he's only just started work... well Seamus and John are really excited... and so is Roy." She added as an afterthought. Mike slumped into his chair. "Mike thinks they should wait just a while before saying anything..." you could hear a pin drop in the studio. "but I know he won't mind if I tell you... you see we get along very well and he tells me lots of things about the horses... and he never said I didn't have to tell anyone... well Storm... that's Rockets son.... He's very special... in fact he's just as special as Rocket but more tractable... whatever that means... though Mike isn't too sure about that! Well last night Seamus and John said to Mike that they thought Storm should win the Derby and just about every big race there is... it's never been done before you know! And if he does then they're going to win the

Melbourne Cup and something called the Triple Crown... I'm not sure what that is but it's very big and it's in America. If you want to know what I think, I think he will... he's a very good horse you know. Oh, and by the way I think he will probably have a girl jockey!" For the first time in history the Channel Four racing crew were lost for words! Seamus burst in Mikes lounge, Mike looked up at him waiting for the apology he was sure was soon to follow.

Seamus was at his most animated and Irish as he spoke. "What a girl! Now let me be tellin' you that's a girl that knows her horses!" Mike sat staring at Seamus in disbelief.

"Seamus." He started sounding slightly weary. "That girl as you put it has just announced the impossible to half the fucking country and by this evening half the fucking world!" Mike's voice rose to a crescendo as he finished the sentence. "That's not all though she's also announced that the horse is going to be ridden by a girl jockey.... I'll tell you what how about I put a fucking dress on and I'll ride the fucking horse! Even better." Mikes voice had risen to a scream. "You and John.... And Roy fucking Winston too for that matter can dress up in a fucking horses costume and I'll ride you in the fucking Derby... we just as well go the full hog in this fucking pantomime you twats have started....!" Mikes voice came down several octaves and he now seemed even more weary. "Fuck Seamus I thought we'd done all this with Rocket... and now you pricks have started again but this time you've really gone flat out.... I just don't believe this is happening!"

Seamus remained totally calm. "Too be sure you do nothing but worry Michael... Ahh... have you forgot what we did with the big fella.... The little chap why he's as quick as can be... you should see him in the paddock.... Why he's just like his dad!"

"Seamus... of all the people I know you know horses and you also know that running round a field is a whole lot different than galloping against a field of highly competitive horses on a race track.... Jesus how on earth am I going to talk my way out of this one!" There was a despairing quality to Mikes voice.

"Now don't you go a worrying about the details... 'twill be easy... you just wait and see... there you go with all that worrying again like you did with the big fella... do you not remember how he showed them all!" John burst in the lounge breathless.

"What a girl!"

"Don't please!" Mike implored. "I've already listened to this Irish dick head... I can assure you I don't need to hear it from another one English or Irish!"

John looked at Seamus. "What's up with him... got a hangover from last night or something?"

Seamus grinned. "I think our young Michael has a touch of the stage fright!" the phone rang which probably saved Seamus from an unfortunate event, Mike picked up the walkabout from the coffee table and put it to his ear, not even saying hello he listened for a second then held the phone out in the direction of John and Seamus, John took the phone. "It's Roy." He said to Seamus. Then talking back into the phone. "He's a bit upset at the moment...... no I'm sure he'll come round eventually.... I know .... You think so.... Bloody hell.... Alright I'll organise things and we'll meet at my place tonight.... Okay that sounds good we'll meet you there. Bye."

Mike sat head in hands. "Don't tell me I've managed to make friends with the biggest bunch of pratts from both sides of the fucking Atlantic!" Seamus and John looked at each other and smiled.

"There'll be no talking to the man when he's like this!" said Seamus, John smiled back and nodded turning back to Mike. "I'll send a car to pick you up at seven, we've a meeting with Roy at eight at the Greyfriars restaurant... foods really good apparently." He pulled a face at Seamus. "See you there." The pair made an exit but not before Seamus threw one small comment over his shoulder.

"And don't you be worrying about a girl jockey... I've got me sights on one!" Mike simply groaned.

Leaning back in his chair Mike started to doze dreaming of pantomime horses, dames and he's won, oh no he hasn't, oh yes, he has! He was rudely awoken by something landing with wind crushing effectiveness on his lap. "Did you record it?... weren't we great... those men were rather rude though trying to look up mummy's skirt!.... when we walked back onto the racecourse there were loads of people!... I've had my photo taken with mummy a million times.... Maybe even more than that... they said I'm going to be in every paper in the country tomorrow and that mummy is going to be the cause of many an argument... though I don't see how if she's here! They said every wife and girlfriend is going to be jealous of mum.... And they haven't even met her!... any way I've got to go and change Seamus is giving me a riding lesson.... Well not a lesson really I'm going to ride up the gallops with him he's going to show me how to ride a finish... I'm so excited I've always wanted to do that!" and before Mike could utter a word the whirlwind sped from the room to change. Kate smiled at him and suddenly all his fears disappeared for a second only to rush back, Kate saw the concern in his eyes. "I think I'll pour us a drink you look as though you could do with one!" By the time she had finished pouring the drinks the whirlwind had hurricaned through the lounge and had rushed towards the yard shouting Seamus name at the top of her voice. Mike looked suddenly fearful. "She doesn't honestly believe she's going to ride Storm... please tell me she's not thinking that... there's no way she can... she's not old enough for one thing!" Kate walked across to where Mike sat put the glasses on the coffee table and placed a finger against Mikes lips. "Shh, of course not she's not silly... she has other plans." Kate put a leg either side of Mikes lap and sat on him. "Just like I have for you...!" she slid her hand under herself and tore at Mikes flies. "You have something I want, and I think you need something to take your mind off things!" she pulled her short dress higher revealing that she wore no underwear and Mike forgot all about horses, jockeys and races.

Kate lay curled up in Mikes lap a satisfied smile on her face. "You realise what you two have done don't you?" Mike asked.

"Of course, I always know what I am doing!.... it did rather catch them all by surprise though didn't it...the look on those guys faces... and then Beck's chipping in not only reinforced my little performance but also threw another cat among the pigeons.... Actually if I'm honest my show really turned me on .... Just thinking about it makes me horny!...." She kissed Mike passionately and the rest of the morning was lost. Mike was standing in the kitchen filling the kettle when Becky burst back through the door. "Wow you should have seen me... where were you... Seamus said I was brilliant... not just good but brilliant... what a rush!" Mike thought that Beck's was spending too much time in the yard and was starting to sound like one of the lads. Never mind he thought there are worse things.

"I rode two lots and did a fast piece against Mel... she's a seriously good rider but I managed to stay upsides..... Seamus said can you go over after lunch because he wants to put Mel up on Storm in the indoor school again." Mike groaned knowing that Seamus, John and for that matter Roy along with Kate and Beck's would be forming the Storm is going to win not just the Derby but every race he enters. It had been done before but never quite on the scale the Storm fan club planned. Becky giggled poking Mike in the ribs as she did so, for a few seconds she reverted to being a little girl. "Come on Mr. Grumpy... smile." She giggled even louder as Mike pulled a face at her. "Oh, I nearly forgot there are loads of people at the gate they want to see mummy mostly, but I think some of them want to see you." Mike looked slightly puzzled. "Reporter people silly." Becky said placing her hands on her hips.

"I spoke to them but Seamus said I'd better leave it up to you because you weren't in a very good mood!"

"That's very nice of Seamus." Mike groaned.

"Don't be such an old grump." Kate's voice echoed from behind him. "Think of all the free publicity you'll get!"

"That's what's bothering me!" Mike complained. "Anyway, I don't think I've any worries... there certainly not going to have any interest in me if you're going out dressed like that!" The sun was beating down outside and it was hot and balmy Mike wondering how hot and balmy it would get if Kate who was wearing an extremely short skirt that rested low on her hips showing off her upper and most of her lower pelvis, the material was tantalising thin and Mike couldn't make out whether she had underwear on or not, she certainly didn't on top as her dark round nipples showed through the material of the white matching tie top she wore. Her tanned and slender form made Mike think that even though she had not yet stood before a movie camera, he was in the presence of a star. An element of doubt started to creep into his mind… how long would she want to be with him when the excitement and the allure of premieres and big parties beckoned. Kate took his hand and walked him towards the door. "Don't look so worried it'll be fine!" She said but in Mikes mind he wasn't so sure.

CHAPTER EIGHT

Mike stood at the top of the gallops, Becky gripping his hand for all she was worth. "Isn't it exciting!" Becky turned her face towards him smiling from ear to ear. "I just know he's going to be fantastic... why I bet he's the fastest horse in the whole world." Mike looked down at the surprisingly strong form of Becky, his knuckles had turned white from her grip.

"Beck's he won't be going fast sweetie." Mike knelt so that he was at eye level, "this is his first time up the gallops and he really shouldn't be here he really should do more in the school before he comes out here!" He smiled. "But you lot have driven me nearly insane over this horse the last twenty-four hours... so against my better judgement I'm going with the majority but he certainly won't be going any more than a very steady canter... if he does that... he's really here to have a look around more than anything."

"He'll still be great!" Becky said almost a little petulantly. "And I think you should have let Mel ride him not Seamus!"

"Sweetheart... Seamus is an exceptional rider and he knows how to get a young horse going... I know Mel's a good rider but she doesn't have the experience yet... let's just see how the little fella does this morning before we start asking too much of anyone... ehh?"

"You'll see in a minute! I just know it should be Mel!" Becky had that determined quality creeping in her voice that meant that no matter how much coercion was given her course was set! Mike said no more.

Storm came onto the gallops looking fit to burst. It was all that Seamus could do to hold him and Mike decided to walk back down the gallops a bit, leaving his truck where it was, the less the horse had to look at the less he could spook at. Seamus turned Storms head up the gallops and tried to get him to trot forward and he did... for about three strides before planting. Seamus turned him back and took him the short distance back to the start of the gallops, again turning him so the he had the gallops in front of him, this time he went about a hundred yards before putting in an enormous buck throwing Seamus completely out of the saddle and onto the side of the gallops. Fortunately, Seamus wasn't hurt but he did have the wind knocked out of him and as he stood gasping for breath Storm turned trotted sedately back to the start of the gallops and stood by Mel who had come to watch. Mike could see or rather feel what was going to happen next and as he shouted as loud as he could, knew it was not going to make a difference, there was no way anyone was going to hear him, even if they wanted too. Becky looked at Mike with such a serious expression that her mature words didn't seem to surprise him. "Don't worry it'll be fine... he's his father's son you know... he'll make his own mind up what he wants to do, Mel and him have an understanding!" Mike just stood open mouthed and wondering.

Mel took hold of Storms bridle and deftly jumped up into the saddle. The horse didn't move, not a jig jog, toss of the head... nothing, she turned him towards the gallops leant forward and stroked his neck put her heels gently to his side and he moved forward. Storm trotted for a few strides before breaking into a canter, not a steady loping canter but one that ate the ground with ease, Mel changed her hands expertly and leaned forward dropping her knees onto Storms withers and he became a blur as his speed increased. By the time he was where Mike stood he was just a formless dark bay shape in a sound of thunderous hooves. "Told you!" Becky said smugly as the horse catapulted by them. Mike looked totally shell shocked. "He's as fast as Rocket." He said as much to himself as anybody.

"Of course he is silly... that's what I've been trying to tell you... why sometimes you're so hard headed... you really do have to learn to listen!" Becky looked so pleased with herself there was a glow that seemed to surround her. Mike never said a word as they walked back to the pickup truck and drove back down the gallops. Seamus had recovered and was in the process of telling Mel off for getting on the horse and telling her how brilliantly she had done. "Jesus Mike!" He said as Mike stepped from the truck. "Didn't I tell you he was a star...? Did you see the little bugger go! Flew so he did!... I tell you we've got ourselves another good un... Why we beat the world with his dad... now we'll do the same with his son... and more!"

"Oh fuck!" dejectedly, was all Mike could say.

"MIKE! Language!" Becky said primly though she had heard far worse in the yard.

"Sorry." Mike took Becky's hand and went back to the truck, driving back towards the yard leaving everyone wondering why he did not feel as elated as them.

Becky raced into the house shout loudly "Mum... Mum." Kate hurried down the stairs. "What's happened." Her face looking concerned.

"You should have seen Storm." Becky gushed. "He was unbelievable... like a proper racehorse and he absolutely flew up the gallops... though Mel had to ride him because he dumped Seamus! I don't know why but Mike doesn't seem very happy but everyone else thinks he's a superstar... I think he'll do even more than Rocket and so does Seamus!"

Kate's face relaxed. "Good grief Becky I thought from the way you were shouting something dreadful had happened! Whatever is the matter with you? You look as though you've lost a pound and found a penny!" she directed at Mike.

Mike look completely dejected. "Oh nothing I just think it's too early to start hyping up the little fella." Was all he said but there was more to it than that and anyone with half an ounce of brain could see it. Kate decided not to press the issue and anyway she was late as Roy had phoned to say an impromptu photo come press conference had been called. Kate explained to Mike and as he was happy to look after Beck's she made her way to the car. Mike watched her walk across the gravel a heavy feeling in his chest. He couldn't understand why because to say that she looked fantastic would have been an understatement. Her long slim tanned legs, hips swaying beneath the short summer dress she wore and blond hair swishing from side to side across her shoulders made a picture any man would wish to look upon but Mike couldn't shake off the feeling of dread that gripped him.

Kate roared off down the drive. "Come on Mr. Grumpy!" Becky said smiling up at Mike. "What shall we do...?" Mike looked at the small up turned face and smiled back his feeling dissipating somewhat.

"I'll tell you what." He said with more cheer in his voice. "How about I take this pretty little lady shopping... we'll go to the saddlery first and I'll treat you to whatever you want for your horses, then we'll go and hit the town and see what we can spend some money on and then I'll take you to the poshest place we can find for lunch!" Becky didn't need persuading, if she was being taken to buy something for her horses she didn't need asking twice. "I've lots of money myself you know... I can spend that... it's from my winnings."

"You hang on to that sweetheart." Mike replied. "I've a few quid myself and I don't very often spend it so today is on me and boy are we going to go wild!"

"Wild in the country!" Beck's squealed delightedly and rushed off to change out of jodhpurs to jeans.

Kate arrived at the press conference to a hail of flashing lights and photographers shouting her name in an effort to get her to look towards them, Kate duly obliged dazzling all before her with her smile. Roy walked over to her ushering her to the small stage that had been set up in front of row upon row of chairs. "You're an absolute natural, I've never had an actress that pulls the crowds like you... and we haven't even started filming yet... I was a bit worried in truth that you wouldn't be able to act but I really don't think it matters... you're a star anyway!" he whispered. Kate gave one of her disarming smiles. That she had found her forte in life was obvious to those around her and she was enjoying every moment of her instant fame. Much to her surprise and a little disappointment the questions thrown at her did not centre solely on her but often a reporter would ask about Storm or Becky one reporter tried to broach the subject of her relationship with Mike but was ignored. The press conference ended with Roy saying that filming would start the following week at a secret location and to remind all present not to forget to mention the fact that the theme park dedicated to The Rocket would be the venue for the premiere. The film he announced would premiere in six months which brought a gasp of amazement from the reporters. How did even he expect to shoot the film in such a short time was the question asked by all but he would give no answer except to say that he had given them the date and the date for release was final.

Kate drove home at a leisurely pace trying to work out how she was going to juggle her life around such a tight filming schedule, Roy having told her that shooting in reality started the following day.

Becky came out of the saddlery shop laden with presents for her horses, Mike had the sense to take the pickup rather than the car having weighed up the odds of Becky's love of buying for her horses. After they had loaded the back of the pickup they decided they would go for lunch before 'hitting the town'. Mike said there was a really good restaurant in the middle of town Becky however had other ideas and asked if they could go and have a proper breakfast in the café they had gone to shortly after meeting. Mike willingly agreed and so after gorging themselves on a large plate of bacon, eggs and all the trimmings they reluctantly pulled themselves from their chairs and moved towards town. Mike bought everything from clothes to computers, in fact there was so much he couldn't get it all in the back of the pickup and had to hire a taxi to take the rest back home. Feeling slightly guilty for spending so much on himself as well as Beck's as they walked down the street he noticed a chap huddled forlornly in a doorway, Becky looked a bit worried as Mike stopped to talk to him. The fellow Mike guessed was about twenty – twenty-five, he was unkempt but reasonably clean, though his clothes looked as though they had been thrown away by Oxfam. After talking to the young man for a couple of minutes Mike reached into his pocket and took out four fifty-pound notes. "Go and get yourself a good meal and find somewhere decent to stay, and if you can buy yourself some decent clothes. If you think you're up to some hard work come along to this address and I'll see what I can do for you, if you're there tomorrow I'll give you a chance, if you're not well good luck in whatever life throws at you." Mike gave the young man a card from his back pocket and Becky and he continued on their way.

"You're a very kind man aren't you." Becky said holding Mikes hand and swinging his arm as they walked along. Mike shrugged. "Well I think you are. You've spent loads of money on me and then you go and give loads of money away to someone you don't even know!"

"Not really sweetheart, tell you what we'll go and have a cup of tea and I'll try to explain to you why I do things like that."

Becky smiled. "And you're a big old teapot. Race you!" Becky said breaking away and running as fast as she could towards the bottom of the street where they had had their earlier breakfast, with Mike laughing joyously as he ran to catch up with her. Both were a little out of breath when they reached the door of the café. They went in and settled themselves at a table. "What do you fancy?" Mike asked when the waitress came to the table. "Could I please have a coke and a piece of cake?"

The waitress smiled at her. "You most certainly can and if it's okay with your dad you can have the cake for free… it's not very often we get a young lady with such lovely manners and I think they deserve rewarding!"

Becky gave Mike a smile and said thank you again to the waitress as Mike feeling as proud as he had ever felt in his life thanked the waitress himself saying he thought it was a very nice gesture. Becky was obviously not embarrassed or bothered that the girl had thought Mike was her dad as she grinned broadly. "Okay dad!" she said, "What were you going to tell me?"

"Cheeky mare!" Mike retorted and they both chuckled. "When I first started out I didn't have two pennies to rub together." Becky looked confused. "I didn't have any money."

"Oh."

"For a long time I begged, borrowed, did just about anything I could so that I could feed my horses, sometimes I didn't have enough money to feed myself…. There were times when I wouldn't answer the phone because I knew it would be someone wanting money and I just didn't have any…. And in all that time I kept hope that one day I would be able to prove myself… get enough money and prove I was good at what I did. It never seemed to happen though… every time I thought things were going well something would come along and ruin it. I knew lots of people who could have helped by saying something to support me, lots of people that could have helped me money wise, a couple of them I had helped myself when they had money problems and put myself in trouble doing it. Yet not one of them offered, not one of them would. In fact, the ones I had lent money too didn't even want to speak to me. I decided that if I ever did make it I would never turn my back on someone genuinely having problems that wanted to do something more than wallow in self-pity. Then John came along and I suddenly found myself not only with an amazing amount of fame but also more money than I had ever dreamed of. So, I reminded myself of my promise and if I think there's a way to make someone's life a little more bearable or I can help someone that's not as fortunate as me then I do. I think that if everybody did the same, rich or poor, then the world might just be a little better…. And any way I now have so much money I would have a job spending it all even if I went shopping day and night, so a few pounds here and there really isn't going to make much difference to me but might make all the difference to someone else." Mike finished.

"Wow! That's really cool and I think you're the best!" Beck's said leaning across the table and kissing him on the cheek. Mike would have given every penny he had for that moment.

It was getting late in the afternoon when they returned to the yard and Seamus was walking around the stables checking the horses, he stopped his inspection and walked over to look in the back of the pickup. "A taxi turned up with a bit of shopping... I put it in the kitchen." Smiling he looked again in the back of the pickup. "Don't tell me that's all the tight old sod bought yuh!" he said in his broadest Irish accent, "why, he can afford plenty... you should have held out for a horse at least!" He smiled again as Mike scowled playfully at him.

Becky grinned broadly. "He said he couldn't afford anymore!" she chuckled.

"Little minx!" Mike said rubbing the top of her head.

Seamus was looking very smug for some reason. "I'll give you a hand to unload and then you'd better come over to the foaling barn with me... I've something to show you!" Becky did her jig and Mike looked at Seamus. "I suppose you'll be wanting to go to the barn first seeing as whilst you two were out gallivanting your old mare produced a cracking little filly foal."

Mike looked stunned. "Tika? But she isn't due for another two weeks and she wasn't showing when I checked her this morning!"

"Well she showed well enough this afternoon! Beautiful little filly, strong as you like and almost as curious as this one!" it was Seamus turn to rub Becky's head.

"Ooohh, come on Mike we can put all this in the tack room later lets go see her!"

Mike was already grabbing Becky's hand and walking quickly towards the barn.

Mike and Becky walked into the barn with Seamus and as they did so the mare looked up and whickered softly. Mike still holding Becky's hand slowly walked up to where the mare stood, a small head popped out from behind her shoulder and looked at them curiously. "She's a bonny little sort." Seamus said to Mike as he spoke softly lifting his free hand to stroke the mares neck. "She is that Seamus." He said smiling moving the hand from the mare's neck to stroke the foal. The foal looked nervous but stood quietly as Mike gently stroked the side of its face. Becky moved closer and the foal reached out its neck and very gently mouthed Becky's nose with a very noisy sucking sound, Becky giggled and the foal did it again. "Well will you look at that!" Seamus declared and both men looked at each other with surprise.

Becky let go of Mikes hand and walked over to the side of the barn where there was a feed bin, obviously with the aim to get Tika a hand full of nuts, the foal gambled after her on unsteady legs. Becky looked round and seeing the foal following her giggled again and broke into a trot. "Do you want to play?" she asked, and the foal kicked up its heels very nearly falling over in the process and took after her. Mike and Seamus watched fascinated as the two ran around the barn playing tag.

"Well I never...." Mike exclaimed, and Seamus answered with a shrug of his shoulders. "Do you like her?" Mike asked as an out of breath Becky re-joined them with the foal still dancing around her.

"Why I think she's even prettier than Sunrise.... And she's so cute!" Becky said reaching out to touch the foal again as it continued its careering around them.

"Okay well seeing as Seamus thinks I'm so tight I suppose you'd better have her.... At least that way you'll have a playmate in the yard!" Seamus looked even more surprised than Becky knowing that Mike had a particular soft spot for the old mare and her progeny. Becky couldn't even speak she threw her arms around Mike and gave him a kiss, then did the same to Seamus and took of round the barn again with the foal in hot pursuit. "Come on Sky!"

"Sky?" Mike shouted after her.

"Sunrise, Dusk, Dawn, Cloud and the bestest of them all Sky!" she shouted back.

It took Mike and Seamus half an hour to pry Becky away from the foal and then only after Seamus had promised he would come to the house first thing in the morning and get Becky so that she could go with him to feed Tika and see the foal. Mike parked the truck in the garage still loaded saying he would put it away in the morning and Becky and he went into the house where he made them a snack sitting down to watch television. Mike sat feeling as though all the goodness in the world had smiled down on him as Becky curled up next to him drifted off to sleep. For the first time in a long time he felt at peace, not just with all around him but with himself. He looked down at the sleeping Becky who had stretched herself half way across his lap, then at his watch. It was ten thirty. "Come on sleepy head! It's way past your bedtime if your mother finds out I've let you stay up this late she'll skin me alive!" Becky yawned and sat up. "Right up those stairs, clean your teeth and get your pee jays on, chop, chop!" Mike said with mock severity. Becky grinned and sleepily wandered upstairs. Mike gave her five minutes and then went up to say goodnight. Becky was obviously shattered but was still wriggling around under the duvet. "Night, night sweetheart."

"I've had the bestest day of my life! Thank you so much for Sky!"

"That's okay poppet, now you go to sleep otherwise you'll be too tired to get up in the morning!"

"Bet I'm not!"

"Go to sleep!" and Mike turned towards the door.

"Love you."

"I love you too sweetie!" and he wandered down stairs feeling euphoric.

Mike woke with that feeling of someone having stuffed one's head full of cotton wool. He wandered into the kitchen in a daze, made a cup of tea took a sip then lit a cigarette. The haze in his head started to lift and he looked at his watch, it was two thirty in the morning. His first thought was he had missed Kate coming home, and he had wanted to be there to hear how her press conference had gone. He crept up the stairs looking through the door of Beck's bedroom as he passed she was sound asleep with just the top of her hair showing from under the duvet, he smiled, walking to Kate and his bedroom he tiptoed in. the bed was empty and for a moment he felt confused. She must be in the lounge he thought and went back down the stairs but there was no sign of Kate. He walked out to the garage and her car wasn't there and a feeling of concern started to rise in his stomach. He went back into the house and wandered aimlessly around for a few minutes before entering the kitchen and making another tea. He looked at his watch again it was three fifteen. He walked back into the lounge and sat on the couch looking at the telephone then his watch. It was three thirty. The feeling of concern became stronger and he reached for the phone starting to think that something had happened to Kate. He was just pressing the last number of Kate's mobile when he heard a car pull into the drive. It wasn't Kate's and he immediately rushed to the front door a feeling of total dread overcoming him. As he opened the front door he could see two people in the front of the car - a black Porsche - their heads were together, and Mike suddenly found the dread being replaced with a feeling of anger. He started to walk across the drive towards the car and the passenger door opened with an obviously half drunken Kate dragging herself from the seat. She closed the door and the car immediately turned and went down the drive. Mike automatically looked at his watch as Kate weaved her dishevelled self toward where he stood. "Christ! Kate it's twenty-five to four, look at the state of you! Where the hell have you been, I've been worried to death!" Mike was starting to get angry.

"Oops!" Kate slurred sarcastically, "Have I upset the poor little farm boy?... if you must know we had a party after the press had gone.... And I've had a great time... it was so nice to be around real people, people with class!"

Mike's temper got the better of him. "Class! You call getting in that state class, real people, my backside!.... And who the fuck was that in the car... I'd like to have a word with him!" Mike was gritting his teeth as the last few words came out.

"If it's any of your fucking business, he's the one who's playing you in the film and he's very sweet."

"Oh, I'll show him fucking sweet when I see him!"

"Why don't you piss off!" and Kate staggered past him waving two fingers in front of his nose as she did.

Mike sat on the settee unable to go to bed for fear of what he would say. He was awoken by a finger poking him in the chest, he opened his eyes to a small face with a look which he wasn't sure was disdain or sympathy. "You're too soft, you know...." It wasn't a question or a statement, Mike was just as unsure of the sentence as he was the look. "I'll make you a cup of tea." The little legs carried the little face into the kitchen leaving Mike to wonder what the hell was happening to his life. Becky came back, a mug of tea carefully carried in her tiny hand, she placed it on the coffee table in front of Mike and unceremoniously climbed onto his lap. "I'm not stupid you know! You two woke me up! I hate it when people shout. You really have to be much firmer with mummy, she's always the same when she has a drink.... She just can't help herself." Mike was a shocked at the way Becky was speaking but did not interrupt as she continued. "Mummy doesn't seem to have any self-respect when she's been drinking and she doesn't care what she does.... I really hope I don't do that when I grow up!" Mike instinctively hugged Becky before he spoke.

"Oh, you won't sweetheart you are far too sensible for that but you mustn't be too hard on mum, she's had a bit of a hard time lately and she's under a lot of pressure. Drink can do funny things to people.... Look what it did to me... I ended up with a broken leg!" Mike tried to inject humour into what he had said but from the look on Becky's face it didn't work.

"You know, sometimes mummy thinks I'm stupid! She thinks I don't know what she gets up to but she's not very good at hiding things. She has a drink and thinks no one sees anything she does.... But I do... I've woken up sometimes and spied on her and she's been very naughty. I still love her loads, but it makes me very cross! Why does she do it?" Mike didn't have an answer… couldn't answer… he could say it was the drink but it wasn't an answer, even from his own experience he knew that drink could turn an ordinarily sane person into a raving lunatic. He knew that wasn't an answer, it was just another excuse. As he knew from his own experience the answer led with the person, it was all about self-esteem and control. He stood up taking Becky with him then turned and threw her onto the settee causing her to laugh and forget the problems that surged around in her small head. "Let's go see how they're getting on with Storm, shall we?" At the mention of Storm, Becky's brain went into horse mode and she ran to pull her boots on. They met Seamus before they got halfway to the yard. True to his word he had come to get Becky. He grinned as Beck's first question was how her new possession was… Sky. He looked towards the house and saw Kate standing at the bedroom window looking out at them. The moment their eyes met she quickly turned and disappeared back into the room. Mike felt something he hadn't felt for a long time as a wave of sadness and despair washed over him, he felt just as he had when his relationship with Ann had broken down and he wondered if the feeling was a pre cursor of how this would play out. Becky's excitement drew him back, "Come on Mr. slowcoach you're holding us up…. You were miles away then." She gripped his hand and hurried him along towards the barn as he and Seamus talked about Storm. Seamus looked quizzically at Mike.

"The little one's right… you're miles away… you haven't heard a word I've said, have you?" Mike looked back at Seamus apologetically. "Sorry Seamus I was thinking about something else… What were you saying again?"

"John thought it would be a good idea to bring the little fella out early rather than leave it as late as we did with his father… Sort of make sure we get all the problems out of the way before they see the real Storm so to speak…. I tell you Mike the little fella's going to be better than his dad… if that's possible!" Mike asked Seamus if he would watch Becky for half an hour as he wanted to go and check on Rocket and Storm, it was a poor excuse and Seamus knew it but he also knew Mike well enough to know that he needed a little time alone.

Mike entered the barn that housed Rocket, Storm and Silver Dollar and was greeted with three whickers. He didn't speak but walked up to where Rocket stood head over his box door. "Talk about Déjà vu old lad." He said as he gently stroked the velvet muzzle of Rocket. "My life seems to be a circle… keeps returning to the same point, just when I think I've put the last brick on the building it all comes crumbling down around my ears." Storm kicked out at the side of his box and Mike looked towards him, it was like looking at a young Rocket. "Stand up you little bugger!" Mike growled and Rocket lent forward and gently nipped Mike on the arm. The voice in his head rang out. "For some life is not made easy… you're given something great, something you've always wanted… only to have something that becomes even more important taken away. Some are born fighters, some with more luck than they deserve. You Mike are a fighter and you'll keep trying to the end… it's the way you are… who knows perhaps you may win, perhaps you won't…. but you'll keep trying. You've achieved an awful lot but still have more to do. You may think you have found what you are looking for but that doesn't mean those around you have. It will come don't worry you just have to look a little harder." Mike stroked Rockets beautiful head before speaking. "That's all I need is a philosophical lecture from you."

"There are more things to heaven and earth than man will ever know." The voice returned and Mike turned and walked back towards the foaling barn to find Seamus and Becky.

Becky was giggling uncontrollably as the foal followed her around giving her a nudge with his nose every now and again. Seamus was looking on but turned as Mike walked up beside him. "Will you look at that! The little 'uns an absolute natural with horses! She's been telling me that she's going to be a trainer…. And if she does when she grows up I think you're going to have some serious competition. She'll get a horse to dance a jig for her that one!" Mike turned to Seamus and smiled but it was the smile of a man forcing himself to even respond. Seamus peered into Mikes eyes. "Mike I've known you a long time now and we've become friends… I'm always here to talk to you know… John's worried about you as well… we've both noticed you're become a bit insular of late. Look I know you keep things inside but you really have got to learn to talk to people… it helps!" Seamus received no reply and so continued. "Mike sometimes things don't go as you think they're going too, I know you and see that this is something to do with Kate. You two have been like two fighting cocks waiting to get in the ring…. Everybody has upsets but you have to talk… you're too much of a romantic… life has ups and downs it's not all about running through a cornfield dressed in white towards the person of your dreams…. There's pot holes to fall down just under your feet!" Mike smiled despite himself, Seamus was a good man and a good friend, but he knew that the potholes he was trying now to miss had become chasms. He had a horrible feeling he was going to slip over the edge and into the depths. Becky asked if she could spend the morning in the yard and though Mike agreed he felt uncertain knowing that the reaction from Kate might not be convivial.

Walking back to the house Mike noticed Mark leading Storm from his barn. Storm was jigging around whickering and shouting, Mike instinctively knew that Mark was in control of the horse but he still changed his direction automatically to lend a hand. He stopped in his tracks as Mel appeared from Storms stable. The horse stood stock still and refused to move until Marks twin was alongside him. Mel took the reins, gently stroked the horses neck leaning forward to kiss his soft muzzle. The horse stood stock still, now silent, Mark smiled at his sister and she moved to the side of the horse and he helped her into the saddle. The moment Mel alighted Storm moved forward like an old hack. There was no touch of the flanks by Mel's heels, no push on the neck, he just did it instinctively. They walked towards the gallops as Seamus and Becky exited from the foal barn, jumped in the pickup and pulled from the yard to watch the first lot work. Mike changed his direction again and walked over to where the old car that was used by the lads sat in the corner of the yard. Jumping in the car he drove off towards the gallops, passing the entrance and going to the top of the hill. He parked the car out of sight and walked over to stand behind the hedge, where he would have a clear view of the gallops but be unseen himself.

Storm jig jogged around in a circle as the other horses walked quietly. Mike didn't know what orders Seamus had given but imagined they would be to take Storm upsides the others at a steady. The other four horses jumped off going at a nice steady pace. Storm continued to jig jog round. He could see that Mel was gently trying to encourage him to follow the others but he was too intent on dancing around the circle looking showy. 'Just like his father!' Mike thought. As the thought came to him Storm decided to work. He turned pawed the ground and took off after the others. Like his father before him he showed blistering speed but there was a difference. Storm didn't seem to be quite as cantankerous as his father because after passing the others without effort he slowed allowed them to catch up and quietly went the rest of the way to the top of the gallops at a swinging canter alongside his stable mates. Mike went back to the stables feeling a little elated at what he had seen even though his overall mood was blacker than the darkest night. The elation evaporated as he walked into the house. Kate stood in the kitchen wearing only a small black G string and matching bra. The sight of her luscious body brought an immediate reaction to Mike but as he watched her walk gracefully around the centre worktop his elation disintegrated as he noticed the red finger shaped marks upon her back and bottom. The effect she had on him took second place as the fires of anger rose within him like the uncapping of a volcano. "What the fuck are those marks?" He practically screamed. Kate turned a look of surprising smugness on her face. "I beg your pardon?" she asked with such condescension it was like spreading oil on Mike's already volcanic reaction. "What the hell has it got to do with you what is on my body?" she continued, "I don't have to explain anything to you!"

Mike nearly lost his control as he stepped closer to her and despite her verbal bravado Kate took an involuntary step backward backing in to the worktop. "It's to do with me because we are fucking living together." He screamed into her face.

Kate laughed. "Tosser!" she said and turned to walk away.

CHAPTER NINE

John Cullen wasn't sure what to do, the phone call and subsequent visit by Seamus had deeply concerned him. For Seamus to phone concerning Mike was worry enough but to follow it with a visit meant his concerns ran much deeper than his loyalty to Mike, which was total. Mike was more than a friend to Seamus he had been his saviour. John sat rubbing his hand through his hair. "You say Mike was not interested in coming over to see the theme park?"

Seamus was surprisingly un-Irish, his voice almost neutral in accent and full of anxiety. "It was like stepping back in time.... He was just like he was when he and Ann split up not as angry perhaps but he looked just as depressed!" the Irish accent returned. "He never said a word too me, just sat there glass of whiskey in his hand staring at the wall. Eventually he turned to look at me and just shrugged, got up and walked out. I followed him but he just got in his car and drove off."

"You know Seamus." John interjected. "Mike is probably the most talented man I have ever met. He can make you smile, make you do things you really don't want to without even knowing he's got you to do it. I know I don't know too much about horses but I am learning but Mike he's a fucking genius! I remember saying to him that Rocket was like all greats they had their foibles.... Take Jimi Hendrix I said to him, Brilliant guitarist but a complete basket case......" John paused... "Do you know what he said to me?...... At least Hendrix could play the guitar!..."

Seamus looked confused. "I'm missing something here!" he said.

"Exactly!" John said triumphantly. "You've hit the nail on the head... We've both missed something... You'd agree with what I said about Mike being brilliant?" Seamus nodded his ascent enthusiastically. "So why then," John continued, "would Mike be any different from all the other greats? Stephen Fry... so intelligent it's embarrassing... manic depressive! Hendrix... Brilliant.... basket case... now I'm not saying that Mike compares but what I am saying is that he is fucking brilliant in his own right so maybe he suffers from the same?"

Seamus looked seriously at John for a moment before replying. "I'd agree with you to a degree... Mike is what you say, and I think you have a strong case for the depression bit, but I've known Mike a long time and this is different....... Vi made a comment the other day about Kate. 'loves that woman more than is right and I've a horrible feeling she'll tear him apart'.... Not the sort of comment you'd normally expect from our Vi, she tends to see the best in everything... always a silver lining. I think our Mike has a serious problem. I've noticed that Kate has become very sarcastic towards him of late and the atmosphere in that house is like the artic. Mike's afraid, I'm sure of it... he loves Kate and that little girl and sees them slipping away. There's a storm brewing John and I think Mike's right in the middle of it... and I've a horrible feeling he's going to be struck by lightning... We've got to do something!" Seamus added but in his heart, he knew there was little if anything they could. They both sat silent just looking at each other. It was a full minute before either of them could think to speak.

"I agree." John said eventually. "But what can we do? You know as well as I do what Mike's like when he gets on a downer.... He won't listen to us.... The only person that could bring him out of this is the one person that has put him there! Kate! It certainly doesn't look like we're going to get much help from that quarter! I don't even begin to know what to suggest. God I'm so fucking angry…. It was so good to see him back to being Mike and now…. And for what… love…!" John spat the last few words through gritted teeth his venom taking Seamus by surprise. "I had an awful feeling this was going to happen Seamus, in fact I told Mike to tread carefully but it was too late he was so much in love with her… you know I think he was from the first time he set eyes on her." All Seamus could do was nod his assertion.

Mike had been looking at the un touched whiskey he had poured into the glass when Seamus entered the kitchen. He hadn't really heard Seamus he felt as though he was in some sort of capsule that kept him in some secret place away from the voices of others, like being in a half sleep when you realise things are around you but can't focus on them. Now as he drove his car back towards the yard the half sleep was replaced by a mixture of absolute rage and desolation. He knew there were tears behind his eyes but would not allow them to show themselves. What he intended to do he had no idea, he felt as though someone had stuck a giant needle in the centre of his chest and sucked the very being from him. Mike was more alone than he had ever been in his life. The car pulled into the drive of the house and he saw Becky running around the garden with her now half-grown kitten and her terrier in hot pursuit of her. Mike sat and watched as she broke off the game and ran towards the car. He was joyous to see the Beck's running towards him her smile with its genuine greeting but his heart sank even lower as he realised how tenuous his grasp upon this little thing he had already taken as his own daughter. Love is a fickle thing, just when you think you have a firm grip on it, it whips through your fingers like a bar of wet soap. Becky wrenched open the door on the car and leapt on Mike's lap before he could exit from the seat. "Where have you been Mr. Grumpy?" Becky said very deliberately. "I've been waiting hours for you…. Seamus had to go out, so I had to come back home and mummy's still in bed… she's a real sleepy head…. and I've had no one to play with…. And I've been desperate to tell you about Storm… and…."

Mike managed to smile at the enthusiastic face that was inches from his own, though the smile wasn't very convincing. "Hold on a second! I'm here now and if you'll let me out of the car you little rat bag, we'll go into the kitchen and you can tell me all about it." Becky was off his lap in a second. "come on then." She said pulling enthusiastically on his hand. "You're so slow Mr. Grumpy!" she giggled pushing her tongue out at him at the same time. They reached the kitchen to find Kate sitting at the table wearing on of Mike's shirts, despite himself Mike couldn't help but admire her she was still in his eyes stunning. Her look towards him dispelled his admiration in a nano second. Becky looked between the two of them. "Have you two had an argument?" She asked.

"Becky!" Kate snapped. "Mind your manners… now you go to your room for an hour and think about why little girls shouldn't be so precocious." Becky looked close to tears and ran towards her room.

"For Christ's sake Kate that was a bit hard. The little girl's not stupid and it wasn't like she was rude. Go and get her back for Christ's sake and give her a cuddle. You can't take your guilt out on everybody else!" Mike's voice was starting to sound angry.

Kate looked at Mike and he was taken aback, her eyes were so cold as to be shocking, their colour had dissipated and they were such a pale blue as to look like ice. "Why don't you mind your own fucking business you wanker!" she was like a striking snake. "She's my daughter not yours so keep your nose out or I'll punch it right off your face!" Mike sat opposite her his anger dissolved and his body felt empty. "When I first met you I thought you were the best thing ever to come in to my life." Kate sneered at him but Mike continued. "And that little girl is as well and you still are… more fool me…. Where's the Kate gone that I fell in love with, I am still I'm sad to say in love with. You can't blame the world for your foolishness Kate… You have, to face up to that for yourself… I had too… you can't go round behaving as though no one is important apart from you because in the end it will catch up with you and it isn't nice when that happens. Shout and scream all you like at me but don't take out your guilt on Titch… she's done nothing." Kate's eyes were still as cold as ice as she held Mike's gaze. Her right hand struck out aiming a slap at Mike's face but he parried the blow. Mike nearly snapped managing God only knows to keep his composure. His eyes were narrowed and as Kate held his look fear began to rise in her stomach at what she saw. "Kate don't you ever try to hit me again…. You've done it once too often now and it's wearing thin. You can only beat a dog so much before it bites you."

Kate's bravado returned she felt rather than knew that although the fire she had seen lying deep behind Mike's eyes he would never let it loose where she was concerned. She felt safe and her taunting came back with a vengeance. "Who the fuck do you think you are telling me what to do? You fucking tosser, what I do has nothing to do with you and I don't have to answer to you or anyone else. Why don't you do us all a favour and fuck off somewhere for good. Go crawl in a hole and die for all I care. You're a jumped up little prick that thinks he's so fucking clever but you're just another country inbred. I fucking hate you… you're a waste of fucking space." She aimed another blow at Mike this time connecting. He laughed. "If that's the best you've got perhaps you should get someone to teach you to hit!" Kate went into a fury grabbing the telephone that sat on the table hitting Mike on the cheek with it. Mike jumped up holding his arms up in defence as Kate continued to try to hit him. There was a cut on his cheek and his lip was split but he still did not retaliate other than to grab Kate's arm to stop her hitting him with the phone again. "STOP IT… STOPIT!" the little voice screamed from the doorway. They both turned to look. Becky was standing in the doorway tears streaming down her face, but she was not crying, they were tears of frustration. "Mike was hitting me darling!" Kate said and Mike stood open mouthed at the bare faced lie. Becky looked at her mother with un-veiled anger on her face.

"That's not true mummy... I saw." She turned to Mike anger still on her face. "Mike just go, you two can't argue then.... Come back when you've both calmed down." Mike hesitated more out of shock at the maturity of the little one in front of him. "Please!" She pleaded. Mike turned and left. He passed Vi as he walked across the gravel towards his car. She paused about to say something as she noticed the smear of blood on his face but refrained as she saw the look off unmasked hurt on Mikes face. Vi entered the kitchen to find Becky in floods of tears and Kate standing by the table telephone in hand cursing everything that came into her line of vision. Vi immediately went over to Becky and wrapped her arms around her, Becky sobs started to subside. "Whatever has been going on." She said towards Kate. Becky tried to answer as Kate stood now silent staring directly at her but her voice came as a choking stutter that had no possibility of being understood. "Right young lady..." she said to Becky. "I want you to go upstairs to the bathroom, dry those tears and wash your face, then you come back down and you can tell me all about what's upset you so much." Becky obediently did as she was bid. Vi turned towards Kate. "As for you young lady you had better sit down and I'll make you a cup of tea and we'll try to sort out whatever this mess is before that little one comes back down!"

"Who the fuck do you think you are!" Kate spat. "You're the fucking cleaner not my keeper." For an instant Vi's face took on an expression of hurt then changed to one of steel. "I said sit down!" she said in almost a whisper. "You might get away with behaving like a spoilt brat with Mike but let me tell you, you won't with me. I grew up in tougher places than you could even dream of.... You can't intimidate me so sit down and let's talk this through, or young lady I will sit you down, don't think my Nick's the only one that can handle others!" Kate sat realising that with Vi her spite might just bring retribution and like all bullies male or female she was in truth a coward. "You and Mike are like my own children and I love you both... and that little one but if you ever speak to me like that again.... just remember I'm no gentleman like Mike.... Is that clear." Her voice had risen to a normal level but there was an edge to it, a calm, that was far more threatening than any shouting could ever be. Kate stayed sat, and Vi made them a tea before sitting opposite her. The new Kate dissolved and the Kate that had moved there returned. Vi moved beside her putting a comforting arm around her as she sobbed. "Come on now that's not going to help is it. Let's try and sort this mess out. Whatever has been going on here this morning?" Kate told her of the argument not omitting anything. Vi sat and listened intently not interrupting as Kate bared her soul, when she had finished she looked up into Vi's kindly face. "Oh dear! What have you done. You, silly girl. Have you told Mike all of this?" Kate shook her head and Vi paused to reflect on what she had just been told. Becky entered the room and walked over to the table sitting next to Vi. Vi inspected her closely. "That's better." She said smiling. "Can't have my favourite little girl looking all tear stained and sad, can I. Now I want you to do me a favour. You go and find Nick for me and tell him I said to take you into town and buy you whatever you want for that new foal of yours." Becky would have protested but 'foal' was the magic word and she beamed. "I have lots of money I can take!" she said her voice now cheery.

"No need for that you tell Nick it's my treat… I've got a funny feeling he might just take the chance to spoil you as well!" Becky didn't need to be told again and raced off towards Storms barn where she was sure Nick would be.

Kate told Vi she would sort out whatever she spent on her daughter but Vi would hear none of it. "I said it was my treat and it is besides I love that little one and Mike looks after Nick and me so well we've more money than we know what to do with. It's my pleasure and I won't have it any other way!" She said firmly but smiling with pleasure at the thought of buying Beck's something.

"You're so kind Vi… I'm so sorry I said what I did."

Vi smiled again warm and comforting. "We all say things we don't mean sometimes sweetheart. God if Nick held all the names I've called him over the years we'd never talk again!" It brought a smile to Kate's lips. "now we had better have a chat I think and see if we can't sort this mess you've got yourself into…. I don't know whether it's better to come clean with Mike or not. My Nick reckons he's got the coldest eyes he's ever looked into when his tempers up… makes even him a bit nervous he reckons. I know Mike would never hurt you but I'm not too sure what he'd do to this other fella. On the other hand sometimes it's better to be up front than to try and hide things… they always seem to come out in the end one way or another! It's definitely a difficult one and one that needs a lot of thinking about!" Kate wasn't sure if Vi was talking to her or more to herself.

"I feel so guilty Vi and it makes me angry. Then I take it out on Mike. Then I feel ten times worse which makes me even more angry and Mike suffers again. He's getting double the dose for something he hasn't done. I really don't know what to do! Things are becoming so bad between us and I really do love him I just don't know what's the matter with me…. maybe it's all this film star stuff going to my head…" Vi and Kate sat talking for the rest of the morning, until Becky returned with Nick who was grinning broadly as he laboured under the contents of loads of bags that had obviously been purchased for Becky. Neither Kate nor Vi had managed to come up with any form of answer or suggestion that would ease or begin to repair the situation. The only agreement was that whichever way Kate decided to approach the problem it was going to get worse before it got better.

"Mummy look at all this stuff I've got for Sky! Nick and I had such fun… and Nick bought some stuff to spoil Storm as well! We had loads of fun… Nick is so funny he put on a lady's hat and walked around the feed store and everybody was laughing." Becky gushed and it somehow eased the tension that was felt by Kate and she smiled.

Mike drove onto the motorway. He didn't have a clue where he was going, neither did he have a clue what he was doing. He drove aimlessly pulling out into the fast lane and pumped the throttle until the needle on the Jag's speedo hit a hundred and forty. It was as though the speed cleared the mist that fogged up his brain and he suddenly backed off pulling back to the inner lane and a more sedate speed. He watched for the next exit and turned the wheel towards it. Mike pulled into the services, parked the car and wandered into the dining area. His entrance started an animated conversation between the waitresses and after a couple of minutes a pretty girl of about twenty wandered over to where he had seated himself. She started without hesitation. "You're that Mike Willett?... The one that owns that famous racehorse Rocket, aren't you?" Mike couldn't help but smile.... Rocket always took centre stage! He nodded his ascent. The girl looked towards the other waitresses who were obviously waiting confirmation eagerly. "I told them you were." She said quite proudly. "Could I have your autograph please." She continued without hesitating to await an answer. "Your girlfriend is going to be in the film about the horse isn't she... Wow I saw her on the telly the other night she is so beautiful, you must be very happy!" Mike smiled again.... 'beautiful... yes'.... He thought... but then at the moment beauty really did run only skin deep. Mike signed his name on the back of a menu card, which the waitress brought back with his order. As he sat there chewing the piece of bacon that resembled plastic he considered his history and his future. Broke... made a few quid.... bad luck.... Lost more than a few quid...... determination.... Struggle... succeeded and lost all in one go.... loads of money.... new beginning.... losing again! He wearily dragged himself from the chair walked over to where the waitress stood asked for and paid the bill, giving her a fifty-pound note and not waiting for the change. "Well' he thought "I don't get asked for my autograph that often!"

He passed over the flyover and exited back onto the motorway thinking how great it was to be wealthy but how sad that love seemed lost. "You know Michael! He said aloud. "Money is important but not as important as having heart and your heart is lost!"

CHAPTER TEN

John and Seamus sat in the office of Hartslock wondering silently to themselves what to do about Mike. He was withdrawing into himself, taking no interest in the running of the horses, the horses themselves, racing... or it seemed life. Neither man made mention of their thoughts they just poured over the Racing Calendar. John was the first to speak. "Seamus, we need to sort out a plan.... I'm worried about Mike...Again. Christ he's starting to withdraw into himself again. I know you are more than capable of dealing with everything but it just isn't the same without that mercurial bugger around!"

"I'd not be disagreeing with you there!" Seamus smiled and paused... "I miss him being around too... I'd be nothing if it wasn't for him and that's something I'll never forget or ever stop being grateful for... Mikes the best friend I could ever have had... I think though I might just have an idea to bring him back into things... even if it means upsetting him a bit!" John looked on his face quizzical but attentive. "I'll enter Storm for the Derby and maybe make a little statement in the racing papers too boot.... Sort of say we don't think there's anything out there that can beat him... better than his dad and all that! Maybe even get Roy Winston involved... be an amazing piece of advertising in a roundabout way for the movie! Imagine what the papers will make of it!"

"Brilliant idea... there's only one down side that I can see......
What will Mike make of it, if he takes this the wrong way......"

"To be sure he'll have a bit of a flid but I'll talk him round...
At least we'll get a reaction."

"It's his reaction I'm worried about!" John said with a concerned half smile. "Alright it's worth a try!"

As Mike drew nearer to the yard his euphoria at being asked for an autograph was replaced by a feeling of despair and his mood quickly changed as he fell into a dark depression.

He pulled the car up in front of the house and slowly exited, walking without enthusiasm towards the kitchen door. Kate and Vi were still sitting at the table as Becky and Nick heaped an increasing mixture of horse paraphernalia, toys, shoes and what looked like a selection from every shop in town. Becky immediately ran to Mike dragging him over to see her new purchases. Kate smiled wanly then excused herself and left the room. The atmosphere was undoubtedly strained but Mike tried hard to keep up the appearance of interest and enthusiasm for Becky's sake. After about fifteen minutes of rummaging through what now resembled a jumble sale table Mike excused himself and went in search of Kate. Kate sat in the lounge and she looked up as he walked in. "I don't want another argument!" he said before she had even finished turning her head. She looked him in the eyes holding on to the gaze and Mike knew something was coming that he would not like. Kate hesitated as though wondering whether she should speak or not, then it just spilled out. "The guy who dropped me off last night I had sex with him!" Mike stood like a statue staring into space, an involuntary tear crept from the corner of one eye and he savagely brushed it away. For the first time Kate felt real fear as she held his stare, his eyes were on fire but it was a cold calculating fire the like of which Kate had never seen or ever wanted to see again. It sent a cold shiver down her spine. Mike made a supreme effort and regained a modicum of composure. He cleared the lump from his throat with what sounded more like a growl. He still hadn't spoken. Kate began to feel uneasier than when she had first blurted out her confession. "It didn't mean anything.... It was just sex.... I was drunk I didn't realise what I was doing... it was just once!"

Mike had still not moved, not spoken, he just stood open mouthed as Kate spoke. His thoughts raced. There didn't seem to be regret in what Kate said, no sorrow for her betrayal, just a portrayal of fact.

"What's his name?" Mike said with shaking voice.

"It doesn't matter... let's just forget it and move on!" Kate's voice was nervous now. Mike never said another word he just turned and walked back through the kitchen and back to his car.

Seamus put the phone down and turned to John. "Well I've entered him, and Roy is going to ring the papers straight away... I think he's going to plug this as much as possible. I hope this works!"

"Do you think we should ring Mike and tell him... forewarning him might just give him time to think it over... I don't really want to have to barricade myself in the house if he goes the wrong way... and you are only a few yards away from him most of the day.... Telling him might just lessen the barrage we're going to get!" John sounded a little nervous now that the deed was done and in truth Seamus had started to look a little pale!

Both men as one suddenly said, "not a bad idea" and reached for the phone. John ended up with the phone in his hand first, he quickly dialled Mikes number. John's face took on a mixed look of horror and concern as he listened to Vi at the other end of the phone. Putting the phone down he turned to Seamus his face full of anxiety. "Oh shit!"

Seamus was also now looking worried. "What is it?"

Apparently Kate's just told Mike she's been unfaithful and Mikes walked out of the house looking like thunder. Vi's found out who the bloke is and has sent Nick to try and find Mike... They think he's on his way to the film set!"

Without even speaking both men hurried towards the door

and raced through jumping into Johns car and spitting gravel as they exited the drive and sped towards the film studios.

CHAPTER ELEVEN

"Hi Mike, how are you? What are you doing here?" Roy's greeting was a mixture of pleasure at seeing Mike and curiosity at his being on the set, as he had never visited before.

Mike smiled his outward demeanour showing no disquiet as he held out his hand to shake Roy's.

"Just thought it was time I came to see how my boy's story is coming along, you know show a bit of interest and all that.... Thought it might help if I met the guy whose playing me... you know give him a bit of close contact with the real thing... give him an insight into the real thing!"

"Great idea third dressing room on the right, his names Scott... better knock first he's a bit of a Prima Donna!"

"Mr. Winston there's a call for you..."

"I'll be there in two minutes."

"It's Kate Stokes sir... she said it's urgent!" Roy's secretary insisted.

"Okay tell her I'm on my way."

He turned back to apologise to Mike but he was already halfway down the hallway walking quickly towards the dressing room of Scott Mackenzie. Mike didn't bother to knock but quietly and quickly walked into the room.

Scott Mackenzie looked up, indignation showing on his young face. "The door is there so that morons like you can knock before you enter... who the hell do you..." Mike reached out grabbing the back of Scott's head, gripping a handful of hair he smashed his face into the dressing table he was sitting at with such force that the lights surrounding the mirror extinguished. Scott didn't have time to scream or shout, simply uttering a muffled groan as he slumped to the floor. Mike calmly walked back to the door carrying the chair that had seconds before been occupied by the now still form of Scott and wedged it beneath the door handle.

"What!.... Oh My God!" Roy Winston threw the phone down on his desk and ran down the stairs towards the entrance hall to the dressing rooms.

The huge form of Nick appeared in reception moving at surprising speed. There seemed to be no need for explanations. "Mike?" Was all that Nick shouted and as Roy pointed towards the dressing rooms, ran in that direction. Nick tried the door and found it jammed shut. He turned to Roy who immediately shouted, "break it down." Nick rammed his huge shoulder into the door and it gave a couple of inches. He could hear half sounds coming from inside the room, and on hearing Mike's voice renewed his efforts.

Mike circled his inert quarry half-heartedly giving the body a shove with his foot as he did. "Come on tough guy... wakey, wakey...I don't want you to miss a thing!" and with that he aimed a vicious kick to Scott's ribs. He walked over to the dressing table leaving Scott half unconscious and groaning. Picking up the bottle of spring water that sat there he unscrewed the top and poured the contents directly over Scott's head. He came further out of his daze and turned to look at Mike's face. It was filled with hate. "Who are you...please don't hurt me anymore...What have I done?!"

Mike smiled, but it was a smile full of scorn. "I'm just about to explain it to you." Mike said, his voice trembling with rage. The door crashed and moved a couple of inches and somewhere Mike heard voices, they were like echoes bouncing around in his head, from another world. Mike lost the plot completely. He dropped his knees into the ribs of the inert but conscious body of Scott, the crack of bone was audible to those outside the room and the scream from Scott ear piercing. Mike had no feeling other than to cause as much hurt to the man that lay beneath him his fist pumping into the face of Scott, blood sprayed across the room. Suddenly Mike was hauled into the air, held in the massive arms of Nick. It was all that Nick could do to subdue Mike and in any other circumstances the punch that connected with Nick's eye might have brought Mike dire consequences, as it was Nick grimly hung on to his writhing form. What seemed like hours but in reality was only minutes, Mike's storm subsided and Nick managed to, without letting him go, get him from the room. Roy ran to his office and dialled for an ambulance then joined Nick in the adjoining dressing room. People were running everywhere. Roy's secretary had rushed off to get a blanket, covering the unconscious form of Scott in an effort to help. Everyone was in a state of near panic not sure of what had just transpired. John and Seamus arrived in the middle of it all. John quickly took charged of the situation, telling Roy to deal with his actor and they would get Mike out of the building. He would ring Roy later when things were a little calmer. John and Seamus took Mike back to Hartslock whilst Nick made his way back to the yard. It took several hours before Nick explained how he had received the cut beneath his fast-developing black eye and the few moments it had taken for Mike to create the devastation caused. Kate stomped about the kitchen a mixture of anger, concern and guilt. Becky was in tears unsure if they were for worry over Mike, her mum, Nick's eye or the overall situation. "Vi will you please look after Beck's for a while whilst I go over to John's. I'd better try and see if I can help sort this mess out!" Vi nodded and Kate turned to Becky. "Now you be good for Aunty Vi, I won't be long." Becky was already in nurse mode tending to a resigned Nick.

Kate pulled into the drive of Hartslock to see Mike being escorted towards a waiting car, his arms handcuffed behind his back a police officer either side of him. Mike looked up from the ground towards Kate and smiled sarcastically. He did not speak but turned his head back towards the waiting car. Kate stood in the drive tears running down her cheeks as Mike was driven away.

Seamus was standing in the doorway of John's house there was anger in his stance. "I hope your proud of yourself. That's the best man you could ever wish to meet and you've fucking destroyed him after he trusted you!" he turned and walked back into the house. John hurried out to where Kate stood tears now running even more freely leaving black trails of mascara as they fell towards the ground. "Don't take any notice of Seamus… he's a bit upset… he thinks a lot of Mike." John put an arm around Kate's shoulders and led her towards the kitchen. Kate sat sobbing for several minutes as John made her a coffee, Seamus rose and went from the room. "He'll calm down by tomorrow." John said in half-hearted explanation. "Now young lady we've got to try and sort this mess out. Mikes in serious trouble… Your friend is in intensive care." John's voice stayed perfectly calm. "Didn't you think about what you were doing? You must know Mike absolutely idolises you. Whatever made you do such a stupid thing?" His voice rose almost imperceptibly. "Christ you know what a temper he's got…. And where your concerned it's ten times worse… shit that poor bastard didn't stand a chance… and I'm not too sure that Mike does now either!"

CHAPTER TWELVE

Mike walked from the cells at ten o clock the following morning. The police had already been to his house and collected his passport. He was bailed to go back in two weeks' time, when he had been told he would be charged. When they had the report from the hospital the police told him they would have sufficient evidence to know how serious the charges would be against him. That they were serious they pointed out left no shadow of doubt... it was just how serious.

Mike knew he was in big trouble.

Mike pulled up at the house walked in without speaking to anyone went straight upstairs and packed a bag.

The morning papers didn't know which headline to print. Storm in the Derby, which had already created an amazing stir with calls from all over the world suggesting another international race with a winner take all, as it had been for Storms father, regardless of a Derby run. It was Mike's other antics that fought for the top billing. The tabloids however seemed to have hit pay dirt, as most attempted to utilise both. One particular journalist seemed to have solved his problem and a full front page read. 'Whilst one Storm is brewing, another breaks!'

Mike didn't tell anyone where he was going, he just walked from the house to the car bag in hand and drove off.

John Cullen slammed the paper down on his kitchen table cursing. Alice looked over towards him sympathetically. "John, you weren't to know! If Mike hadn't have gone off on one... Well who knows it could have been just the kick up the backside he needed!"

John smiled at Alice as she prepared 'young Mikes' breakfast. "How can such a talented guy have such an uncontrollable temper? I just don't understand it, he's such a great friend, kind, helpful but Christ when he loses it he's like a man possessed! He should be ranting and raving at us this morning instead he's God only knows where. At least I suppose we know he can't do a runner like he did last time because the police have collected his passport."

"Don't worry he's obviously cooled down or we'd hear the sirens going from here!" Alice tried to make light of the situation in an attempt to nullify her husband's feelings. "He'll be back in a day or two as soon as he's got his head around things... You know what Mike's like he'll be feeling dead guilty now and probably angry at himself for doing something so stupid. Look, why don't you drive over and talk with Seamus, maybe have a word with Kate as well.... I don't know that it will do anyone any good but at least she might understand that where Mike is concerned you're as near as damn it, dealing with a sort of modern day cowboy, come knight who believes that unprincipled behaviour has to be dealt with a showdown at noon. He forgets there are consequences to going around like a gunslinger... not least that someone is going to be faster to the draw than you one day!"

John looked up surprised at Alice's comment and Alice smiled at him. "I've got a soft spot for the silly sod too you know, he's really a nice guy... it's just he seems sometimes to belong to another age."

John rose from the kitchen table. "I'll pop over to the yard then." He said walking over to kiss Alice and young Mike. "I'm a very lucky man!" he added and turned to leave.

The same conversation had taken place in Seamus house except Seamus was a bit more vociferous and a little harsher on Kate. Mary had tried and succeeded in calming him down slightly, but he was still quite vocal as John tapped the door and entered the kitchen. "Any fool could see how much he thought of her... loved the air she breathed so he did... she should have realised, she knew him well enough to know he has high morals and that something like that would crack him up...!"

"Seamus," Mary said quietly, "We all make mistakes I'm sure you did at some stage in your life just the same as I have. The thing is you must take circumstances into consideration. Just imagine what it must be like to suddenly find yourself surrounded by all those people treating you like a demigod, telling you how wonderful you are, hanging on your every word and action? It wouldn't be too hard to forget yourself now would it.... and let's be honest Kate was married herself when Mike met her!"

Seamus face held its look of stone and it was enough for everyone to know that his mind was set in the defence of Mike.

CHAPTER THIRTEEN

Mike drove, he didn't drive in the normal purposeful way one drives when one is aiming for a destination he just drove. The only thing he was aware of was that he had to get as far away as was possible, and he did. Seven and a half hours later Mike crossed the border of Scotland an hour later and he pulled off the main road and followed a sign to Canobie where he found a small but comfortable hotel that offered bed and breakfast. He signed the register and went to the bar. He looked at his watch it was nine thirty. He ordered a whisky and dry, wondered at the strange look he received from the barman, decided it was for asking for the dry to go with his whiskey. "I suppose that's bordering on sacrilege." He mumbled and for the first time in the last few days smiled to himself, asked the barman if it was possible to get a sandwich or something and after receiving an affirmative nod from the barman wandered over to a table. He casually picked up the paper that laid on the edge of the table. It was well read and folded backwards but he noticed it was today's. He folded it back meticulously attempting to shake out the creases as he did. He turned to the front page and immediately recognised why the barman had looked at him so strangely. WHILST ONE STORM

IS BREWING ANOTHER BREAKS. Mike almost put the paper down again but there is something we all have, some macabre streak that forces us to read something we know is going to be bad, something we know is going to hurt but we do it nonetheless. Mike read the 'article' slating him as an uncontrollable freak, a man that was lucky by having 'obtained' the Rocket and then his son Storm. Mike could cope well enough with being called a freak but the suggestion that there was something amiss in his purchase of Rocket infuriated him immediately. He waited for his sandwich, forced himself to eat it and made his way to the bedroom.

Mike woke to a surprisingly warm Scottish morning. He meandered down the stairs bag in hand walked to the reception asked if they could prepare his bill ready for him to settle after breakfast, then took a place at a well laid table in the dining room. Mike's breakfast came and although the food was delicious he found he had to force himself to eat. His mind was racing with thoughts of the previous newspaper headlines his problems with Kate and his own inability to cope. It was a tired and weary soul that rose from the table to pay his bill. Mike thanked the receptionist, complimenting her on the Inns standards and left. Turning the Jag towards the main road he hesitated for a moment before pulling onto the highway and accelerating away.

Seamus stood on the gallops cursing as Storm bucked, plunged, ducked sideways until the rider that was precariously holding on was thrown from his back and plummeted to earth. The rider picked himself up brushed the woodchip from his jodhpurs and marched towards Seamus. "Sorry Seamus, you're a good chap and all that but if you think I'm riding that nutter on a racecourse you're sadly mistaken... I don't care what he's by or if he's got gold plated shoes... he's a nut, if I were you I'd put him in a field and forget he's there before he fucking kills someone!" Finion Mars was one of the best jockeys around and

Seamus had wanted the best for Storm's coming races and it was with sinking heart that he watched Finion's back disappear towards the yard. He stood watching long after he had gone, in fact until he heard Finion's car roar off down the road before he made a move towards Storm who contentedly grazed at the side of the gallops. Storm twitched an ear in his direction as he approached. Seamus picked up the reins and swung up into the saddle. "Oh. You're, your father's son alright and make no mistake... Now you get me home safe you little bugger... I've only got one good leg left thanks to your old man and I want to keep it just as it is!" Storm gave a mini rear, turned and walked back down the gallops towards the yard. Storm entered the yard at a prancing jig jog gait and a disconsolate looking Seamus aboard. Seamus jumped down out of the saddle and before he had walked three paces Mel was there fussing the horse and taking the reins from him. Storm nuzzled her neck and she smiled, it seemed as though Storm was encouraged by her smile and snorted loudly following her as she silently turned with him obediently following.

Seamus dialled Mikes mobile number and was more than surprised when it was answered. So much so that for a moment he was so taken aback he did not speak.

"Hello.... is that you Seamus?"

"Uhh! Yes.... Mike Storm is being a pratt he's doing a Rocket with everyone but Mel.... I'm at a bit of a loss..."

Seamus was stunned into silence as Mike told him he was on his way back and though he wouldn't be back until late, he would sort it all out in the morning. Seamus put the phone back in his pocket and with a feeling that wavered between jubilation and trepidation walked over to Storms stable.

Mike chatted away to himself as the Jag cruised at eighty down the M56. he wasn't sure why he had changed his mind and turned back for home but somewhere deep inside he knew he had to see Kate again. 'This is stupid' he said to himself. 'If she wanted you then ...' He couldn't bring himself to think of her infidelity. 'I just want to see her smile... how can I hate her and love her all at the same time?' He paused his thoughts feeling anger build inside him and tried to set his mind on other things. 'I'll sort out Storm... then I'll decide what I'll do.' He laughed emptily... 'If I'm honest with myself I think that's already been decided ... and not by me!'

He flicked off the cruise control and pushed his foot on the accelerator pedal firing the Jag forward. Mike drove hard for about ten miles then relaxed and flicked the cruise back on. He'd be home soon enough he determined.

It was five thirty when he pulled into the yard and Seamus was busy checking that evening stables had been completed to his satisfaction. He walked over to Mike and warmly shook his hand "Jesus I was worried you would be off again, so I was!"

Mike smiled in return. "Not this time Seamus... I've done all the running I'm going to be doing... Right what's this little bugger of a horse doing?" Seamus suggested they go up to the house and surprisingly Mike agreed. As they entered the kitchen Kate was stood at the Rayburn making supper for Becky. Becky leapt up and threw her arms around Mike's neck, clinging to him like a limpet. "Whoa... steady up ... you're strangling me." And Becky laughed. "We were all very worried you know..." she said in her most serious tone.

"No need to worry Titch I'm here now... just needed a little thinking time... it's one of those boring grown up things."

"Becky let Mike sit down I expect he's tired... Would you like some supper... I can soon make something?" Kate's voice held a nervous edge as though she was waiting for an explosion. It didn't come. "Just a tea will be fine, thank you." Mike's voice was almost sad, yet calm and neutral as he looked at his beautiful Kate. Seamus was sure there were tears in his eyes.

Kate made the tea and sat at the table the awkward silence that dwelled between Mike and Kate was almost unbearable. Seamus took a sip of tea and tried to make the running. "He's just like Rocket... being a right little bugger dropped Eddie this morning and he reckons he won't sit on him again, Finion Mars reckons there's no way he'll get on him again. Word will get round quick

Mike, you know that as well as me and we'll struggle to find a jock that'll ride him in his first race... well one that's any good that is."

"I think I might just have the solution to that!" Mike said rather smugly.

CHAPTER FOURTEEN

Mike sat looking at the panel of three that sat in front of him headed by Sir Alfred Mapperton s they whispered from one to the other. It was Sir Alfred that spoke first. "Mike... I think we all know each other well enough to forego the formalities, don't you?" and it was with some surprise to the others two sitting on the panel that Mike replied using the Christian name of Sir Alfred. The large woman dressed in tweed sitting to Sir Alfred's right interrupted. "Sir Alfred, surely we must maintain a standard here... we are after all an official body... it could look rather contrived if we treat this matter with such informality."

Sir Alfred Mapperton turned towards the tweed lady an almost patient look upon his face. "Come, come, Daphne. I have met Mr. Willett on numerous occasions and have always found him to be honest, forthright and if I may say so a man that speaks from the heart... I can assure you that on all of these occasions both formal and informal I have referred to Mike as Mike and he, in return has called me Alfred... he is a man of integrity and I am certain that even if the outcome of this meeting does not fall in his favour he would never use an informality to oppose the result..." He looked towards Mike for his assurance and Mike nodded. "Good then I suggest we carry on and hear what Mike has to say on the matter." He looked towards Mike.

Mike cleared his throat. "Well as you know the Rockets son is proving to be as popular as Rocks himself, sorry that's his stable name. Storm... that's the lad, is just like his father, shall we say a bit of a character. He's taken a shine to one of our lasses and I'd like to get her a license. You are aware that the young lady in question is mute, hence my being here to represent her. There is no question whatsoever of her ability and I would like to point out that she has already completed her nine-week course at the racing school and is booked in for her apprentice course for next week!" Mike noticed that Sir Alfred Mapperton tried to hide a smirk as Mike finished his speech. The Tweed lady however was not going to be so easy on Mike.

"Mr. Willett!" She said with a rather pointed look towards Sir Alfred. "This committee has been convened not just to decide on ..." She looked at the papers lying before her on the huge polished Oak table. "Melanie Stokes... but also about your own behaviour and of course the furore you've again caused not only in your private life but with another of your horses." She looked towards Sir Alfred and the other members of the committee for effect. "We are not here solely for the benefit of your stable..." Sir Alfred noticed the rigidity creep into Mikes stance but the tweed lady seemed not to have noticed and made the error off continuing. "Stokes...?" she said. "Isn't that the name of the woman you are living with and whom the papers seem to be unable to refrain from placing on the front page everyday, all rather contrived wouldn't you say?" The word woman came out acidly and the sarcasm was plain even to Mike.

Mike tried to breathe, tried to stay calm, tried to relax his tensing body but then Mike never was much good at that his heart was far too imprinted on his sleeve.

"Madam!" He spat. "My private life has nothing whatsoever to do with the Jockey Club and as for Melanie's surname I have never connected the fact that she and Kate share it... It is therefore something I have never questioned and as far as I am aware there is no relationship, just the sharing of a name... I do of course expect to be penalised in regards to my behaviour as I would agree that does bring the reputation of the racing industry into disrepute but my personal life does remain my own."

"You have never questioned the fact…. I find that hard to believe." Tweedy interrupted.

Mike felt the mist descending on his brain. "Madam… I have no real interest in what you believe." He hissed. "I have come here to present a case for Melanie and you have done your best to poke holes in me… I will walk from here with a licence for this young lady or I promise you that tomorrow the newspapers will be screaming your name from the front pages as the person that not only refused to help someone less fortunate but as the person who is trying to stop one of the world's most famous horse from emulating his father." The committee went very quiet and it was a full fifteen seconds before anyone spoke . It was Sir Alfred. "Mike…I am certain that any offence was not intended… As I know you do… We simply want what's best for racing." He turned to the tweed. "If we take a step back from this it actually presents us with a golden opportunity… the Jockey Club can not only present the world with two of the greatest races in history… the profile would be immeasurable and to top it off we can do it by offering a person that is less fortunate than ourselves to not only take part but to potentially win." He smiled at the tweed. "Tell me where or how we can get better advertising for British racing?" Sir Alfred looked at the tweed meaningfully and suggested they retire to discuss the matter in private. The three members of the committee rose and walked into an anti-room. Mike was left alone in the committee room. It wasn't long before the committee returned with a smiling Sir Alfred leading them. They sat and Sir Alfred very formally addressed Mike. "I am pleased to inform you that after careful consideration it has been decided that the license for Melanie Stokes will be granted. There is however another matter I must deal with… this is off the record however but nonetheless is something that must be addressed… Your behaviour of late has not been that of a… what shall we say someone with such a high profile within the ranks of the racing industry and it must stop." Mike was sure that Sir Alfred winked. "We are all only too aware that you have a temper but because you are in the public eye so much at the moment you really have to learn to control yourself a little more. You have a responsibility having brought two such horses to the fore and now have a responsibility to the young lady you are so keen to support. I would ask that you consider your actions. In short please put your brain in gear before your temper in the future!" Mike nodded and the meeting was called to a close. As he was making his way from the building he heard Sir Alfred's voice. "Mike..." He turned to face Sir Alfred. "look old chap I just wanted to say that I have the utmost confidence in you... I do believe you must take a step back on occasion so to speak, that temper of yours will get you in a lot of trouble... I'll have a word with the Chief Constable he's a personal friend of mine maybe he can sweep your latest debacle under the carpet. No promises mind but I'll try... you however must stick to doing what you are good at...... training horses. Now are we going to show the rest of the world that we are the best with this young horse of yours? He finished with a smile.

Mike automatically shook the hand of the man in front of him. "Thank you... as for Storm I don't know... he's as good as his father, of that there is no doubt whatsoever but he does have the same personality and will only do what he wants when he wants. I was lucky with his father I'm keeping my fingers crossed that I have the same luck with his son!"

"Luck has nothing to do with it. It's the training!" Alfred Mapperton answered. But Mike knew it was all to do with luck, having two such horses was nothing to do with training.

CHAPTER FIFTEEN

For the next few weeks the yard buzzed as Melanie was prepared for her baptism into racing with Seamus instructing her on race riding. Becky was never far away from the action and watched as Melanie began to improve her technique. Mike however was seldom seen and seemed to spend most of his time away from the yard only showing his face when Storm made an appearance on the gallops, disappearing like a will-o-the-wisp as soon as Storms work was over. On the occasions when he did not show his face Storm became intractable and though he never showed any malice refused point blank to work.

Sir Alfred Mapperton true to his word spoke to his friend the Chief Constable and it seemed that after looking into the matter there had been a glitch in the computer and the records pertaining to that particular case seemed to have been wiped from the database, the statements had to be scrapped as it appeared the policemen that had arrested Mike, suddenly remembered that they had forgotten to read him his rights. The actor in question was given a straight one million and told to forget the incident or any work he hoped to get in the future would prove extremely difficult to obtain and the whole thing was consigned to the bin.

Mike only went to the house when he had to, he was courteous to Kate but despite her efforts to engage him in serious conversation and to attempt to get close to him again he would have none of it. It had been over three weeks since Kate had admitted her mistake and Mike had taken such drastic action. As Mike walked with the kettle, he filled it to make tea, having come in to see what post there was and to have breakfast. Kate walked into the kitchen and put her arm around him. Mike's voice was totally flat emotionally, "Please don't do that Kate." He said moving away from her.

"Mike please talk to me... I am so sorry... can't we put this behind us and start again. I miss you and so does Becky."

Mike's emotions may have been a boiling pit of lava, but his voice remained flat and emotionless. "That is low even for you Kate. You know I think the world of Becky and to try and use her for your own selfish gain shows me just what sort of person you really are, I'm sorry I would never be able to believe you again or to trust you and trust is the most important part of a relationship. I am happy to train Becky's horses and to have her here whenever but you and I are not going to be together. I love you but do not trust you. You can stay here as long as you like but even if I am here we will never share the same bed or for that matter the same space."

At first Mike thought Kate was going to burst into tears but her face changed from sadness to anger in a flash and she suddenly started screaming at him for all she was worth. He was everything bad, lower in the food chain than slime, a worthless lover, a useless trainer. She would move out as soon as she could and she would also arrange for Becky's horses to be moved to another trainer. She aimed a vicious kick at Mike's crotch, catching him on his upper thigh, spun and marched out of the room. Turning momentarily, she threw the Jags keys at him, "And you can keep your shit car..."

Mike stood for a few seconds before grinning to himself despite the pain he felt. "I think it might have cost you quite a lot in every way but sunshine I think you have nonetheless had a lucky escape!"

Much to Mike's surprise the following morning Geoff Stokes arrived greeting Kate as though she had just been shopping. Becky was full of tears but calmed a little after Mike told her she could come and see him or the yard anytime she wanted. Geoff Stokes walked over and shook Mike's hand. "We'll keep the horses here for Becky's sake." He turned to walk back to the car then changing his mind turned back to Mike, "I told you Mike you were not the first and you will not be the last… me I don't care, she is shall we say, convenient for me, if at times annoying." And he strode to the car and they drove off. In that last comment Mike knew that he had been a fool but wondered if the bigger fool was not Geoff.

CHAPTER SIXTEEN

John and Seamus stepped around Mike like they were walking on broken glass for the next few days. Everyone it seemed was waiting for his reaction but it didn't come. Mike walked around like nothing had happened, he threw himself back into the yard and the horses and much to the surprise of them all seemed to be the old Mike. He was back on form.

Mike stood looking over the box at Rocket, Storm had reached over the door of his stable next to Rocket and was nuzzling Mike's pocket. Mike laughed. "I know you have mints stop teasing you know I love them." Mike reached in his pocket and brought the packet of polos out. "Okay half each!"

That's not fair I should get more I'm the one that is in training, the old chap is retired… all he does is sleep all day!" the voice had a cheekiness to it.

"And think yourself lucky you are in your box or I would teach you just how good the old chaps is!"

"Okay guys enough, half each and that's an end to it." Mike shared the mints which were crunched up quickly by both horses. "Well Storm I am going to enter you for your first race so you had better be good, Mel will be riding you and I expect you to look after her."

Mike said goodnight to the two and wandered out into the

yard. Just as he got to the door the voice of Rocket sprang into his head. "Don't worry Mike, I know you are hurting but remember I told you keep trying that you would find what you are looking for… I was wrong, it will find you… looking too hard sometimes means you take a wrong turn. Wait and see it will come and you will trip and fall flat on your face!"

What are you on about… can't you speak plainly?"

"You'll see, and I do speak plainly it is just that you find it hard to listen! Everything happens for a reason!"

And it went quiet.

Mike was sitting in the lounge when the shout came through the kitchen door. It was Seamus and Mike shouted back and walked to the kitchen. "Hi Seamus, tea? Or something a bit stronger?" Seamus smiled in answer and Mike pulled two glasses down from the cupboard and poured a generous measure of Jameson in each.

"I think we should give Mel a ride on the track before Storm? We have Dusk running in a Maiden at Lingfield on Thursday I think we should put the girl on board it will give her a bit of race experience before the lad… I think we have to put her on Storm because I don't think he'll accept being ridden by anyone else. If you would rather I will ring and tell Becky we are going to put Mel up on Dusk?"

Mike smiled, it was a nice thought on Seamus' part but as much as he appreciated it he knew it had to be him or he would look like a complete coward.

"Thanks Seamus but no worries I'll do it, I'll ring in the morning. Went down and looked at the theme park today… bloody hell they are getting on with it. I never thought it would be possible to get it done in that time but it's like watching an ant colony working. George reckons he'll be a couple of weeks in front of schedule. That would be great as it would mean we could open at the same time as the film premiered."

"Yeah, that's one of the things I wanted to talk to you about. Roy wants to know if you can take Rocket to the set as they want to do the scenes with the boy? He asked for you as John told him the horse behaves a lot better when you are around… look Mike if you'd rather I did it we all understand!"

"No Seamus it's no problem." Mike smiled, "I've come to terms with my problems and things look a whole lot different to me now. I just want to put myself back on the map." Seamus looked at Mike with scepticism. "Yeah, I know Seamus, but believe me I have done a lot of soul searching and look what my temper has done… and my pride… I lost Ann who stuck with me through thick and thin but I couldn't forgive her a stupid error, I have done the same with Kate… both caused by drink perhaps and I sink into the bottle myself and everyone suffers… which makes me no better! Time for a change I think… I intend to make a concerted effort to control my emotions and who knows as Rocket keeps telling me maybe I will find what I am looking for? Or maybe if I stop looking so hard it will find me. I don't know now I am just having a drink or two I actually enjoy it rather than feeling like I have given myself the flu. Look at where we are Seamus, I have been a fool, we have so much now. I'm not saying I'm becoming a saint but I am going to try to be a better person."

Seamus looked at Mike his face serious. "Michael we all love you and all we want is for you to be happy and be more like the old Mike… with a little less temper." He laughed and raised his glass. "Here's to a new beginning and to the Storm that's brewing and about to become a cyclone on the race track!" they clinked their glasses together and drank.

Mike watched the horses the following morning feeling like it was the first time he had seen them, his old enthusiasm seemed to have returned and his elation at watching them work lifted his spirits higher. As Seamus pulled his horse up at the top of the gallops Mike walked over and suggested they should go to the film set together. Seamus agreed saying that he thought it would be nice if Nick came as well, Mike looked a bit suspicious and Seamus was quick to point out that it was for Nick's benefit knowing how possessive he was over Rocket.

Mike went back to the house and walked into the kitchen

where Vi seemed to be preparing a mountain of food. "Now I've done you a few sandwiches and a few snacks to take with you, I don't trust those catering things they have at them sort of things." Mike grinned. "Thanks Vi though by the looks of things there is enough there to last a week, we'll be back before six I should think," he paused, "I don't know where were going to put Rocket though because there won't be any room in the lorry with all that food!"

"That's enough of your cheek Michael Willett. Now you go and wash up and put on some decent clothes and I'll do you some proper breakfast." Much to Vi's surprise, Mike walked over gave her a hug, kissed her on the cheek and said. "I don't know what I did to deserve you Vi but it must have been pretty damn good." Vi fluffed up like a bantam hen over her chicks. "Away with your nonsense… go on get and clean yourself up and out of my kitchen so that I can do some work," her eyes were like diamonds and her cheeks pink and Mike smiled to himself as he walked to do his mother hens bidding.

Rocket loaded easily and with the huge hamper loaded into the compartment Mike Seamus and Nick made their way to the racecourse where the re-enactment of Rockets derby win was going to be filmed. The three were a little taken aback when they pulled up it was like a race day but with absolute mania, as people milled around waiting for the filming to start. Seamus pulled the lorry into the lorry park and shrugged his shoulders as they saw many of the normal emblazoned lorries that would be there on a normal race day. He switched off the engine and before they had even managed to open the doors an old trainer appeared. "I owe you a thank you Mike," he almost shouted as he stood by the cab, "I'm earning more today than I would winning a good race and I haven't even got to win."

A sarcastic voice rang in Mikes head. "Lucky that because you would have no chance of winning… oh and by the way if they think I am going to let one of those things bite me again they have another think coming." Mike burst out laughing but manage a spluttered. "No problem Charlie glad you could do it."

CHAPTER SEVENTEEN

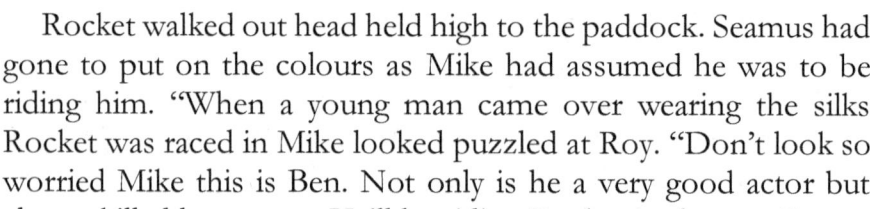

Rocket walked out head held high to the paddock. Seamus had gone to put on the colours as Mike had assumed he was to be riding him. "When a young man came over wearing the silks Rocket was raced in Mike looked puzzled at Roy. "Don't look so worried Mike this is Ben. Not only is he a very good actor but also a skilled horseman. He'll be riding Rocket in the race."

"Roy, I had assumed that Seamus would be on board, not only is Rocket very valuable but he is not the easiest of rides."

"I beg your pardon." The voice in Mike's head rang out. "I'll have you know I'm very easy to ride… leg the man up I'll show you."

Mike turned to Roy "Okay lets leg him up and see," Mike hiked Ben up into the saddle and Rocket looking very smug Mike thought, almost tiptoed around the paddock, Ben grinning confidently, as they reached the exit to the race course Rocket suddenly jinked sideways and the moment his feet touch back down took off around the racecourse like all the hounds of hell were after him. Ben hanging on for dear life. Everyone seemed to be holding their breath as Rocket tore round the course coming to a skidding stop as he reached the paddock gate. Ben not very elegantly shot over his head and landed with a thump on the grass, he lay there for a minute as a surge of people rushed to help him. Rocket walked back into the parade ring and stood stock still by Mike. Ben eventually rose to his feet and hobbled through the paddock. "Sorry Mr. Winston but you can't pay me enough to get back on that lunatic." He continued his hobble towards the line of actor's caravans that were parked by the stable block. Seamus wandered out to the parade ring, looking at all the people standing there. "Did I miss something?"

"No just Rocket being his old self." Mike smiled.

Seamus was legged up onto Rocket and along with the other horses went down to the start. As had happened in the Derby Rocket stood casually in the stalls as the others were released with Seamus surprisingly doing an excellent job of acting as he pretended to be re-enacting Williams ride. Seamus suddenly realised just how far away the other horses had become and started to try and get Rocket to move forward in earnest. Rockets feet remained firmly planted on the spot. "Come on Rocks Don't make me look a fool they're getting too far you'll never catch them and we'll have to do this all over again."

Mike stood watching thinking this may take a long time if Rocks was up to his old tricks. All the feelings he had felt when he was training Rocket came back and his stomach sank to his boots. Suddenly there was an explosion from the starting stalls and Rocket burst onto the track with Seamus clinging on desperately. Rocket stuck his head out and like a Ferrari chasing a moped ate up the ground between his and the horse's way in front of him. Mike knew it wasn't a real race but the euphoria of seeing his horse perform made it just like the real thing. He literally ran to the winning post pushing the extras out of the way as he did. "Go on son, go on." he screamed at the top of his voice. Rocket looked to be really enjoying himself as he virtually cruised passed the other horses and passed the winning post in front. Mike found he was so elated. Roy Winston walked over to him and patted him on the shoulder. "Boy oh boy can that horse run! Why the hell don't you race him again he's phenomenal! I have my take in one… brilliant." He was breathless as he finished. Mike stood stunned Rocket was as good if not better than he had ever been and hadn't even trained.

The voice behind him made him start. "Mike let's run him again!" it was John. Mikes heart fell to his boots the I Love Rocket fan club seemed to be making a comeback.

"I didn't know you were coming," he said to John who was grinning broadly.

"You didn't honestly think I would miss the chance to see the boy run on the track again did you?" A jubilant Seamus interrupted further conversation. "Did you see that? The boy obliterated them, didn't even break a sweat. No training and he destroys them… and let me tell you there were some good horses out there and they were trying… they all wanted to say they beat The Rocket… you know what Michael me boy…" Mike raised his hand… "Don't tell me we should run him again?" Seamus smiled from ear to ear. "Oh my God… I'm surrounded by fucking idiots! We have a horse that you couldn't even put a value on as a stallion… everybody and his uncle want to use him he earns us so much money we can't even count it if we lived a thousand years and you two daft buggers want to risk him by putting him back in training?" Seamus and John looked at each other conspiratorially. "Well now," Seamus said, "you have to admit he was seriously impressive, and he did enjoy himself and…"

"Enough! We are not racing him and that is final!" Mike said but John and Seamus simply grinned inanely. Nick walked over to where they were standing, he had put Rocket in the stables, made sure he was safe and that the security guards Roy had employed knew exactly what would happen if one hair was missing from his boy when he returned and went off to find the others.

"Did you see him go? Is he some racehorse or is he some race horse?" Nick said proudly. Mike threw his hands in the air. "Not you as well?" he leaned forward and spoke quietly to the three grins. "He is not a fucking race horse he is a stallion at stud!" the other chuckled and Mike walked away muttering under his breath.

"You know what Seamus, I'm beginning to wonder how the world would react to a race that had a father and a son in it?" Seamus grin widened.

Mike wandered over to the stables and stood outside the box that held Rocket. He told the security guards to go and grab a coffee he would watch Rocket until they returned. "Well son that was pretty damn impressive, it still looks like you have it. I wish you wouldn't show just how good you are though... I'm going to be harped to death by your fan club to race you again, and I'm not going to risk your old son!"

The voice in Mike's head spoke. "We'll see." And Mike groaned.

The security guards returned, and Mike wandered back to the racecourse to look for the others. He found them in deep conversation with Roy but as he got close their talk ended abruptly, they looked around guiltily. "Do you want me to come back seems I have interrupted something?"

"No... no we were just talking about the theme park," Roy said though it sounded totally lame, "George says it will be finished two weeks ahead of schedule as long as they don't come across any problems."

"Mmm," was all Mike replied.

"Come on Mike, let's all take, a look around, never been on a film set before." John said more in, an effort to take away from the awkward silence that had loomed over them all.

John, Seamus, Mike with Nick at the rear moved off across the stand area looking at all the paraphernalia that came with making a film, lights and cameras were everywhere as people rushed around dabbing a bit of makeup on a face here, styling hair and straightening clothes as others preened themselves ready for their part however big or small.

Mike had forgotten that Kate was the star of the movie and when he saw her stepping out of a trailer being fawned over by half a dozen minions he surprised himself. He would have thought the effect of seeing her would be painful but it was not. He actually found himself amused at how she seemed to be soaking up the attention. He realised even more just how false and self-centred she really was. He looked around for Becky but she was nowhere to be seen, he was so intent on looking that he didn't see the young woman who was crouched down in front of him writing on her clipboard. He crashed straight into her knocking her over and falling on top of her. "I am so sorry are you okay." The young woman looked at him she was obviously dazed her green eyes unfocussed. Mike had a thing about eyes and it took all his willpower to focus on the problem and not her eyes. he jumped to his feet and helped the woman to hers still apologising profusely. She spoke her accent strange but assuring Mike she was fine. "Sorry I didn't see you… are you sure you are okay."

"I am fine it is no problem." The accent Mike thought Polish?

"Are you Polish?" the woman smiled.

"No, I am from Ukraine, I come to work for Mr. Winston, I help with the scripts. You are Mr. Willett, I have seen your picture in the paper… I love horses could I come to see your horse Rocket sometime please? He looks so beautiful."

"Please feel free to come and see him anytime… it is the least I can do after knocking you over and then falling on top of you!" The woman laughed and Mike passed her his card telling her to call him when she wanted to come to see Rocket, adding he would show her Storm as well. "My name is Natalia." "I'm Mike." They shook hands seeming to hold each other's hands a little longer than necessary before Mike walked off with the others.

"Seems a nice girl?" Mike said casually to the others.

"We noticed you thought so." Seamus said grinning. Mike started to splutter an answer but before he could Seamus continued. "Seems rather odd though, don't you think boys that the Rocket is only, what two hundred yards away and yet our Michael here invites, I have to say the very beautiful young lady to visit us all at the yard… or perhaps it is not a visit to us all or even Rocket… perhaps it is Mikey boy the visit is for!" John,

Nick and Seamus went into spasms of laughter as Mike continued spluttering his face glowing red.

The rest of the day went well with though a great many jibes at the expense of Mike and it was a happy crew that left the film set and headed for home.

Mike felt relaxed as he walked into the kitchen, he missed Becky and her chatter and missed Kate, but had though he did not think it possible, he had resigned himself to the fact that it was not to be. Vi did her normal fuss and presented Mike with a huge plate of food before cocking her head to one side looking at him with a smile and saying. "Well I'm off now… got to go and feed that big lummox of mine! you look different Michael, more relaxed, it's good to have my boy back." She leaned forward kissed his forehead and went to feed her lummox. Mike felt so warm inside as he watched her leave and the realisation came over him how lucky he was to have such wonderful friends.

Mike managed to finish about half the food which was quite an achievement, in itself and thought perhaps he should get himself a dog. It had been six months since his beloved Jody had passed on and he started to think that now for some inexplicable reason he was more settled, it would be nice to have the company. It was strange but watching Rocket on the racecourse was so exhilarating all Mikes worries seem to have dissipated. He poured himself a glass and sat back comfortably in front of the tv. He had just settled himself and started watching a program on how desperate the poaching situation was becoming of endangered species and started thinking that he would do something to help and would speak to the others about it when he heard the bell ring on the front door. It was strange as most people just came to the kitchen door and wandered in or shouted his name and wandered in. Unusual for someone to call in the evening, he looks at his mobile, it was 8.30, not late but certainly not normal for someone to call at this time. He hoisted himself from his chair a little reluctantly and walked to the door. Roy Winston stood ginning like a Cheshire cat. "Sorry to bother you Mike can I come in for a minute or two? Something I would like to discuss with you... oh and I have someone in the car if you wouldn't mind?" Mike looked towards the limo that had brought Roy but couldn't see through the smoked windows. "Yeah no problem. I was only watching the tv it will be nice to have a bit of company for a while do come in." Roy Winston beckoned towards the car and Mike saw a very nice pair of ankles appear. His surprise must have shown on his face as he saw Natalia walk towards him. Roy grinned, "I think you have met Nat, the lads told me you two fell for each other," he chuckled. "Nat is here for two reasons, one to help me in what I am about to say and two she is desperate to see The Rocket," he ginned wildly and moved a bit closer talking in quiet tones. "Mind you from what the lads told me I am not sure if it is the horse." He threw back his head and laughed loudly. Mike found himself grinning despite. "I'll bloody murder those buggers when I see them!"

After the normal pleasantries and Mike supplying Roy with a glass of Bourbon, Nat with a glass of red wine and topping up his own glass he sat down to listen to what Roy wanted to ask. He couldn't help sneaking a look at Nat every now and again, she had the most incredibly green eyes, her hair was died snow white she had a gorgeous smile he thought, she didn't have the stunning beauty of Kate but there was something about her... she had class, charm, she had inner beauty as well as a very attractive outer shell Mike decided. He suddenly realised he was staring as Nat caught his eye. "Umm I thought before we get down to discussing whatever it is... maybe we should go and take a look at the horses before it gets dark?" Nat smiled and without saying a word rose. "Good idea, if you don't mind though I'll stay here I saw Rocket at the races and I'm sure he won't want my ugly mug staring over the box at him... anyway I think Seamus and John are one their way, I'll play butler." Roy laughed as Mike gave him a withering look.

Mike and Nat walked in silence towards the stables until Nat spoke, "I love horses," she pronounced it "harses" which made Mike smile, "In Ukraine I used to go to a how do you say riding school? I used to help the children, teach them to ride. I was very lucky I grew up in the countryside and did not move to the city until I was older."

As they entered the stable block horses started looking over the doors and whickering. Mike automatically reached to his pocket before realising he had no mints. "Sorry guys I have no mints!"

Nat touched his arm and a shiver ran down his spine, "May I? I brought some mints!" she produced several packets of mints from here pocket. Mike watched her as she handed out the treats to each horse in turn, she seemed very comfortable around them and the horses obviously thought this new person was wonderful with all the mints she was handing out. Mike walked up to her side. "The next box has Rockets son in it and then the massive box at the end is Rockets. He insists on being with JC at, all times but then when you have a horse as special as Rocket he tends to get a little spoiled." "I would agree with the special but definitely not spoiled!" the voice rang in Mikes head. Mike looked, and Rocket had his beautiful head out over the box door.

Storm was sprawled out in the middle of his box and Nat chuckled and turned to Mike, "What have you done to poor boy he is so tired!" Storm lifted his head as though to say 'you don't know the half of it and flopped back down on the straw again. "Poor baby," Nat said, she moved smiling to Rocket. "And this beautiful fellow must be Rocket? He is handsome man." She ran her hand down his sleek neck and Rocket nuzzled her bringing another chuckle. She turned and looked at Mike. "Mike, I miss to ride so much, maybe one day you let me come and sit on one of your horses?"

"She can ride me!"

"WHAT!"

Nat looked crestfallen, "Sorry I did not mean to offend."

"No… no you didn't, yes, yes of course you can I was just a bit surprised you want to ride a racehorse… they are a bit different than a riding school pony."

Nat smiled again. "Do not worry I not ride racehorse but I have ride show jump horse many times."

"Well in that case how about this weekend?"

"Yes, and she can ride me!"

"Rocket!"

"You let me ride The Rocket!" Nat leapt forward throwing her arms around Mike's neck and kissed him.

"Sorry to be a party pooper!" Seamus said trying hard to hide his mirth, "but we were getting worried you guys had got lost." He turned and hurried out trying unsuccessfully to stop chuckling.

"It isn't how it looks..." Mike said as they caught up with Seamus and received a knowing look from Seamus and more chuckling.

By the time they had reached the house Seamus had managed to get his mirth under control but still seemed somehow to pass on telepathically what he thought he had seen and the others grinned broadly as Mike and Nat entered the lounge. Maybe it was the inane grin on Seamus face, it just felt as though everyone in the room knew and Mike felt himself blush for the second time in his life. It was strange Mikes lips were still tingling and his stomach still churning. It wasn't the same feeling he had with Kate, it was, he didn't know how to describe it to himself, sort of more comfortable, warmer, slower, a glow. Don't be so stupid he thought to himself the girl is half your age.

"Well," Roy said, "you two seem to get along well together and that is a good start as that is part of what I came to see you about... a small part but nonetheless a part." They all grinned widely as Mike blushed for the third time in his life. "So, I'll start with the small bit! I need Nat to understand more about the racing here, she is pretty good around horses by all accounts but in a different field apparently." Roy held his hands out as a demonstration that he lacked any idea of exactly what that meant. "John, Seamus and I had a bit of a chat earlier this evening and they suggested that Nat should come and stay here for a couple of weeks, sort of get the feel of a British racing yard. She isn't needed on set for a few weeks and the boys said you had plenty of space and could perhaps accommodate Nat?" John and

Seamus were grinning so much it was like watching a toothpaste advert. "Okay to the second point." Roy paused, "actually I think I'll let John and Seamus explain that, if you don't mind I'll pour everyone a drink." Mike looked from one to the other a feeling of doom hovering over him as he looked at the nervous faces in front of him. John and Seamus sat looking back at each other then at Mike. "For God's sake spit it out will you. I'm not about to bite anyone…" it suddenly dawned on Mike what the possible conversation was going to be about. Seamus jumped in quickly. "Now Michael I would like you to remember that we have been friends a long time," he gulped.

"Seamus!" Mike said his exasperation rising.

"Now don't be doing anything silly!" Nick suddenly appeared looking sheepish from the kitchen.

"What the hell is happening." Mike said impatiently.

"Well after seeing the boy go today we thought… I rang up and put Rocket back in training, John rang the jockey club and ask them to put forward a race for all comers, in which Rocks and Storm would also run in!" he blurted out, "Oh and Roy rang a few people he knows and it seems it might… might mind you be in the papers tomorrow… and maybe on the television… and it looks as though CNN are going to feature it… maybe." Mike sat open mouthed, he was totally lost for words, he could not believe what he was hearing. The silence hung over the room like a guillotine waiting to drop. It was Nat that tried to break the silence.

"Mike said I could ride Rocket! Isn't that great?" it was John and Seamus turn to sit open mouthed. Nick was shuffling nervously from foot to foot obviously expecting to have to jump in at any moment. "Vi said she is coming up to make you all some supper." He said lamely, and they heard the kitchen door and Vi humming. Walking into the lounge she took one look and in typical Vi fashion went into mother mode. "Well I've seen happier funerals. Right you lot don't sit there moping I'll have some supper on the table in about ten minutes," she looked at Nat, "And will you boys have some manners and introduce me to this lovely young lady." Mechanically the introduction was made and Vi tutting at the men ushered Nat into the kitchen, turning as she left the room to say, "play nicely children!"

John broke the silence. "It's a great idea Mike think of the publicity it will create, the income and what it will do for the theme park." Mike looked at John, then to Seamus and then at Roy. He spoke quietly and much to everyone's surprise with a small semblance of calm. "John, Seamus, you would understand, Roy you can't even begin to, but I will say this to you all. It is insane! Rocket to train is an entity all to himself, he will only work when he wants to, yes, he is exceptional but he is older and is the leading worldwide sire… he doesn't need to race he has nothing to prove. It's nuts I'm stunned you even considered it… let alone went ahead and did it. We have only just managed to get Storm working, now you want to bring Rocks in, Seamus have you forgotten the headaches we had with him?"

Seamus smiled at Mike, "Ahh Michael have you forgotten how talented he is and how talented you are."

Mike threw his hands in the air it was useless he knew. The I love Rocket fan club was back! A voice came in his head. "Don't you worry I still have it and remember time is man-made and age just a number." A lighter voice said, "Yeah but the competition is greater this time!" there was laughter and then silence. Vi called them to the kitchen and Mike rose from his chair, tripped over the edge of the rug, and fell flat on his face. "Whoops" the voice came back and more laughter.

CHAPTER EIGHTEEN

Vi was in her element, she had taken to Nat like a duck to water and the two seemed to spend every spare minute whispering and giggling to each other. Nat had settled in and Mike looked towards the calendar and wished the days to stop, not only was Nat great around the yard but she was also good company in the evenings. She became really excited when Mike said he was thinking of getting a puppy and asked if she could go with him when he finally decided. Rocket was behaving himself and Seamus was thoroughly enjoying riding him. "You know," he said, as they walked towards the house after the horses had just done a strong canter. "Me boy just seems to stay fit... I know it's too soon to be cantering him but I just take a wise old trainers advice I was given many years ago," he grinned, "he told me to let the horse do what he wanted and that's just what I do." Mike couldn't help but smile. "Less of the old I still have a mile or two left in me yet!"

Seamus continued, "And I'll tell you this Michael, there is nothing between them the young fella is just as good as his old man!"

Mike had been plagued on the phone, wherever he went, the

papers seemed to have forgotten the world existed and everyday there was a report on how father and son were doing, whichever channel you turned to it seemed they were the topic of discussion and it was five months away from the date set for the race by the Jockey Club. There had been literally thousands of entries from all over the world. 23 of the best horses ever had been chosen to take on the most famous horse in history and his son.

Mike sat on the settee and Nat came in with the coffee she had made for them, under her arm she had a magazine. She sat next to him which was unusual she normally sat in the chair opposite, Mike could feel the warmth of her leg close to his but didn't move. "Mike? Can you help me please? My old car it falling apart, and I need to buy a new one... I bought magazine thinking that you might help me pick which is the best to buy?" She opened the magazine and spread it over both their laps. "I like this one she laughed but I think too much money for me, it was a rather nice Nissan 370z, maybe this one though? She pointed at a Seat Ibiza. I have good money from Roy but I send much to my parents back home, and my flat in London cost me so much money I have little savings. This car looks nice though, you agree? Maybe you can come look with me, I know nothing of cars." Mike looked, into her emerald eyes and his impetuous nature kicked in. "No problem, of course I will help you. Tell you what, why don't we take a walk around the horses, I feel like stretching my legs?" They both rose and wandered out through the kitchen door. As they walked around the yard Nat was telling Mike how in her own country she struggled to survive. She loved her home but there was so much more opportunity here if you were prepared to work hard. She said she felt like she was in a fairy tale, first she had by pure chance at a talk he was giving, met Roy and he had given her his card and told her to send him her CV. She was stunned she said when he offered her a job, and now she was if only temporarily living in a beautiful house in the country and riding horses when she wanted. it was wonderful. Mike stopped in front of the barn they were walking past. "I just want to check something in here," Mike said pulling the roller door back and the sweet smell of hay wafted in the air, he moved to his left, and switched the lights on. sitting at the side of the barn there was a car with a cover over it. Mike walked over and pulled off the cover. Nat ran her hands over the sleek bodywork of the purple Jag. "Wow she is beautiful... why do you have two though? Is this one different?" Mike smiled. "I suppose you could say it was different... I bought it for someone in honesty but... well it doesn't matter. it has been sitting here and I have been wondering what to do with it."

"Maybe you should sell it... it must be worth a lot of money?"

"Oh, I don't need the money and I don't know that I can be bothered with all the fuss of showing people the car then haggling over the price... too much hassle."

"I don't understand hassle."

"It means bother, the trouble of doing something. Any way it isn't a problem as I have solved it now." Nat looked puzzled. Mike smiled again, "Its simple you need a car, I have one spare, so she is yours, my thank you for your help and for being such lovely company."

Nat stood stunned, "Mike I couldn't, she is beautiful but it is far too much..."

"Well its either that or it will sit here forever and that won't do anyone any good,"

Nat burst into tears and threw her arms around Mike's neck kissing him soundly between thank you's. Mike's knees went weak.

Nat spent the next few days between the horses and cleaning the car which had accumulated a lot of dust in the barn, until it was spotless. She was due to move out the following day and Mike had organised a small farewell dinner for her. He had to explain to Vi again why he had employed the Thai couple. How could she cook and be at the dinner at the same time? Nat had organised to ride Rocket and was out with Seamus, so he was feeling a bit down as he entered the kitchen on his own. He found it strange, he always felt happy and comfortable when Nat was around, he found her extremely attractive but she was so much younger than him he hadn't considered, well not for long, anything other than a friendship. Vi plonked his breakfast in front of him unceremoniously and Mike started. "Have I done something wrong?"

"Nope!"

"Vi what have I done… I know you well enough to know when you are not happy."

Vi clattered a few things on the worktop before turning to face him. "It's not my place to say. I'm just the housekeeper is all." Mike was worried there were tears in her eyes. "Vi you know better than that… whatever brought this on… I would be lost without you, you're like a mum to me… is it money… I don't really pay you enough I'll sort it out," he rose from the chair and put his arms around her. "You can have what you want Vi, if you want a Rolls Royce you'll have one…"

"You are such a fool." Vi sobbed," Mike just stood there with his mouth open not knowing what was happening. "You're going to let that beautiful girl slip through your fingers!" Mike was aghast.

"What beautiful girl… Kate and I are over…"

"See stupid… totally stupid… that's what you are… you can't see it can you," Vi's voice was getting higher. Mike guided her to the table, "come on sit down and I'll get you a tea, don't upset yourself, it took me a while to realise but Kate was just an infatuation, Becky was a star and I loved her but I also had to realise that in the end she was her mother and fathers daughter not mine. Come on now have some tea and don't upset yourself, its fine I'm okay."

"You're as daft as my Nick. Not Kate… Nat."

"Wha…!" Mike virtually feel back into his chair. Regaining his composure, he spoke again. "Nat? Vi she is beautiful, but she is half my age, she wouldn't be interested in me… she is a friend… I… I think she is wonderful and I am going to miss her like crazy, but she is half my age and… well…"

Vi looked up her tears stopped. "If ever there was a man with a thick skull it is you Michael Willett… you look after me and my

Nick like we was family but you can't see the wood for the trees… that girl is in love with you… not infatuated in love! I have become very close to her and she tells me everything and she doesn't know what to do… she can't make a move on you… it has to come from you, it's her culture, she would jump at the chance to be with you!"

"Well I… I… well… I."

"That's it you sit there stuttering while that wonderful little slip of a little thing slips right away from you… she'd make a thousand of that Kate. Eat your breakfast!" Vi rose and went off busying herself in the lounge leaving Mike speechless.

John walked in the kitchen. "Bugger!" he said, "I was hoping Vi would be here I'm starving, and no one makes a better breakfast than Vi!"

"I heard that John Cullen and you had better not let Alice hear you say that. sit down I'll be there in a minute." John pulled a face. "And don't pull faces!"

"How does she do that?" Mike simply shrugged. "What's wrong with you everything is going tickety boo and you look like you have the weight of the world on your shoulders? Rockets flying and so is Storm. The little fella has his first race coming soon and I think he'll romp home. The garden couldn't be rosier… so what's wrong?"

"Don't ask… Vi just told me something and I'm a bit shocked."

"Nat." Vi said as she re-entered the kitchen.

"Oh." John offered.

"Does everyone here know everything before me?" Mike snapped.

"Was pretty obvious old man!" John said kindly.

"That's exactly it isn't it?" Mike pounced. "Old man… what would a beautiful, kind amazing person like that want with an old man."

"It's just a turn of phrase Mike!"

"Perhaps you should ask her!" Vi's voice chipped in and Mike looked up to see Nat standing in the doorway. He slapped his forehead and groaned. John and Vi suddenly found something very urgent to attend to and both hurried from the kitchen. John exited the front door and Mike heard his car move off down the drive.

"So, who is this beautiful, person you are talking about?" Mike groaned again, "and you say she is kind... and what was it... amazing?"

Mike looked up. "I was talking about... you. Because I do think you are all those things."

"Why you not say these things to me?"

Mike voice sounded professorial. "Nat I am twice your age, you are young, beautiful and I adore having you near me, but what would you want with an old man like me?"

"First maybe you should ask me before you make up my mind for me... you agree... you would want to make up your own mind... you agree me? As for age... time is man-made and age is just a number."

Those words seemed spookily familiar. Mike's mouth fell open and as he looked, into those green eyes with the tantalising and confident smile she had, he knew that this was real, not infatuation, not a fling, it was real. Mike wasn't sure what he was doing it was like someone had taken him over as he rose from his chair. Nat rose and he reached out and cupped her face in his hands. "Nat I can't promise you anything other than I will love you until the last breath leaves my body and then some more, I don't want you to leave... ever. Will you stay?"

Nat leaned forward and gently kissed him, "Yes, but not as just your friend, I want more than that. I want to be a part of you."

Mike couldn't really say if he was being influenced but he did know that he couldn't let this woman leave his life. "Then marry me!" the words came out before he even knew he had thought them.

"Yes." And she fell into his arms. The voice in Mikes head rang like a bell. "AT LAST!"

Vi came rushing in the kitchen and grabbed Nat in her arms

sobbing buckets. "Ooh I'm so pleased. I'm going to make the best cake that has ever been seen!"

That evening Nat and Mike sat curled up together on the settee, the remains of a takeaway sat on the table and an empty bottle of wine. Nat stretched kissed Mike on the cheek, "Well my future husband, today has been very exhausting! I am go to bed, I see you in morning." She rose and walked to the bottom of the stairs. "I am happiest woman in the world Mike!"

Mike took out the empty takeaway containers and put them in the bin and went to his room. As he walked up the stairs he thought how different this all was, he and Nat had become friends and were not even lovers yet she lifted his spirits and fulfilled him, she was like a soothing waterfall gently cascading over him relieving the pain he had felt for the past few years.

He walked into his bedroom and switched on the light Nat was lying in his bed the duvet up to her neck her eyes shining. "I think you surprised? But I think I have long time to spend with my man so maybe start now!"

There was not the urgency about their love making that there had been with Kate or even Ann, Mike thought it was like the world had slowed down, each kiss, each touch was like it lasted for years, and when Nat pushed him onto his back and straddled him Mike thought the world had stopped turning and he hoped it would never start again.

The next few weeks were a haze for Mike, everyone thought it was because of Storm though they couldn't quite make out why Vi was walking around like the cat that had got the cream, even Nick couldn't find out why she was so pleased with herself. Storm was to have his first run and the excitement of that coupled with his as, yet secret, took him along in a blaze of euphoria. Nat had taken a flight to her homeland to inform her parents and Mike already had the idea of a surprise waiting for her when she returned.

Mike sat Mel down at the kitchen table, the race was today. "Now young lady don't go looking to do anything spectacular. This is just to let the boy see the racecourse. No heroics and just make sure you both come home safe." Mel frantically scribbled on her pad. "Don't worry I would never do anything to hurt Storm, I will take care of him."

"Just make sure you take care of yourself as well Mel."

The racecourse was packed, and everyone had forgotten just how popular Rocket had been and it seemed Storm was literally creating the same storm. The traffic was appalling with a five-mile tailback there was no way they were going to get there in time. Seamus rang Mike who was travelling to the races with John. "Michael, can you get hold of someone and tell them if I don't get on the hard shoulder and someone clears the junctions they won't be seeing our boy race today. The traffic is at a standstill."

"You just do it Seamus, come up the inside nice and slow mind I'll see if I can get us some help."

Mike telephoned Sir Alfred Mapperton and he in turn telephoned his friend the chief constable, who immediately sent squad cars to make enough room for the lorry to get through. There would be riots if the horse didn't make it to the course! Seamus arrived at the course with an hour to spare and Nicky and Anita, who was now running the satellite yard unloaded the horse. Seamus went off in search of Mike and John. He found them in deep conversation with Sir Alfred Mapperton. "Hello Seamus," Sir Alfred said warmly. "Your jockey career seems to be doing well and it seems you are as good a trainer as you are a rider from what Michael here tells me!"

"Now Sir, don't be telling me that or me head will grow so big I shan't be able to get in the cab of the lorry to get home!"

"Now Seamus I have to ask… how good is Storm?"

"He'd be as good as his father Sir!" Seamus replied.

"Surely not… his father was exceptional! Unique even!"

Seamus smiled. "Well Sir there'd be nothing to choose between them and that's for sure. The only thing is Storm loves young Mel… won't have anyone on his back but for her he is a Christian. He seems a bit more tractable than his father though… but we'll see today if he is anything like as good as I think!"

Anita and Nicky brought Storm into the parade ring to tumultuous applause. Storm looked around unfazed and Mike went back in time to the first time he raced Rocket. He was so focussed on watching Storm he didn't notice Roy Winston until a hand slipped into his and he looked round and Nat was standing beside him. She gave him a coy smile stood on her tip toes and kissed him chastely. Mike hugged her so tightly she thought he would break her ribs. She laughed. "I have someone I want you to meet later... Roy flew me back..." and she reached up and kissed him again as cameras flashed everywhere. For once Mike was going to make the front page for the right reasons!

Mel was legged up and Mike leaned in close to speak with her, Kevin Stokes stood beside him with tears in his eyes as he proudly looked at his daughter. "Thank you, Mike... if I can ever do anything for you well it goes without saying!" Mike smiled at him he was almost as proud of Mel as her father was. "Right young lady no heroics just let him enjoy himself and come home safe."

Anita led Storm out onto the track and whispered. "Good luck Mel, we're all so proud of you."

Storm cantered past the winning post, turned and with elegance cantered down to the start. Mike was so tense he couldn't stand still, and Nat had to let go of his hand as he nearly crushed her fingers without knowing. "Mike don't worry they are fine."

Mike watched as the horses loaded, and the commentator said, "Three to go, two to go, one to go and they're all in... AND THEY'RE OFF..." Mike was dumbstruck as the horses burst from the stalls all except Storm who walked out leisurely looked around with interest as Mel urged him to go forward. The racecourse was in uproar as Storm took three strides forward then looked at the fast disappearing rumps of his competitors and decided he might just give it a go himself. With a massive surge he took off after the rest of the field Mel clung on for dear life as Storm ate up the ground. Mike had not seen any of this as he had sunk his head in his hands when Storm casually walked out of the stalls. "Mike… Mike look at him go!" Nat screamed in his ear and Seamus grabbed his arm nearly tearing it from its socket. Mike stood open mouthed as Storm caught up with the rest of the field. There were three furlongs to run. "He can't do it Seamus… he's used up too much to get back on terms he'll hit a wall." But Storm didn't, he passed the rest of the field with disregard it appeared. Flashing by the leading horse to win the race by a neck.

It seemed the only one that wasn't crying for joy was Storm himself! Storm walked into the winner's enclosure like he was a king, Mel was in floods of tears as was everyone, she was hugging Storm around his neck and it was all that Mike could do to get her to let him go. "Mel, you have to weigh in!" Storm had just like his father made sure he would be front page news along with Mike.

Everyone was thrilled having won not only the race but having lightened the bookmakers pockets considerably. Mike was almost crushed by the hug given him by Mel's father and organised for him to come to an impromptu celebration party that would be held that evening. Nat came rushing up to him, throwing her arms around him again. "You are so clever, they said you would do it and I won two hundred pounds!" She kissed him fervently and the cameras flashed again.

CHAPTER NINETEEN

Mike nearly had to drag Vi from the kitchen to allow the caterers access. It was only after he told her that she had to be at the party. After all he said she had to be there as tonight he was going to make it official. Vi rushed off grabbing a confused Nick who was just entering the kitchen. She ushered him out saying they had to get to town quickly as she must get something special to wear this evening. Nick turned in the door, shrugged his shoulders and grinned at Mike.

Nat asked Mike if she could bring two extra guests to the party and though he pushed her, she would not tell him who it was. She went off in the car and told Mike she would be back at six that evening as she had to go to town to get some clothes as she only had jeans and casual wear here, and she wasn't going to embarrass him by being under dressed for the party.

When she returned just after six a taxi followed her up the drive, Mike walked out to meet her and her mysterious guests and Nat immediately said, "Mike this is my mama and my papa, I am afraid they only speak little English but what they do not understand I will translate." Mike was at first nervous and thought it must be difficult for Nat's parent to accept that she was to marry an older man but they seemed overjoyed at the prospect and although they found it a little difficult with a bit of help over language they were soon laughing together and getting along far better than Mike could have hoped.

The caterers that had been brought in laid a lovely buffet it, seemed as though everyone was having a marvellous time. The room was quite crowded with all the staff and their guests as well. Mike tapped the side of his glass with a knife and said he would just like to say a few words, the room went silent. "First I would like to thank you all for the support and effort you put into the yard. I think you may be getting a small bonus this month." A small cheer went up from the staff members, "We have been blessed I believe in having Rocket... and now we have his son who, it would appear could well emulate his father. Now thanks to my friends here he pointed to John and Seamus, with a little help from our American friend we have an all comers race coming! Rocket and Storm will be facing the best horses in the world." A lad chirped up from the listeners. "What do you mean Guv... Rocket and Storm ARE the best horses in the World!" There was tumultuous laughter and a rousing cheer from the rest of the staff.

"I agree but that doesn't mean we can be complacent, we must give them every chance, this is not going to be an easy ride, for the next couple of months everyone has to be at the top of their game... not only for the boys, sake but for the rest of the yard... and remember we will be under the spotlight, so even I have to be on my best behaviour!" This elicited a lot of mirth. Mike signalled to Nat to come beside him. "Right before you go back to getting a hangover I have something else I would like to say. You have all met Nat as she has been helping out around the place... well you're going to be seeing a lot more of her because..." he put his arm around her shoulder... "I am pleased to say that we are getting married!" There was a moments silence then the room burst into a mixture of shouts of congratulations, applause, and a lot of back slapping. Nat stood on tip toes and whispered in Mike's ear. Mike's mouth dropped open and his eyes went wide, Nat looked concerned but then a smile as wide as the Grand Canyon spread across Mike's face. He put his hand up for quiet. "Well this one is a bit of a surprise, but I have to say two minutes ago I would have told you I couldn't be happier... I was wrong... because I am also going to be a DAD!" Everyone went crazy. If they could have remembered anything the following morning, they would have known they had had the greatest party in history.

Mike had to be virtually put in a muzzle for the next couple of days. Nat only had to blink and he was like a mother hen, but after several talking too from Vi, Seamus and Mary and Nat herself, he started to calm down. As Seamus told him and nearly got a whack around the ear from Mary for his troubles, "You don't stop a filly kicking up her heels now do you when she's in foal?"

Mike had told Nat he had a surprise for her when at the races and as they walked down through the yard he decided to show her. They walked up the short track that spurred off the main drive to the cottage he had done up for Kate. "I know you think a lot of your parents and if we can get all the necessary visas I thought it would be nice for you to have them close... so if you want they can have the cottage?" Nat threw her arms around his neck and kissed him passionately. "You are a wonderful man Michael!" and she skipped to the front door of the cottage.

CHAPTER TWENTY

It seemed that the world news had taken a back seat and that the only topic of conversation was the race which was to feature Rocket and Storm and the wedding. *Hello* magazine had offered a ridiculous sum of money to gain exclusive rights of the wedding and it was decided that the money would be divided between several charities.

Nat had gone back to the film set for a few days and Vi and her mother had formed a tight bond and were showing each other different styles in the kitchen, language didn't seem to be a problem, with the little English her mother had, and the secret sign language Vi and Svetlana had developed they giggled their way through the day. Alexi Nat's father had found a friend in Nick and spent his day helping to repair fences sitting with Nick when he was watching over Rocket and Storm and joining him on the gallops when they worked.

Mike, John and Seamus were walking around the theme park site with George. The transformation was astounding, most of the rides were finished but George wanted them to look in as he said he had an idea for The Rocket. It would he said add to the cost and would put a month on the finish date, but it would still be finished in time for the film premiere. Roy was waiting for them in the office, he was a little overwrought. "Hi Roy," John greeted, "you don't look too, happy... something wrong!"

"You could say that... look can we get this sorted out with George and then perhaps go back to Mikes and grab some lunch or something..." he whispered to John, "you might want to get that big fella of yours close by..."

"Roy this place is bloody brilliant, your guy has done marvels!" Mike half shouted across the office, he was studying the map of the facilities on the wall.

"Yeah, he sure has..." he leaned close to John again, "just make sure the big fellas there!" John looked concerned and signalled Roy to go outside with him.

"Mike I'm just going to take another look at the Rocket ride, I think Seamus is still mooching around there. Roy and I will be back in a moment."

"No problem, I'd like to take, a look at the old stable block... George told me they have built a special trail ride for kids and the hostel is finished." Mike's grin was from one ear to the other, "You and I are going to start looking for ponies next week! I'm really looking forward to seeing kids that have so little suddenly have a good time... and think of what this will do for the poor little buggers that are ill... I bet they'll be so chuffed it will take their minds off, of their problems if only for a while!" John grinned and Roy couldn't help himself. "You're an odd one Mike, one minute you damn near beat a man to pulp and yet to see you now you wouldn't think there was an ounce of spite in you!" Mike strode out of the room grinning wildly.

John and Roy wandered over to the Rocket ride. "This is going to be a huge success John!"

"Can't disagree with that, but what is all this about getting Nick to be around, sounds a bit serious?"

Roy looked tense. "Could be I'm afraid... bit of a problem on the film set. I'm in a real dilemma, if I don't concede then the film will be held up and the whole shebang will fall around our ears. And it might be Mike that brings it tumbling down when he hears!"

"Hears, what?" Seamus had wandered to join them.

"Spill the beans Roy." John interjected, "we've come too far to let this fall apart now...there's too much at stake."

"I have had to sack Nat!"

John and Seamus both spat. "Fuck!"

"Why the hell would you do that?" John asked incredulously, "you said she was brilliant at her job!"

"She is, it's Kate. She has become a real Prima Donna, has to have the right flowers in her trailer, the right wine... which she seems to get through at an alarming pace. The trouble is she has become a complete pain in the ass, but we are so far into filming that if I get rid of her it will cost me so much time and money it will put the film in jeopardy. Nat was showing off the ring to everyone on set and she came over and... well she wasn't very nice. She and Nat had a huge row and Kate refused to work unless I got rid of Nat. Nat understood and of course I will make sure she is well looked after but what worries me is how Mike is going to take it.... I saw what he did to Scott, and I really don't fancy the same happening to me, or worse Mike pulling out of our deal!"

"Don't worry about the deal I know Mike he won't go back on his word. The problem is going to be his temper!" John replied, Roy gulped. "Is there any way you can keep Nat on set?"

"Not unless I want to start the filming all over... and that just wouldn't be commercially viable!"

"Okay we need to think about this, find a way to keep Mike from losing the plot when he's told. How does Nat feel about it... is she pissed off? Silly question really!"

"Strangely enough she isn't. I thought she would be furious but either she should have been an actress, or she is genuinely okay with it. I gave her a huge settlement but Nat is normally about the job not the money."

Seamus piped up. "I think there might just be a way to stop Mike, it isn't Nick. What we need to do is to have Vi and Mary close at hand. You know Mike might just listen to them rather than us… he's a soft sod around women!"

"Seamus, you might just have found the answer. Right, tight lipped chaps until we get back… Seamus find an excuse to get Mike to the yard and delay him whilst we get things in place. I'll have a word with Nat as well and explain that Mike really can't get into any more trouble!"

They found Mike and as they drove back Seamus was saying he thought Mike should take, a look at a new filly that had arrived. At first it didn't look as though he was going to succeed but came up with the excuse that he thought the filly had a problem in her back, Mike couldn't resist taking a look and the moment they pulled in the yard he and Seamus wandered off to take a look. John and Roy rushed into the house.

CHAPTER TWENTY-ONE

Nat and Vi were sitting at the kitchen table giggling like two school girls. Roy went straight over and started to apologise for the hundredth time to Nat. She stood cupped his face in her hands and told him it was not a problem and that she really wasn't bothered. Roy started to splutter that he was worried about Mike's reaction and both Vi and Nat started giggling again. Vi spoke, "I don't think you have any worries on that score. We'll make sure our boy behaves!" and the giggling started again. Mary arrived and there was a huddled conversation between her and the other two women and again the giggling. John overheard... however did you get it done in a day? He looked at Roy. "I don't know what worries me more Mike or those three!"

Mike walked into the kitchen, saw Nat and immediately walked over and kissed her. "You look gorgeous... you've changed your hair... I like it!" Nat did a twirl.

"Mike sit down, I have something to tell you."

Looking puzzled Mike sat down and Vi brought out the compulsory cake and tea. "Are you going to stand there like the lummocks you are or sit and have some of my cake... I don't just cook for fun you know!" Nick had come into the kitchen and cautiously moved and sat beside Mike making sure he was close enough to grab him if necessary, Seamus sat on his other side while Roy and John moved to the opposite end of the table.

Mike sensed the atmosphere and turned looking questionably at the others. "What is going on?" The others looked sheepish especially Roy.

"Wha..."

Nat stood at the worktop. "Mike, I want you to listen to what I have to say you agree?"

Mike looked almost as worried as Roy. "Roy had to sack me today..." Mike leapt from his chair and it was with great effort that Nick and Seamus held on to him. Nat jumped in front of him. "Mike Willet you sit back in that chair and listen! Roy had no choice, it not his fault. Now I am as it happens quite happy about it because I have plans, so stop being an idiot and listen to what I have to say!" Mike slid back into his chair looking thunderous. "Kate kicked up a fuss and Roy had no choice... she refused to stay on set if I was still there and there is no way that she could be replaced at this stage in the filming."

"I'll kick her skinny little ass right across the county." Mike growled.

"You will not do anything! You will behave like grown man and stop having temper tantrums like little boy!" Mike had never seen Nat angry and it sort of made him want to hug her for some weird reason. "Now you haven't got anyone to run the kid's stables... I would like to do it, I love kids and horses and think I could do a good job. It will be different and interesting, and I have decided I would like to write a book, so I can do both. Oh, and I am sure when your daughter arrives she will want her papa to be here and not locked in a jail!" Mike stared at Nat. "How do you know... what...?"

"I had scan a few days ago and they told me I am having a girl and we are going to call her Amber Michelle Willett. Oh, and you had better go and see what was in your dressing room of our bedroom... I have had it converted to nursery for our daughter."

Mike seemed as stunned as he was when he first found out he

was to be a dad, "Amber," he kept saying, "what a lovely name. And she is my daughter." Everything else was forgotten much to the surprise and relief of Mike's friends.

Nat showed Mike the changes she had brought about to the dressing room and he was amazed. She had got the builder to bring in a team to get it all done and they had made a splendid job. It was like walking into a fairy tale, unicorns, rainbows, horses, puppies had been stencilled on the walls the room had a beautiful cot sitting in the middle it was Mike thought the perfect place for their baby, he did have one reservation though. "Don't you think Amber should be in our room? This is beautiful, but she is only a baby and...?"

"Mike, Amber is only three metres away. Promise me you won't spoil her too much she has to learn a bit of independence." Nat stood on tip toe and kissed Mike on the cheek. "I know she will have so much from us, but I don't want her to grow up a brat that thinks life is one big bank account." Mike grinned and nodded. He knew he would be a soft touch but he also knew that Nat was right and Amber, when she came, would need to be able to stand on her own two feet and to be able to appreciate that she was fortunate.

Nat grabbed his hand and pulled him towards the stairs. "I think we should go and look at the riding school yard, that is if you are okay with me giving it a try?"

"I couldn't think of anyone I would rather give a try."

Seamus rode Rocket beside Storm up the gallops, both horses seemed to be taking their work seriously. Mel crouched over Storm's shoulders, her knees dropped onto his withers and toes just sitting in the irons, her face almost touching Storm's ears. Seamus was sure he saw her lips move but then thought he must be imagining things as Storm suddenly surged forward, Rocket reacted immediately keeping level with his son. There was a look of euphoria on Seamus' face as both horses raced to the end of the gallops neck and neck. As they circled before walking the horses back, he patted Rocket's neck telling him what a star he was. He looked over at Mel again and she seemed again to be whispering in Storms ears. "You know Mel that little lad loves you." Mel smiled. "Now I don't know if you are speaking to him," Seamus spoke gently, "but if you are then perhaps you could speak to me?" Mel looked at Seamus and then burst into tears.

Nat skipped around like a child as they walked around the riding school. "Mike can we make different?" Sometimes Mike had a little trouble and had to build on Nat's English but her excitement seemed to reduce her English ability and this time he had no idea of what she was talking about. He looked at her puzzled. "Disabled and poorly children come, yes? We make this for children that have no disabled or ill, we need make for them as well, so they have same! Maybe we can make a what you say track? Like a small racecourse but safe so that the kids can go around and think they race?" Mike looked a little dubious. "We can make safe, not really fast but…" She smiled, "I know how to do!" She linked her arm through Mike's and pulled him close, snuggling into him and worming her way beneath his arm. "But maybe you have to pay." She looked, into his eyes and he melted, "And I be very nice to Michael when we get home!" Mike was already on his way back to the car. "Mike, you are bad man!" Nat laughed.

Seamus and Mel were side by side walking back down the gallops, Seamus was looking a little confounded at Mel, "Mel I saw you talking to the boy, now I don't know what is going on here but you and me, are going to sit down, just you and me when we get back and…" He tailed off as Mel's mouth opened and she haltingly started to say something. He could only pick out a few words it was like a listening to a child trying to form words, but he understood a little. she had always tried to speak but no sound would come but it seemed that since she had been working at the yard she could make noises more than words. She was embarrassed that it sounded silly not like words at all, she was also concerned how her twin brother would feel. Seamus thought about this and could understand a little. It was a difficult position to be in. "Right young lady, for the moment we will keep this between you and me but when we get back we are going to sit in the office and see what we can figure out." He smiled, "I won't say anything if you don't!"

The kitchen was empty when Mike and Nat returned and Nat had to remind Mike that Vi had taken a day off to go shopping with her mother, Nat started to fill the kettle and Mike put his arms around her waist and pushed himself against her from behind. He kissed her neck and she sighed reaching back and pulling his hips tight against her. "Mike, we have a lot to do," she said unconvincingly as she pushed herself tighter against him.

"Yes," Mike breathed heavily, "but first you have to keep your promise and be very, very nice to me!"

Nat turned, kissed him and grabbing his hand led him up the stairs.

She pushed him onto the bed and stood before him and Mike realised that this was not about the sex, it was about being together. He watched her smiling at him, she was not classically beautiful he decided, but exceptionally pretty, it was her charm that drew him. He noticed the way her mouth turned up at the corners, her eyes like two emerald orbs, her neck slender, she peeled the tee shirt she was wearing over her head revealing her small pert breasts and slim waist, sliding her jeans down Mike reached out but she smiled and stopped him as he reached forward. She moved onto the bed straddling him, Mike reached between her legs stroking the neatly trimmed light brown triangle. Nat grabbed his manhood and sunk herself onto it. They both orgasmed within moments, giggling like naughty school children before making love slowly. Mike felt so deeply emotional as he kissed her, he had found himself again and he knew this time it was forever.

As they lay spent, Nat lying with her head on Mike's shoulder, she reached up and touched his lips with her finger. "I love you Mike, I don't want a big wedding, just a few people we care for, it is for us not for the world."

CHAPTER TWENTY-TWO

Sir Alfred Mapperton could rightly pat himself on the back. He had against his colleague's opinions turned the racing world upside down and it had given racing the greatest lift it had had for years. Epsom had been chosen to host the race and preparations were already underway. It was still a month away from the actual race and already every hotel and bed and breakfast for miles was booked solid. Mike, with the help of John and Seamus, had unwittingly created an economy that would make countries blush and it had all begun through one very special horse Rocket. Sir Alfred had driven up to the downs and was watching the horses due to take on The Rocket and Storm, what he saw gave him a sense of pride. Win or lose the two horses would face the world's best. There were horses from America, Australia, Japan, the Middle East, Europe, Sir Alfred smiled as he wondered at the countries that were represented. He was pleased that Epsom had been the choice, at least the expected crowds could sit on the downs and watch even if from a distance they would still be a part of what promised to be a momentous day. His only niggling doubt was whether Rocket and Storm really were good enough against such amazing competition.

Kate Stokes sat fuming, Geoff had taken her back but had made it perfectly clear he had done so only as a convenience for himself and for the sake of Becky. Now she a film star in the making no less had been humiliated by some stupid little foreign cow showing off her ring from that bastard who had the nerve to have found another woman after only a few months! And to top it all she had just discovered that Geoff's estranged brother who she hated. It was her fault the brothers were estranged though no one knew, she had at the funeral of Kevin's wife made a play for him and had been flatly refused. Her attempt had been brazen and Kevin had made no bones about how disgusted he was. It had taken her a couple of years to drive a wedge between Geoff and Kevin but she was very good at being manipulative and eventually they had drifted apart. She now discovered that not only had that bastard found himself another woman. how dare he, he should still be grieving over the loss of her! But he had the nerve to employ Kevin's dopey children. Well today she had a bit of her own back. She was the important one and had gotten that little foreign bitch the sack, it was a start, but she had no intention of leaving it there! Just wait. If those two donkeys managed to win the race it would be a miracle with that idiot behind them and if they did then she had already overheard Roy talking about a sequel. She was no longer a part of it all. If a new movie was planned she would not be a part of it so she would have to make sure there was no sequel.

Kate walked onto the set to every man turning in her direction. It was quite strange really as most of them had been on set during her nude scenes so she had nothing they had not already seen but she knew how to make use of herself. She was wearing a very light white cotton mini dress that was as near see through as cotton can be. It was obvious that she wore nothing underneath and she accentuated the sway of her hips as she walked across the set to her caravan. She opened the door and smiled at herself. She knew just how easy she could grab most men and it still rankled that Mike had not chased her... she didn't want him, he was just another passing ship, but he should have turned and kept sailing in her direction. He had been too ready not to chase her and her pride hurt. She despised him even more for not chasing her, she would not have succumbed… might have dallied with him for a little longer just for fun, but that was all. She dialled Scott's number and he answered within a couple of rings… "Hi sexy… are you in your trailer?" Kate almost purred down the phone. "Why don't you come over? We aren't due on set for a couple of hours…" she paused for effect. "I was thinking that maybe we could continue getting to know each other better… last time was such fun." She didn't wait for an answer but hung up. Within a few minutes Scott was knocking on her door, bottle of champagne in hand. Kate opened the door and the light shone through the material of her dress outlining her naked body beneath. She smiled and beckoned Scott into the trailer. Grinning at him wickedly she put her fingers to his lips and with her other hand grabbed his crotch, pushing him back onto the sofa, tore at his jeans pulling them down only enough to allow his hard penis to spring free, lifting her dress over her head she almost jumped on him pushing him hard and deep into her. She slammed herself against him thrusting herself up and down wildly and as she did, looked into his eyes and knew that she now had Scott just where she wanted him, eating out of her hand or wherever she wanted him to eat. When the sex was over, it was nearly time for the makeup artists to arrive and Kate told Scott he should meet her after the shoot and they would have a quiet intimate dinner. She knew he would agree, he had been like a lamb to the slaughter. She had been so confident she had already made her excuses to Geoff saying she had to work late so she had no timetable to follow other than her own.

For the first time in several weeks, much to the surprise of the camera crew and set workers, Kate was the pleasant malleable character she had first been and the filming went well with only one extra take. It was with a feeling of relief that the crew packed up for the day and muttered to each other the hope that Kate, being a Prima Donna, was a thing of the past. After all, said one young girl as she hung clothes on a rail, "We can all hope… but

I personally wouldn't want to put my wages on it!"

Kate and Scott drove to an exclusive restaurant where the menu didn't list the price. It was assumed by the management that if you had to know how much you couldn't afford it. The food was fantastic if grossly overpriced. As they were eating, Kate removed one of her stilettoes and pushed her foot between Scott's legs, at one point pretending to drop her phone under the table and unzipping him, she took him in her mouth. Scott nearly choked on the piece of turbot he had just put in his mouth and she came out from under the table laughing. They didn't bother with desert. Paying, they left the restaurant and hurried to the car. They hadn't driven more than two miles before Kate had stripped naked, laying in the passenger seat, her hand busy between her legs, she moaned and turning to Scott said, "Find somewhere to pull over I need you to fuck me now!"

Scott lay exhausted in the driver's seat, he wanted to pee but was afraid to step out of the car for fear his legs would give way beneath him. He had been with a lot of women but this one was a complete entity to herself. He listened as she spoke her tone cajoling at first. "How would you like to get that Bastard Willett back for what he did to you... to us really because I had to stop seeing you for fear he would hurt you again!"

"Whoa!" Scott was defensive, "I'm not going up against that lunatic... he's a fucking animal, there's no way..." Kate placed her finger to his lip.

"Listen, I have an idea, you don't have to face him... I know what he's like, he is you're right an animal, but I know a way where you, we, can get our own back and he'll never know. And trust me this will hurt him more than a dozen beatings!"

Scott looked a bit dubious and Kate leaned forward and kissed him passionately. "You would be doing it for us!" she crooned and Scott was hooked.

CHAPTER TWENTY-THREE

Nat sat in the lounge a Jack Russell puppy on one leg and a Rottweiler puppy on the other, she was kissing each alternatively and fussing over them like a broody hen, which they both seemed to be enjoying immensely. Mike came in the lounge and smiled, "Okay time for these two troublemakers to go to bed," he reached forward to remove them but Nat threw her arms around them protectively. "No! You cannot take..." she kissed each puppy. "Do not worry bad, Papa not take you from Mama, you stay with me!" she looked at Mike a determined fix on her face.

"Nat, let me have them and I'll settle them in the barn!"

She slowly placed the puppies carefully on the sofa and stood, squaring her shoulders. "You bad man Mike Willett, you put my poor babies in BARN? You not do... they my babies, they stay with me!" she stamped her feet and Mike burst out laughing.

"You VERY bad man Mike Willett, you trick me! You not really put in barn?" Mike put his arms around her and went to kiss her. "You no kiss me bad man until you promise my babies not go to barn!" Mike laughed again.

"Okay... they can sleep in the kitchen, they'll be nice and warm in there and if they make a mess it will be easy to clean it up." Nat walked over to the kitchen which, although she knew as well as anyone, seemed to want to reassure herself it was suitable. She noticed the newspaper that had been laid on the floor and a rather comfy looking dog bed in front of the Rayburn. She huffed. "You very, very, very bad man to trick me so…" then she smiled, "now you have to be very nice to me, bad man!"

Seamus called Mel into the office, Mark automatically went to follow her and Seamus smiled, "It's okay Mark, go and tack up Storm for your sister, she just has a few papers to sign." He excused. Mark reluctantly made his way to Storm's stable. Seamus signalled Mel to sit. "Now young lady you and me had better have a chat." He smiled, "And I mean a chat." Mel looked at the floor for a moment and then like a small child trying to sound the words in their head spoke to Seamus. It wasn't much, just a few words, she haltingly explained that for some reason she wanted Storm to know how much he meant to her and the only way she could do it was to speak. She didn't understand how or why it just came to her. There were tears in Seamus' eyes, "Well holy mother of Jesus. If ever there was a miracle it was them two horses! What does your brother think?" Mel told Seamus he was the only one that knew and Seamus, though he didn't know why, thought it might be wise to keep it that way just for the time being, he would give it some thought before deciding on a course of action.

Rocket and Storm worked in perfect harmony neither giving quarter to the other, neither slacking off as they raced head to head up the gallops. They didn't do enough for Mike as in typical Rocket fashion. Once the pair had done one trip up the gallop, no amount of cajoling would get them to do another. Rocket still seemed to have an unerring sense of where the best dandelions were and would select the one he thought was the choicest morsel once they had reached the top of the gallops, whilst Storm looked on with great interest as his father relished every mouthful. Once he had finished eating, he would leisurely lead his son back to the yard regardless of whatever Seamus promised or threatened him with. This morning Rocket had decided that the dandelions were not to his standard and so had selected a considerable patch of cow parsley of which long fronds hung from his mouth as he chewed with a look of total ecstasy on his face. "Did you see them go?!" Seamus blurted at Mike. "There's no way they get beat, I tell you Michael these two have a bigger engine than a Ferrari!" Mike still had a look of concern. "Yeah! That's fine here Seamus but you know, and I know the race course is different, and these two chaps are up against the best there is." Seamus was again the number fan of the I Love Rocket Fan Club. "I'm telling you Michael the boy can't be beat! Why look what he did before and with less work in him than he does now." Mike smiled but it was a smile that held concern.

"I know Seamus but you seem to be forgetting he is considerably older than when he raced last. Look I love the lad, but I am worried, I don't want him hurting himself. I think we should consider withdrawing him… make an excuse say he has damaged a tendon or something." The voice rang angrily in Mikes head. "Oh yea of little faith… you will not, you are as young as you feel, you want to be an old man fine but me I'm just a foal." Rocket took off down the gallops like all the hounds of Hell were after him and Mike could hear Seamus who seemed to have lost his enthusiasm for the I Love Rocket Fan Club shouting "Whoa, you stupid bastard, whoa!" Mike smiled to himself and a lighter voice rang in his head. "Don't worry about the old man I'll look after him!" Then laughter and Storm turned and took off after his father.

Mike sat at the kitchen table with Vi fussing over breakfast, Nat sat opposite him and not for the first time he looked at her amazing smile and those deep green eyes, he felt a warm comforting glow in his stomach as she smiled back at him and reached over to hold his hand. "the puppies were sound asleep in the bed by the Rayburn and Vi had become almost as broody as Nat over them. Nat looked towards them then back at Mike smiling. "I not forgive you yet bad man… you still have to be very nice to me, trick me, poor babies!"

"Well Michael Willett, I sure I don't know if you deserve breakfast!" Vi scolded, "Fancy playing such a joke on my little girl and her having your baby and all… look at them little darlings, put them in the barn indeed!" Nat suddenly winced and held her stomach, "I think Amber try ride horse she kick me!" Then she slid from the chair onto the floor. Both Mike and Vi leapt towards the prone form of Nat. Mike was nearly in tears and immediately reached for his mobile dialling 999. He cradled Nat's head in his lap as Vi ran out to get Seamus and Nick. Nick immediately ran to the end of the lane to signal the ambulance and Seamus hurried into the kitchen consoling Vi who was in a total state of panic. Mike was sitting on the floor despair written over his face as he whispered to Nat, tears streaming down his cheeks. Hearing him saying over and over "I love you, I can't lose you, I have only just found you, please come back to me." Seamus found that tears were streaming down his own face he moved to help his friend. The paramedics arrived within fifteen minutes but it seemed like days. Seamus managed to prise Mike away from Nat and the paramedics placed an oxygen mask on her face and a drip in her arm before placing her on the stretcher. Seamus knew Mike was in no state to drive it was like someone had stuck a needle in him and sucked out his life force, he just stared vacantly at Seamus. Seamus guided him to the car and they raced off after the ambulance. "What's wrong with her Seamus." He almost whispered. Seamus took one hand from the wheel and patted Mikes leg. "I don't know Mike, but she'll be alright, you'll see." Though his tone was unconvincing.

It was several hours before the doctor walked into the small room they had placed Mike, Seamus sat opposite him talking quietly as Mike sipped at the coffee he held in his hand like an automaton. As soon as the doctor entered Mike leapt to his feet. "Can I see her, is she awake?" the doctor indicated for Mike to sit and the room was in silence. "Your wife is very poorly, you may stay with her if you wish. She is in a coma and it may help for her to have someone close by. We find it often helps if there is someone that can talk to the patient."

Mike face looked as though someone had thrown whitewash over him. "Is she going to be okay? Money is no object whatever she needs…" Mike swallowed the lump in his throat made the words almost guttural.

The doctor looked at Mike sympathetically, "Mr. Willett, it isn't about money, your wife has eclampsia. We don't actually know what causes it, all we can do is monitor her closely and pray. We will do our best of that you can rest assured, everything that can be done has been. I'm afraid it is now a matter of time we have to wait and see, she is a healthy young woman and the baby's heart beat is still strong." He put his hand on Mike's shoulder. "Be there for her Mr. Willett, and let us hope it is not too long before she wakes." There was nothing more the doctor could say, and Mike came out of his reverie a little. Seamus stood patiently as he listened to Mike's instruction before saying. "Michael, you have nothing to worry about now you go and be there for that young woman and we will make sure everything else is done, you just worry about her. I'll come back later with some clothes, toothbrush and whatever you need. Just stay calm Mike, I'm sure she will be fine." Mike gave Seamus a weak smile and mechanically walked towards the room where Nat laid connected to a bank of machines.

CHAPTER TWENTY-FOUR

"This is so perfect!" Kate declared, she threw the newspaper casually on the coffee table in the centre of Scott's trailer, Scott looked puzzled as he read the headline. Mike Willett keeps vigil at the bedside of what was to be his future wife. The story went on to say that Nat was in a coma and Mike had not left her bedside. "He hasn't left that little sluts bedside idiot! Which means the yard will be off its guard... everyone will be more concerned with Mike and his little bitch than the yard... it's perfect! And what a bonus that little cow is in serious problems!" she laughed.

"Come on Kate she was okay it isn't very nice she didn't really do you any harm!"

Kate's face was aflame. "Don't even go there... she is a whore, little slapper got what she deserved." Her mood changed and she became placatory. Moving over to where Scott sat she slowly eased her skirt up her legs." She leaned forward and kissed Scott, her hand searching between his legs, "Come on big boy mummy has a nice warm play room for you."

That evening Scott listened as Kate told him exactly where to go and what to do. He tried to get her to go with him but she said it had to be him, if she thought anything of him then... Scott crept across the yard. He entered the barn Kate had told him to and walked on tiptoe to the second but last box. Very quietly he pulled the feed tray out as Kate had told him to do and poured the small phial of liquid into the feed bowl. He was shaking so much he nearly spilled it and it seemed as though it was an age before the thick liquid trickled out. Scott wanted to run but he wouldn't have been able to he was shaking so violently it was all he could do to walk. Staying in the shadows he made his way to the end of the lane another few yards and he slid breathless into the passenger seat of Kates car. She didn't wait for him to settle. "Well did you do it?" Scott could only nod. Kate leaned over and kissed him.

Mike sat talking to Nat his hand gripping hers, every few seconds he would lean forward and kiss her. "Oh, Nat I should have told you how important you are to me. please wake up I just can't be without you!" Nat did not stir.

Storm ate his food up almost before Seamus had finished putting it into his bowl, "Good lad." As he reached and stroked his sleek neck he moved to the next box and the new filly came over to look for her breakfast. "there you go lass." The filly dug her nose deep into the feed bowl and munched away happily. Seamus finished putting the feed in as Nick strode done the alley dragging a huge bale of hay behind him. "You'll have to just park that in the third box up Nick. Once they've had their breakfast and settled a bit they can go be tacked up and go on the walker whilst the yard lads muck out. it you leave it there it will block the alley." Nick dragged the bale into the box next to the filly. Made a fuss of Storm walked to the end of the alley where Mike had converted the end of the barn to house Rocket and JC, made a fuss of them both and started to walked back. "Seamus this filly doesn't look too well!" He said loudly to catch Seamus attention. "I just saw her Nick she was fine!"

"No, you had better take a look Seamus, she doesn't look good." Nick opened the stable door and Seamus knowing that Nick was a bit protective over the horses and that he would get no peace until he looked walked back to the box. "She dead!" Nick shouted and Seamus sprinted into the box. The filly laid on her side froth covering her lips and her legs curled up as though all her muscles had contracted. Seamus couldn't believe what he was seeing. He checked the fillies feed bowl and noticed it had a sweet sugary smell, a bit like honey. "Nick!" He shouted turn all the feed bowls round so the horses can't get to them and he started spinning the bowls himself so that they latched on the outside of the box where the horses couldn't get the feed. He looked at Storm and Rockets bowls, both were empty. They had eaten everything. He sniffed the bowls but there was no sweet smell as there was with the filly's bowl. When all the bowls had been turned around he looked at Nick. "Nick I'm going to get the vet here we need a post mortem done. No one gets in this barn!" Nick ominously squared his massive shoulders and nodded his head. "They won't!" he said simply. Seamus raced off and phoned both the vet and John. by the time the vet had arrived John was already in the yard. Staff were milling about waiting to find out what had happened and Seamus called everyone close. "Right there has been a bit of bother which I will explain to you all later but for the moment those that normally do this barn help out in the other barns." He waited for a response, but everyone still stood about. "Get a fucking move on you, lazy sods!" he shouted and they all hastily made their way to another barn.

It took the vet just a few minutes to come, to a conclusion. "Poison without a doubt, but I have never heard of a poison that could knock a horse down that quickly. has this horse been turned out at all?" Seamus explain she had been on box rest for three weeks and had been put here to keep Storm company, the only move she had made was from the box next door. Seamus went on to say about the sweet smell in her feed bowl and after the vet spent a few seconds sniffing agreed with Seamus it was honey. "I think to be on the safe side we should get the feed tested… I suggest you call the merchant ad get a new lot delivered until we are sure it is okay. Though it seems odd that only one horse is affected. I have to say that I think you have been the target of sabotage." The vet organised for a trailer with a winch to come and pick the horse up so he could do a proper post mortem, and John rang the security firm that had been used to protect Rocket. "Somebody got this wrong… it wasn't the filly they were after it was Storm!" Seamus said, "Nick I'll get someone to bring you breakfast and a cup of tea… don't let anyone and I mean anyone near the boys!" then almost to himself, "We have to keep this from Mike… he has enough on his plate and this might tip him over the edge!"

John and Seamus walked to the house deep in conversation, Seamus signalled to one of the lasses just before they entered the kitchen. "Tell everyone to drop what they are doing and come here straightaway. No excuses, everybody!" Five minutes later the lass poked her head around the kitchen door. "Everyone's outside Guv." Seamus and John walked out to the garden where the staff now stood. "Right!" Seamus shouted across the babble and it immediately went silent. "I'll not beat around the bush, yesterday Nat fell ill and has been taken to hospital, she is very poorly and Mike is staying there with her." There was an audible intake of breath. "on top of that last night some sneaky bastard tried to poison Storm." Everyone started shouting and asking questions most of which centred on Storms well-being. "Storm's okay they must have got the wrong box and sadly the little filly next door to Storm ended up being the one poisoned. I'm afraid she didn't make it. Okay I don't want you talking to anyone about this, not anyone, if I find out that someone has said a word of this you will be out of a job and I promise they will never work again… I will make sure of it! Right off you go there's still horses to do, Nicky make sure everything is done, I am not going to be around much today. No one goes in to Rocket and Storms barn not even you Mel."

Within an hour a van pulled up and two security guards stepped out moved to the back and removed a German Shepherd and a Rottweiler. As they approached Seamus and John they looked down at the dogs, "Friend." They said and the dogs stopped looking a little less menacing. "sorry to hear you have problems Sir," the elder of the two said. "We've organised three shifts Sir, there will be two of us here twenty-four hours a day until you longer require us." John and Seamus thanked them and led them over to the barn that housed Rocket and Storm. They were obviously impressed with Nick he even towered over the two of them and they were not exactly small. "Okay Nick you can leave it up to these guys now." Nick looked at them dubiously, "You sure?"

"It'll be okay Nick we have a lot to do and we need to go see Mike and Nat…. Vi wouldn't forgive you if we didn't' take her."

Nick still looked a little doubtful. He took a step closer to the two men ignoring the dogs who seemed as much in awe of him as their handlers. "You make sure you don't go sleeping or nipping off somewhere… make sure you look after my boys!" Both men nodded quickly.

Mike was sitting in a chair at Nat's bedside stroking her hair with one hand and holding a book in the other as he read to her. Vi watched him from the doorway un-noticed, he stopped leaned forward and gently kissed her and she heard him say, "Come back to me Nat, I can't be here without you!" He had only been there 24 hours but looked as though he had been there a month, his face was drawn and haggard. It was all Vi could do to stop herself from bursting into tears. She moved to Mike's side determinedly. "Right young man, you get and find a shower and tidy yourself up if you think I am going to let my little Angel wake up and see that I haven't been taking care of my boy, you have another think coming. Now get up and go and make yourself look presentable and you can take my Nick and he WILL make sure you sit and have something to eat… No arguments now off you go." She finished briskly and Mike nearly managed to smile at this wonderful woman that had come onto his life in the most unusual of circumstances. He went to the door and the huge arm of Nick slipped over his shoulder and squeezed reassuringly. The second they were out of sight Vi grabbed Nat's hand and through a flood of tears said. "Now young lady, you are far too precious not just for our Michael but for me… I can't lose you either, so you damn well get better!"

After visiting and trying to reassure Mike, Nick and Vi made their way back to the yard and John and Seamus took their turn to visit. On the way they discussed the problems that seemed to have come in a landslide. They knew they could not tell Mike as it might just be enough to send him over the edge and if he lost the plot in these circumstances they were sure the damage he would do would be catastrophic. They decided that they should let Mike worry solely about Nat and they would worry about the yard. They found Mike just as Vi had and both their hearts went out to him, he had showered and changed but the drawn look was etched onto his face as he clung to Nat's hand. Staying with him for a few hours was as much a strain for them as they watched their friend sink deeper into despair. The only thing Mike had said apart from thanking them for coming was "Why doesn't she wake up doesn't she know how much I love her!" Seamus and John left the hospital wet eyed and it was several minutes before either could speak.

"Are you sure you put it in the bowl of the second box?" it was a snarl rather than a question.

"Just like you told me the second box from the bottom of the alley."

"Why the fuck is there nothing in the papers... all there is, is more about that little tart, and POOR little lost Mikey Wikey sitting at her bedside. Pathetic wanker!"

Scott was an arrogant sod, a Prima Donna but he wasn't a total ass, he did have some feelings and was beginning to wonder what he had got himself involved in. "That's a bit harsh babe... I have reason to hate the guy but the girl well..." Kate wasn't listening. "you say the second box up the alleyway?" she asked calmly and Scott nodded. "was there a stable next to the one you put the stuff in? and was it really big"

"No same size as the one I did."

"How many horses in the box next door?"

"Just one of course."

Kate smacked her hand across Scott's face. "You, fucking idiot you put it in the wrong box!" she screamed. "You'll have to do it again!"

Scott had enough. "You can do it yourself I'm having nothing more to do with it… you need to see someone and get sorted out… and if you ever hit me again I will knock you on your pretty little ass!"

Kate grinned and it was a grin of pure malevolence. "You'll do as your fucking told! What do you think Mike Willett would do to you if he found out you had tried to poison one of his precious horses?"

"What do you think he would do if I told him it was you?"

"God, you are fucking thick aren't?" she sneered. "do you think he would believe you over me?" her smile was cruel, she spoke again in a wheedling tone "Mike darling, I only stayed away from you because I love you and was worried you were going to ruin your life because of me… as soon as I found out I came to tell you that Scott tried to poison your horse to get back at you for beating him." Her tone became malicious. "You'll do what I tell, or you'll have that lunatic Willett hunting you wherever you go… and when he finds you what he did to you last time will seem like a good night out!" Scott went silent.

Kate went home well pleased with herself. She had Scott exactly where she wanted him. He was just another pawn she could use as and when she pleased.

Scott sat holding his head in his hands before opening a bottle of champagne, he didn't even bother to get a glass but sat drinking from the bottle.

Roy was not in the best of moods. He was really angry with himself for getting rid of Nat, her replacement was nowhere near as good and he felt as though his getting rid of her might be partially to blame for her falling ill. He thought that maybe she had been really upset by the sacking and the stress had got to her. His misplaced guilt moved his mood down several notches on the smile scale. When Scott walked in his office he was met with barely concealed contempt. "What's wrong now… toilet paper not soft enough for you." Roy barked at him. Scott looked both worried and sheepish.

"Look Roy, I know I haven't exactly been the easiest of people to work with but something has come up that has made me realise what an idiot I've been, and I need your help." Roy scowled at him thinking Scott was going to come up with an even more ridiculous demand than normal. "Serious Roy... this is serious, I don't even know where to start." Roy sighed the day was just getting better and better.

"Sit down, I don't have a lot of time so you had better get straight to the point."

For a few seconds Scott sat half stuttering trying to say something but not succeeding. "Get on with it or get going." Roy said brusquely.

"Look you have to tell me you will help me I'm in big trouble!"

"How much?" Roy snapped.

"No, it isn't money... Christ I have never complained about that, my fees are very generous!" Roy looked flabbergasted Scott had never done anything other than complain about everything else, so it had to be money! "Roy you really need to tell me you will help me, this is deep shit!" Roy was getting impatient but he was intrigued as well. "Okay I'll help you spill and I'll see what I can do."

Roy sat open mouthed as Scott told him of his visit to the stables in unadulterated detail.

For a few minutes Roy couldn't even speak. He just sat there his mouth wide open and a look of disbelief across his face. "You, fucking idiot!" He suddenly exploded. "Wasn't the beating you had before enough... do you have a death wish... you try to poison one of Mike's horses... and not just any horse but Storm? Are you fucking insane? Who the hell is going to stop him? How the hell we're going to get past this one I don't know; the man is sitting by the bedside of the girl you helped get the sack with that fucking nuisance you've been humping... I wish I'd never met the bloody woman... I'm telling you neither of you will ever work in the film industry again... I hope you've had the sense to put some money away because you are going to need it, or you'll have to get a job in a burger bar, and that's if you're lucky. Fuck you were unconscious when they pulled Mike off you I saw what he was like, he'd have killed you and if we're not careful he'll be finishing the job!"

Scott covered his face with his hands and muttered "Oh my God!"

"I don't think he's going to help you. Go on fuck off out of my office. You had better get every take right and get this film finished and I'll try and sort this mess out." Scott rose and made for the door. "And if you as much as smile at that fucking whore off set you'll be gone! Tell Stephanie to come in."

Stephanie had replaced Nat and she hurried into the office looking worried, she tried hard but Nat's shoes had taken a lot of filling. Roy looked up and smiled it was strained but he had been around enough to see the concern on her face. "Steph would you do me a favour and find Kate, tell her I need to see her now don't take an excuse tell her I said immediately."

Kate strutted in the office like she owned the world not just the space she stood in. Roy didn't bother to look up from the papers he was studying "Sit."

"I'm not a dog Roy." Kate laughed and Roy looked up and pulled a face.

"If this movie wasn't near completion I would have you off the set so fast you would catch fire!" Kate looked shocked and went to speak but Roy stopped her. "Don't even bother to open your mouth Kate, just listen." He paused for a moment and looked her up and down. She was wearing a light white cotton tee shirt and her nipples were fully visible through the thin material. "Let's start with your tee shirt Kate! Look I know you are doing nude scenes in the movie and so have nothing to hide but off set dress up a little bit… this game is all about appearances… that is not a request by the way and it stands until we have finished the movie… after that you can walk naked down Bond Street for all I care as long as it doesn't affect the box office but when you are on my set you will do the right thing. Now we come to the crunch! I know what you have been up to." Kate tried to look innocent. "Don't even try to deny it." Roy had been around actors long enough to know how to act himself and to lie. "Your car was caught on CCTV just down the road from Mikes lane!" Kate gasped. "I didn't mean anything I was angry with him." She tried, "Kate I told you listen, so shut up and do just that. You know damn well if Mike finds out he will kill your little part time lover." Kate smirked, "You think it is funny? You stupid little harpy. What do you think would happen to the person responsible for trying to poison one of the most loved animals in the world?" Roy's voice was rising, "Not the country you stupid little cow but the fucking world... I bet they would be queuing up outside their cells waiting for your arrival, a movie star and a looker... you would end up everybody's bitch! Now there might be a way out of this but I am going to tell you don't think that this is a career launch that it should have been, you are going to the bottom of the Abyss, you will finish this movie on my terms, you will get paid as I agree but all your plans for a future in this industry and any other I can assure you are over. The moment I see you trying to get in on any spin off from the movie I shall make sure it doesn't happen... when this is done you are going to be one of those actresses... "That just wants to be alone" and definitely will be... I shall personally make sure you are the first female hermit in history... is that clear?" tears were streaming down Kates face and she nodded sheepishly "Right you can cut the waterworks for a start. I will try and sort this mess out and YOU had better hope I succeed, now get out of my office the only time I want to see your face is when it is on set, and you had better get that right or I will replace you regardless of what it costs me financially or in time." Kate started to walk to the door. "Oh, and if you do think you can mess up, read your contract because if I have to replace you, you won't get a bean! Now get out of my sight!

CHAPTER TWENTY-FIVE

There was an aura of sadness over the yard. Everyone did their job just as they always had but the last week they all seemed to feel Mike's pain. Vi in particular was suffering, she had lost weight and looked tired and drawn. Everyday Nick drove her to the hospital and she would chivvy Mike into showering and shaving. She would make him sit and eat the food she brought before letting him back to his bedside vigil. The stress seemed to be melting him. Everyday Vi would sit with Nat as Mike took his shower and she would cry and tell her how important she was… she was the daughter she never had, she loved her. John and Roy had organised to bring her parents over. Vi had taken it upon herself to organise getting the cottage finished for them. John had pulled as many strings as he could, and had brought Sir Alfred in on the case, he proved to be an absolute superstar. He had badgered his friends in high places and two permanent resident visa were sitting on his desk waiting for Nat's parents. Nat however stayed with her eyes firmly shut and showed no signs of recovery. Mike resumed his vigil refusing all attempts to get him to go home if only to get a good night's sleep. Vi sat beside him. "You know Michael you are nearly spent! You are no good to her if you kill yourself before she wakes." Mike looked at Vi the tears streaming down his face.

"I can't leave her Vi… I love her too much she is just my love she is me!" Vi hugged Mike and he sobbed uncontrollably into her shoulder "Look Michael you are as much my children as if I had given birth to you and I love you both, but do you think this little Angel would thank either of us if you didn't get out there and continue… can you imagine what she would say if you weren't a part of the greatest race in history and just sat here by her bed… it isn't you it is her she would never forgive herself!" Mike pulled himself together and looked at Vi. "Okay Vi I'll be there at the race but that's all Seamus and John can manage the rest, I'll not leave her, she's mine and I know I have to be here for her."

"You're not quite right Michael! It isn't just Nat who needs you, Seamus and John do as well… we all do, the staff, the horses. I know this little slip of a girl and I can tell you she loves you more than the air she breathes, she knows as well how much you love her. She wouldn't want you to sit here, she would want you to get out there and do what you are good at… when she wakes don't you think she is going to want to see you win? Now young man you had better make some time to make sure you please this young lady and make sure you do your job." Vi's voice softened. "Michael you don't have to be away from her for long, just an hour or two a day, make sure everything is running properly. If you just show your face it will make all the difference." Mike reluctantly agreed that he would put in an appearance the following morning.

John and Roy finished the press conference, answered questions on Rocket, Storm, the theme park, the movie and on Nat's progress. For once the press showed a sympathetic side and every day the papers would print a small piece wishing Nat a swift recovery.

Roy took John to a restaurant he liked for dinner and as they ate he told him the story, of Kate and Scott. Although John was appalled he surprised himself at not being shocked. It seemed that he had secretly harboured some doubt over Kates character.

John knew that if Mike found out at this moment in time that it was Kate and Scott let alone that one of his horses had been poisoned he would be berserk, but he also knew they somehow had to break it to Mike there had been an attempt on Storm. They had to somehow make sure he never discovered Kate and Scott were behind it. John made, a decision and picked up his mobile. It was a long conversation. Roy overheard him saying, he knew whoever it was he was talking to had a nice mare and wouldn't it be something to have a foal out of her.... Then either you choose... no charge. There was a lot of thank you at the end of the conversation and when John put his phone back in his pocket he gave Roy a smug grin! "Well?"

"Solved! It has just cost me a free service to either Rocket or Storm when he stands but it is worth it."

"Yes but..."

"The vet is going to write a post mortem report saying the horse had a hypersensitivity to insect bites and it appears the filly was stung in the throat by something like a wasp and had an allergic reaction which closed the airways. It will say it is very rare almost unheard of and that it was just an unfortunate accident. We can cover the security guards by saying we thought the horses had to be protected because of the high profile of the race... Mike will swallow that if I say it was me... he knows I am a bit paranoid over Rocket sometimes. I think we can get away with it, and the beauty is even the staff will have to buy it!"

"And I thought I was the master of devious!" Roy said with a grin. "Now the only other thing we have to solve is getting that little lady to wake up. And I have to say I am really very concerned. She is a great girl and if you want the truth I feel I might be responsible in sacking her... sort of stressed her?"

"Look Roy you told me what you gave her as a gratuity and it was an awful lot of money, far more than you needed to and I'm sure Nat appreciated that, we have all become fond of her... you can't help it she is just so likeable. I don't think you can blame yourself, I just think it was one of those things. I hope and pray though that for once Mike gets the break I see just how much he has fallen for her. I have known him for a long time now and believe me he loved Ann, but what I see he thinks of Nat pales that into insignificance. I dread to think how he will cope if he loses her. I took the liberty of asking the doctor if there was anything I could do and all he said is hope and wait!"

When Mike entered the yard at seven the following morning he was greeted as a hero, everyone was ecstatic to see him. They were surprised at how thin and drawn he looked but still thrilled at his presence. He drove up the gallops and watched as Seamus and Mel took off at a strong canter and although he felt the familiar tingling in his stomach his normal euphoria at watching Rocket was not there, all he could think of was Nat. Halfway up the gallops the lots that had set off just after Seamus and Mel came level with Storm and Rocket. Seamus felt Rocket's muscles bunch beneath him and knew he was about to experience something special. "Easy now son, you have nothing to prove, we're just doing a steady to pick young Michael up a bit." But he knew Rock's had a different idea. Rocket's hindquarters seemed to come right under him and he sprung forward, his stride lengthening instantaneously. Storm followed suit and the two took off hell for leather, each stretching his neck trying to get in front of the other. Both Seamus and Mel frantically pulled on the reins trying to slow them down but they would have none of it and they went past Mike as a blur locked head to head and disappeared around the bend. Seamus and Mel came back around the gallops grinning from ear to ear. "Michael me boy I think the boys are pleased to see you… I have never been so fast in me life… what a horse!" and Mike had to smile. Rocket walked over to where Mike stood and pushed him with his head. The voice rang in his head. "Sometimes it is the little things in life that matter." Rocket turned with Seamus looking puzzled and trotted back down the gallops closely followed by Storm. Mike got back in the Land Rover and drove back home all the way thinking what the little things in life mattered meant. He parked the Land Rover and Vi came out of the kitchen and walked up to him. "You will eat something before you go back to the hospital." Mike knew it was an order and followed her into the kitchen. He wasn't paying attention and hadn't noticed the puppies rushing towards him to say hello and he tripped over them, making the pair of them yelp and run for cover as he tried to regain his balance unsuccessfully and fell flat on his face. Mike jumped up almost whooping with joy and Vi turned a look of sheer amazement on her face. "That's it why that horse has to talk in riddles... I know what to do!" And he raced over to where Vi was standing kissed her on the cheek and hugged her. "I need a box Vi, about this big and sturdy can you ask Nick to find me one please?" he held out his hands to show her the size he wanted. Vi looked completely puzzled and realising whatever it was that had brought Mike back into the land of the living it had to do with the box she hurried off to find Nick. Nick returned carrying a strong cardboard box. Mike was sitting eating the bacon and eggs that had been prepared by Vi. "Perfect." Mike smiled. "Oh, and I'm fed up of seeing you and Vi in the yard pickup!" Nick and Vi looked at each other with concern, "Sorry Mike I didn't think you'd mind us goin' to town in it!" Mike laughed. "Course I bloody well mind! Should have thought to say before!" Nick now looked at Vi with dread. "I want you to drive over to John's place in the Land Rover, you and Vi, and tell him I said he is to ring his mate and organise for you to go and pick up whichever model you want at his showroom and I will sort it out with him. And don't come back here with a load of rubbish... new and the best they have." Vi burst into tears and Mike laughed. "Bloody hell I thought you would be pleased!" Vi threw her arms around him. Nick before you go there's a throw on the settee, can you put it in the box please, then catch them two little buggers and put them in the box." Mike finished his breakfast picked up the box as Nick and Vi watched him opened mouthed. "I thought I told you to go and buy a car? So, what are you still doing here?" and he waltzed out to his car placed the box on the passenger seat and roared off down the road.

When John opened the door and saw both Nick and Vi there his face was panic stricken. "What's happened?"

Nick looked at Vi and she explained what had transpired. "Well I can see the car bit, no problem, but the box and taking the puppies… that would worry me! Look you know where my friends showroom is you've been there with Mike, Nick. Just go and ask for Simon and tell him I sent you and will sort it out with him later today. I'm going to the hospital and make sure our boy hasn't lost his marbles." John didn't wait for an answer but jumped straight in his car and spitting gravel roared off down the drive.

John found a spot and hurried into the reception area right into the middle of possible chaos.

Nick and Vi stood looking at a new Land Rover Discovery sitting at the front of the showroom. "This!" Simon said, "would be perfect for you, fantastic headroom, which looking at you Sir you are going to need! It's top of the range."

"It's an awful lot of money Nick!" Vi said and Nick nodded, "I think we should look at something else?"

"Madam, John told me that my instructions are to get you the very best car we have in the showroom and he also said you would be worried about the price and told me quite definitely it is not an issue. The price does not matter one iota, that you are happy is the only consideration, if you like it I am told you MUST have it, no arguments and once you are happy I am to arrange for it to be delivered to you by this evening!"

"Well it is lovely." Vi said coyly, "What do you think Nicholas!" Nick simply smiled. "Then this one it is!" Vi said much to the joy of Simon.

CHAPTER TWENTY-SIX

Before John had taken a step into the hospital reception he grabbed his phone from his pocket pressing the speed dial for Nick, as soon as Nick answered he simply said come to the hospital straight away and hung up. There was a cardboard box on the floor with the two puppies yapping frantically and trying to jump over the edge, a security guard sat with his back to the wall obviously winded but otherwise seeming unhurt, there was another security guard holding his hands wide shouting "Sir please calm down... this is a hospital you cannot bring dogs in here." As Mike advanced on him with both fist clenched. John jumped in front of Mike and tried to get through to him but it seemed hopeless, Mike just walked kept walking forward he eyes wild and unfocussed. For an instant John thought he had made a dreadful error as it seemed he had become the target. Then from out of nowhere the huge figure of Nick loomed in front of him. Mike actually growled and advanced even more. There was a split second that seemed to go on for an eternity then Vi stepped into the fray, "Michael! You stop this at once!" Mike shook his head as though trying to understand where he was and Vi immediately hugged him and his eyes return to normal looking around as though he wasn't sure where he was. "Now my lad... what's this all about?" and she lead Mike to a row of chairs by the wall and sat him down. "They tried to take Nat's babies!" Vi looked puzzled and then realised he was talking about the puppies. Nick and John had told the standing security guard not to do anything and they went over to the guard sitting against the wall. "You okay?" Nick asked and the security guard paled a little as he looked at the huge figure leaning over him. "Yeah caught me a corker just under the ribs, took the wind right out of me. Bloody hell I thought a train had hit me!" there was a smile on the guard's face now. "I only reached out to take the box off him and bam!"

"Are you sure you're okay?" it was John asking now. And the security guard smiled and with the help of Nick rose to his feet. "No real harm done. I tell you what though I wouldn't want to meet him on a dark night! I didn't even know he had punched me until it connected, Christ he's fast!" John held out his hand and there was two hundred pounds in it. "Look what's say we forget all about this wipe the CCTV, you take the wife or girlfriend out to dinner and we'll put it all behind us?" John gave the other guard one hundred pounds and the same to the receptionist to settle the problem. Fortunately, there was no one else in reception. Mike apologised to everyone and the doctor was called who had been looking after Nat and it was explained by Mike that he thought the puppies might help her, and the doctor agreed that anything was worth a try. Nick had hold of the box containing the puppies and Vi stood lecturing them about making so much noise in a hospital! Mike grabbed the box and raced to the room that held Nat. She was lying just as she was when Mike had left her first thing that morning. The machines beeped relentlessly a few feet away. Mike put the box at the side of the bed and lifted the two puppies out, Vi, Nick and John stood in the doorway watching enthralled. John felt a tear course down his cheek and he certainly wasn't alone as they watched Mike gently pick up the puppies, kiss each one, whisper "please" desperately to them both, and placed them at Nat's shoulders. The puppies immediately wriggled free and their little tails wagging with abandon started to enthusiastically lick Nat's face. Apart from the wriggling little puppies it was deathly silent it seemed, as though everyone's breath was held. Mike held Nat's hand "Please!" he implored, "please." Vi choked back a sob. It was heart wrenching to watch Mike's despondency as his shoulders sagged. Vi took a step towards him intending to comfort him when a weak voice said "Babies!" and Nat opened her eyes. Mike thought he would explode with joy. The voice in his head rang... "It's the little things that matter!"

It was several days before Nat was allowed a discharge from the hospital, even though she felt perfectly well 24 hours after waking up. Mike still spent his time fussing over her and though she made a show of complaining she lapped it up. Her parents had arrived and Mike thought she would burst when he told her that John and Sir Alfred had managed to get residence visas for her parents. Her homecoming was not just an ecstatic moment for Mike but it seemed everyone in the yard. Nat was home! She held up the paper at breakfast. "Michael Willett's wife recovered from her illness and has returned home much to the joy of the irascible Mike Willett... Mr. Willett didn't try to punch anyone as he left the hospital to his wife he in fact smiled for the cameras!"

"Typical of the papers, they always have to have a pop at me."

Nat laughed. "They wrong though I not your wife!" Nat chuckled, "What they mean irascible?"

"It means really nice." Mike said straight faced.

"Mmmm, I not sure, I think maybe I look up!"

"Nat your parents are here and I don't want to wait any longer to get married to you. Look we can get married the weekend after the race if we get organised, I know we were going to wait but your parents are back here and well..." Nat jumped up from her chair and threw her arms around Mikes neck. "I marry you tomorrow bad man if I could!" she kissed him then realising to herself the kitchen was empty. "Where my babies?" she said sternly to Mike. Mike looked puzzled.

"You had them on your lap a few minutes ago they must be here!" they searched the kitchen and there was no sign of them then a little yap came from outside. And they looked out of the kitchen door to see both puppies making a gallant effort to worry a curled-up hedgehog. Mike and Nat put their arms around each other and laughed as they watched the two puppies jumping up and down as the hedgehog remained in a tight ball ignoring them both. "You come here naughty babies, poor hedgehog you frighten him!" Nat scolded with a grin. The puppies ignored her and continued in their attempt to worry the hedgehog. She walked over and scooped them up giving each a kiss as she did. "Ooh you smelly I think you go for bath!" She went off toward the shower laughing as her two bundles squirmed in an attempt to get back to their game. "You, wriggly little things, but you have shower," Mike heard as she disappeared upstairs. Mike had never been so happy.

It was a beautiful morning, the sun shone and lazy wisps of mist rose from the ground as the sun rays warmed the soil. Nat and Mike stood at the top of the gallops, Nat's "babies" were alternating between frantically scratching and desperately trying to remove the collars she had put on them, they were struggling to understand why every time they tried to get away they were jolted to a stop as their little leads ended their escape bid. "You learn naughty babies… have to be good puppies." Nat said adoringly

"I think it's about time you named these two," Mike said and they decided that they would agree on a name for each puppy before they returned home. They stood arm in arm the puppies still tugging determinedly at the end of their leads. Nat leaned her head onto Mikes arm and looking at the large bump showing beneath Nat's coat he realised he was a part of a family and he felt as good as you can get.

Rocket and Storm had been jumped off behind the others as Seamus had hoped to settle them into a steady canter. His idea was in vain as the others jumped off Rocket and Storm both took off together surging past the others nearly knocking them off the gallops. They tore up the gallops and Nat jumped up and down with excitement which worried Mike to death. Nat laughed at his protestations. "Don't be silly man I fine," she said after the horses had blasted by them. "They very good, no horse will beat my boys!" There was another member of the Rocket and this time Storm fan club!

Seamus and Mike watched as Rocket with the ever-present JC munched at the tufts of grass that grew around the fence posts, whilst Storm sprawled out beneath the branches of an oak tree. "Well Michael, just think in a month you'll be a married man, and not long after that a Dad! I am so happy for you." Seamus said patting Mike's back. "Seamus I can't tell you how happy I am… God I love the ground that girl steps on! I just don't know what I would do without her. It's odd really because it all happened quite quick but from the first moment she walked into the house I just knew she was perfect… and if it hadn't of been for Vi I would have let her go!"

Seamus laughed, "She's a canny one is our Vi, she's a very special lady! Have you ever wondered Michael? We spent all those years struggling to make a go of it and every time it seems we couldn't quite get there, then along comes saint John and saves the day and our fellow here," he pointed towards Rocket, "Suddenly produces and stuns the world! I think the good Lord must have looked down on us and decided it was time to give us a break! Mind you this wild trainer I know nearly threw it all away a couple of times!"

"Cheeky Bugger! But right if I am honest!"

"Mike, I just want to say thank you for all you have done for me, you are a great friend and I know you think I have too much faith in the boy there, but I am telling you I don't know which of them will win, but for sure it will be one of them."

As the days went by the excitement almost reached fever pitch in the yard and a week before the race, staff were already preparing. It had been organised that no one would be left out. Everyone was going to come in early, feed, muck out, get changed and off to see the race. A day's holiday for the horses would not do any harm. Mike was getting nervous and it was only the presence of Nat and Vi that kept him calm. Nat would kiss his cheek each time she saw his cool slipping and say... your daughter says for Papa to be good and Mike would be like a puppy. Nat's babies were never far from her side and no longer tugged at their leads, finding it far better to be out on the leads than shut in the kitchen. They were as besotted with Nat as Mike was. She had given them each a name, she had called the Jack Russell *Poppy* and the Rottweiler *Jude*, they were already learning their names as everyone in the yard spent at least five minutes fussing them, which they thought was great. If someone came within a hundred yards of them they seemed to find an excuse to divert and crouch down to ruffle their ears, pick them up or play with them. Mike would pretend to be cross and say to Nat, "They should be in the kitchen, they're time wasters, cost me a bloody fortune stopping people working."

"Ooh you are hard boss man Michael Willett... they my babies, they with me! You be nice to them... and I be nice to you!" Then she would go up on her toes and kiss his cheek tenderly. "Why I fall in love with such a bad man I not know!" she would say laughing.

CHAPTER TWENTY-SEVEN

The day of the race came and there was not a person in the yard that was not shaking with excitement. One young lad shouted across the yard on seeing Mike, "Guv we have the best horses, the best trainer and the best jockeys… we don't get beat today… or any day for that matter… Hartslock is the kingdom and Michael Willett the King!" and despite his reservations on the amount of work or rather lack of work Rocket and Storm had put in he couldn't help but smile. Rocket and Storm were brought out and walked to the back of the lorry, both planted and refused to walk up the ramp. Seamus walked over to them and tried but they refused to move. Mike strode over to the horses. "Don't start playing up you buggers walk on!" Neither moved. "Come on boys, don't be messing me about… now WALK ON!" Still they didn't move. Mel walked over and took Storm's lead rope. He didn't move, she tried again but he just stood looking at her. She gritted her teeth and tried again giving him a slap on the shoulder, he didn't budge. The whole yard had congregated looking worried. Their stars were not going to be stars anymore if they didn't walk into the lorry. "Come on you daft buggers walk on you are always good to load!" Mike said, but still they didn't move. Mel suddenly burst into tears and though it was halting it was distinct. "Storm this is our chance, please." As everyone stood in the yard their mouths wide open disbelievingly at hearing Mel speak, Storm and Rocket casually walked up in the lorry together. "Well I'll be…" was as much as Mike could manage. No one was sure what they were more excited about the race or hearing Mel speak. Mark had raced over and hugged his sister his hands working at supersonic speed as he told her how pleased he was. Mel looked him straight in the eye and again though the words were similar to a child trying to get their tongue around the syllables said, "Your turn next, at the races." Mark smiled signed and walked round to jump up in the compartment behind the cab.

Mike walked across the yard in a state of wonder, Seamus by his side, he looked at Seamus, "You knew, didn't you?"

Seamus winced a little, "Yeah, but only a few days ago mind you… I promised the little maid I would keep it quiet, I tell you Michael it's the horses they heal people you know!" His voice had become broad Irish. "she only started speaking a few days ago and she didn't want anyone to know… she said she was going to tell her dad she had won! I told her she should tell him before the race because for sure she was to be second, my boy doesn't get beat!"

Mike grimaced "Okay I suppose I would have kept the secret as well if I'm honest. But you know Seamus, they haven't done enough work, the horses they are up against are super fit and are as good as anything Rocket has raced against and he's older now, Storm only has one race under his belt…"

"Now there you go having no confidence, I'm telling you we are in the winner's enclosure!"

They had reached the door of the kitchen before Mike had a chance to answer. His breath was taken Nat was standing at the table a glass of wine in her hand, she was wearing a dress with an oriental print that came an inch above her knee and she looked incredible. "Wow you look beautiful," he gushed and she gave him a girlish smile that would melt rocks. "Do you think you should be drinking though?" he said.

"We win best race of course I have drink, it is fine, silly man…" she did a twirl "you like my dress?"

"I like your dress and love the person inside it."
Nat walked over to him, "Sometime, you very nice man!" and kissed him soundly.

"Well we had better get going. The cars are waiting, and we have, as this gorgeous young lady said a race to win. And I have a gorgeous young lady of my own to attend to!" John said offering his arm to Alice and kissing her cheek as she slid her arm through his. "Right let's hit the road!"

John, Alice, Nat and Mike rode in one limo and Seamus, Mary, Vi and Nick rode in the other. "Ooh this is nice!" Vi said and settled back in the seat with a glass of champagne Seamus had just given her. They had the sense to leave early it was still only seven in the morning and it was just as well they did; the traffic was appalling. Mike started to fret over whether the lorry had beaten the queues. The last thing he wanted was his boys standing in the back of a lorry for hours and arriving at the races with no time to relax. He phoned Anita who had been placed in charge of things Seamus being given royal treatment for the day. "No problem Guv," Anita's cheery voice came back, "we must have missed the worst of it the road is fairly clear here, we'll be at the racecourse in plenty of time. I'm putting my savings on the boys, half on each… the odds are crap only got two to one on Rocks and threes on Storm but at least I'll double my money. The American horse must be getting a lot of support though he has gone odds on favourite!" Mike groaned at the thought of Anita putting all her money on the boy's and Anita must have thought it was because the American horse was so well fancied. "Don't you worry Guv our boys don't get beat!" Mike groaned again.

It wasn't that Mike didn't have absolute faith in his horses it was simply that he was concerned they would be injured, it was a big field, twenty-five runners over a mile two, Rocket was a lot older than any of the other horses and Storm a lot less experienced. He wanted desperately for them to prove themselves but deep down he had doubts and concerns.

Mike had never seen so many people in one place. He thought of Rocket's previous races and how crowds had flocked to see him, but this was something completely different. Cars reflected the sun people milled around and it was the same as far as he could see. There must be hundreds of thousands here he thought. There were hundreds of brightly coloured brollies under which harassed bookmakers struggled to take the money from the huge queues that formed in front of them. "Fancy a bet?" John grinned at Mike. "I like to have bet!" Nat chirped "I have bet on my poor baby Storm, my bad husband, make him very tired he always have to sleep, but he good boy and win! I have some money from Roy I going to spend some today!" she looked at Mike with a determined look. "Okay how much do you want on Storm?"

"Fifty thousand of your pounds," she said confidently passing over a shoulder bag she had been carrying. She poked her tongue out at Mike who was standing open mouthed, "I have lot of money Roy pay me so I think I spend a little and then have more money!" he moved forward kissed her and gave her back the bag. "I'll tell you what, I'll put your bet on as a bit of a wedding present how 's that?"

"See, I always right my husband. Sometime, you very nice man, and I have very special wedding present for you. I love you so much my Michael Willett, " she winked at Vi, Vi ginned knowingly and hiccupped.

Mike, John and Seamus walked toward the rail bookmakers. "Michael you know the rules, so will you put 50,000 on The Rocket for me? I'll sort it out with you tomorrow you know I'm…"

"Seamus shut up… if you asked me to put my life on him I would for you!"

Mike put the bets on he had promised and placed a half million bet on Rocket if he won he told John he was going to donate it to the hospital that had cared for Nat. the race time was getting closer and Mike walked over to the saddling boxes to help with the boys but they were already saddled both looked as calm and composed as could be. Mike went on and spoke to them in turn. He said the same to both, of them but with a small addition to Rocket. "Whatever you do I am proud of you and love you, you are special and I am honoured to have you." to Rocket he added, "Rock's thank you not only have you given me so much but you gave me back Nat." He kissed Rocket on the side of his face and left the box.

Rocket and Storm walked around the parade ring almost disdainfully. They looked at the other horses as though they were beneath them. The jockeys came out there bright colours almost a mini carnival as they made their way Indian file to the parade ring then dispersed to find their owner and their mount. Slowly the jockeys mounted and the trainers whispered instructions. Mike didn't worry telling Seamus anything other than good luck he knew he was as good a jockey as he could get and as good a horseman, he patted Rocket and said, "Just be careful old lad!" he walked over to where Anita held Storm. "Mel the only thing I ask is that you and Storm come home safe... I don't care if you are stone wall last, just both of you come home safe!" Mike was visibly shaking. Nat walked over to join him and linked her arm in his. "Do not worry my husband, my boy will win." She kissed Storms nose and pulled Mike away. Mike watched the two canter down easily to the start, his stomach churned and his heart was in his mouth. He watched as the horses were loaded and stood almost frozen waiting for the commentator. "And they're off!" The crowd roared, "and its Sapphire Blue that takes the lead and Plains Drifter..." the commentator, the crowd, in fact the world went silent for several seconds. Rocket and Storm ambled out of the stalls and broke into a leisurely trot. Laughter echoed across the Epsom Downs. Mike was heard to say by John who was looking totally bemused, "That's okay boys you just come home nice and steady!" What John did not hear was the voice in Mikes head, "I don't think so!" Mike whispered, "Oh fuck!" Rocket and Storm took off after the fast disappearing horses in front of them. the commentator very nearly gave birth which was pretty impressive as he was a man and tried his best to catch the flow of the race... he didn't! "Sapphire Blue leads the field and... what the hell Rocket and Storm are neck and neck fifteen, no ten lengths off the pace and closing, my God I have never seen speed like it!" Seamus and Mel toes in their irons crouched over the withers and neck of Rocket and Storm, they looked at each other and grinned. "Time to go?" Seamus shouted across to Mel and she turned her head and pushed her hands up Storm neck. It was like pressing your foot to the floor on a Bugatti Veyron. The commentator kicked back in. "Sapphire Blue holds the lead, Plains Drifter tracking closely followed by Orange County and Kanga. Two furlongs to race and Sapphire Blue kicks for home." The commentator seemed to forget that his was probably the most important and the most watched race ever as the crowd start to sing… Come On Baby Light My Fire, "And Storm and Rocket behind the leaders going at an unbelievable pace, they seem to be actually taunting the other horse! a furlong to go and Rocket and Storm are neck and neck, they pass Orange County, pass Sapphire Blue half a furlong to go," The commentator broke down but it didn't matter the crowd were roaring so loudly they wouldn't have heard him, "And it's The Rocket and Storm that pass the line together, too close to call, too close to call!" the announcement came "Photo, photo."

Mike was as exhausted as he had ever been. Nat raced up to him. "I tell you my boy win… you, clever man my beautiful husband, I win much money!" She kissed him soundly and cameras flashed. Mike tried to calm Nat down. "just hang on a minute sweetheart it's a photo finish we don't know who won yet." Nat stamped her foot "My baby win!" Mike wrapped his arms around her "Nat, I know one thing for sure I won when I met you. We have to go to, come!" He pulled Nat with him as he hurried his way to the exit of the race course to meet the horses. Anita was there with Nicky waiting to lead their respective horses to the enclosure, Mike heard Anita say, "I think my boy got it on the nod!" and Nicky reply, "No way Rock's got it!" the stewards were taking ages over the photo and the crowd was virtually silent as they waited for the announcement to come over the tannoy. "Dead heat, results of the photograph, dead heat!" and the race course erupted. People laughed and cried, people jumped for joy and sat on the floor head in hands. Mike smiled! He walked into the paddock and Kevin Stokes stood waiting for his daughter tears streaming down his face he saw Mike and rushed over to him grabbed his hand. "Thank you, Mike, thank you!" he choked. "Dad!" an almost strangled voice said. "she did it our Mel did it!" and Kevin turned and hugged his son unable to speak.

CHAPTER TWENTY-EIGHT

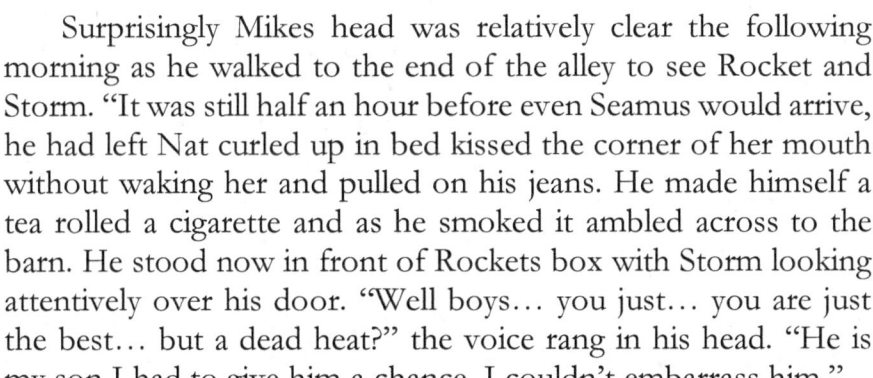

Surprisingly Mikes head was relatively clear the following morning as he walked to the end of the alley to see Rocket and Storm. "It was still half an hour before even Seamus would arrive, he had left Nat curled up in bed kissed the corner of her mouth without waking her and pulled on his jeans. He made himself a tea rolled a cigarette and as he smoked it ambled across to the barn. He stood now in front of Rockets box with Storm looking attentively over his door. "Well boys... you just... you are just the best... but a dead heat?" the voice rang in his head. "He is my son I had to give him a chance, I couldn't embarrass him."

"Hah old man!" the lighter voice rang. "I slowed down, so you could keep up!"

"You will never be as good as me my son, if I wanted to pass you I could, if I was trying my tail would have been all you saw!"

Mike jumped in. "Whoa boys! Storm no one will ever emulate your father, he did more than any horse in history, you are good but well Rocks is just...."

The lighter voice rang in Mike head, "Then are you man enough to let me prove it?" Mike quietly left the barn.

CHAPTER TWENTY-NINE

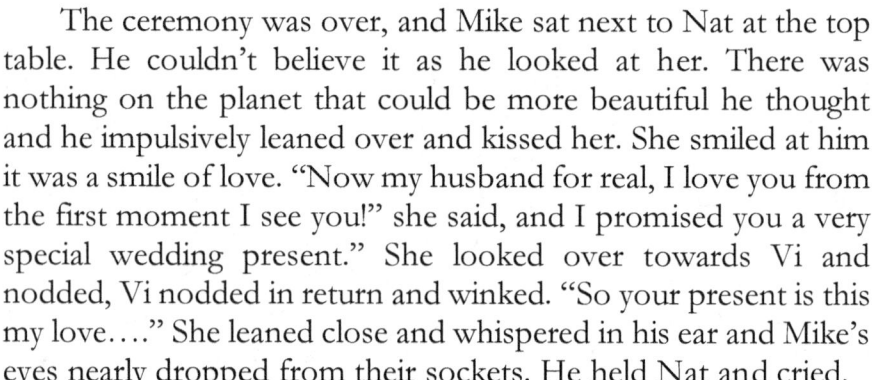

The ceremony was over, and Mike sat next to Nat at the top table. He couldn't believe it as he looked at her. There was nothing on the planet that could be more beautiful he thought and he impulsively leaned over and kissed her. She smiled at him it was a smile of love. "Now my husband for real, I love you from the first moment I see you!" she said, and I promised you a very special wedding present." She looked over towards Vi and nodded, Vi nodded in return and winked. "So your present is this my love…." She leaned close and whispered in his ear and Mike's eyes nearly dropped from their sockets. He held Nat and cried.

Vi tottered towards the Discovery with Nick steadying her. "What was that all about between Mike and our Nat? He asked.

Vi smiled knowingly. "Nothing for you to worry about my Nicholas, you'll find out soon enough!" she giggled and slid into the seat of the Discovery.

ABOUT THE AUTHOR

Chris Dyer has spent most of his life around horses. Described by one of his friends as "the man that doesn't fit in" he is never afraid to voice an opinion regardless of the consequences. Disparaging of bureaucracy and unpredictable – the probable cause of "not fitting in!" He has without credit worked on many horses from unknown ponies to well-known racehorses without bothering to attention seek. He has trained Arabian racehorses and pre trained thoroughbreds. His knowledge and occasionally his opinions are evident as he weaves his tale around the books characters.

A man of extremes Chris is either irritatingly happy or manically depressed (though more often than not the former). To describe Chris is almost impossible - he is a bit like pulling a Christmas Cracker… you never quite know what you will find on the inside!

A close friend.

For more information about Chris and a list of his other books, visit www.chrisdyerauthor.com